Praise for the
Werewolves of Grundy, Alaska

The Art of Seducing a Naked Werewolf

"Your spirits will automatically be raised if you read a novel by this author. . . . *The Art of Seducing a Naked Werewolf* is comedic entertainment at its best, where the characters are appealing and the plot is intriguingly original."

—*Single Titles*

"Harper's gift for character building and crafting a smart, exciting story is showcased well."

—*RT Book Reviews* (4 stars)

"A charming story that straddles several genres."

—*Fresh Fiction*

"Another great girlie read with a paranormal side by Molly Harper."

—*Rabid Reads*

"Once again, Molly Harper has worked her magic and gives readers what they want to read . . . sarcastic yet strong heroines who try to 'deal' with amorous heroes with sexy banter thrown in between each other."

—*Romance Bites*

How to Flirt with a Naked Werewolf
RT Book Reviews TOP PICK!

"A rollicking, sweet novel that made me laugh aloud. . . . Mo's wise-cracking, hilarious voice makes this novel such a pleasure to read."

> —*New York Times* bestselling author Eloisa James

"Harper is simply fantastic. . . . The story is a page-turning delight and the main characters are fraught with sexual tension."

> —*RT Book Reviews* (4½ stars)

"A light, fun, easy read, perfect for lazy days."

> —*New York Journal of Books*

"Riveting suspense, hilarious dialogue, and lusty love scenes make this first of a new series a winner."

> —*Fresh Fiction*

"Ms. Harper certainly has an extremely vivid imagination, and her skill at creating off-the-wall incidents has never been better."

> —*Single Titles*

Praise for the
Nice Girls of Half-Moon Hollow, Kentucky

"Terrific vamp camp. . . . The stellar supporting characters, laugh-out-loud moments, and outrageous plot twists will leave readers absolutely satisfied."

> —*Publishers Weekly* (starred review)

books by molly harper

In the land of Half-Moon Hollow

Nice Girls Don't Have Fangs

Nice Girls Don't Date Dead Men

Nice Girls Don't Live Forever

Nice Girls Don't Bite Their Neighbors

Driving Mr. Dead

The Care and Feeding of Stray Vampires

A Witch's Handbook of Kisses and Curses

The Naked Werewolf Series

How to Flirt with a Naked Werewolf

The Art of Seducing a Naked Werewolf

How to Run with a Naked Werewolf

The Bluegrass Series

My Bluegrass Baby

Rhythm and Bluegrass

Also

And One Last Thing . . .

Available from Pocket Books

How to Run with A Naked Werewolf

molly harper

POCKET BOOKS

New York   London   Toronto   Sydney   New Delhi

Pocket Books
A Division of Simon & Schuster, Inc.
1230 Avenue of the Americas
New York, NY 10020

This book is a work of fiction. Any references to historical events, real people, or real places are used fictitiously. Other names, characters, places, and events are products of the author's imagination, and any resemblance to actual events or places or persons, living or dead, is entirely coincidental.

First Pocket Books paperback edition January 2014

POCKET and colophon are registered trademarks of Simon & Schuster, Inc.

For information about special discounts for bulk purchases, please contact Simon & Schuster Special Sales at 1-866-506-1949 or business@simonandschuster.com.

The Simon & Schuster Speakers Bureau can bring authors to your live event. For more information or to book an event, contact the Simon & Schuster Speakers Bureau at 1-866-248-3049 or visit our website at www.simonspeakers.com.

Designed by Leydiana Rodríguez-Ovalles
Cover photograph by Claudio Marinesco; wolf © Anna Henly / Workbook Stock / Getty Images

Manufactured in the United States of America

10 9 8 7 6 5 4 3 2 1

ISBN 978-1-4767-0599-6
ISBN 978-1-4767-0602-3 (ebook)

For Amanda Ronconi.

Thank you for giving my characters your voice.

Acknowledgments

A great big thank-you to the readers who contacted me, encouraging me to continue the Naked Werewolf series. And an even bigger thank-you to those same readers, who didn't get cranky with me for refusing to tell them which of the Grundy, Alaska, characters I was writing about. It was a surprise!

I could not get through the writing process without the saintlike patience of my agent, Stephany Evans. And to my fantastic editor, Abby Zidle, thank you for publishing this work, despite its distinct lack of possums. (Werewolves in Alaska? Sure. But possums in Alaska would be pushing believability.)

Thanks to Yaya and Papa for their endless support and enthusiasm. To my husband, David, thank you for providing the inspiration for my badass, snarky wolfmen. And for my children, who suffer the embarrassment of having book covers featuring shirtless dudes delivered to the house while their friends are over—and the additional humiliation of having a mother who has the gall to call this "business correspondence"—I'm sure you'll turn out just fine.

And to the meteorological community at large, every time I write a Naked Werewolf book, there is a huge snowstorm that traps me inside my house with my family for extended periods of time. A heads-up would have been nice.

I'm just saying.

How
to Run
with A
Naked
Werewolf

1

All the Pretty Pintos

If Gordie Fugate didn't hurry the hell up and pick out a cereal, I was going to bludgeon him with a canned ham.

I didn't mind working at Emerson's Dry Goods, but I was wrapping up a sixteen-hour shift. My back ached. My stiff green canvas apron was chafing my neck. And one of the Glisson twins had dropped a gallon jar of mayo on my big toe earlier. I hadn't been this exhausted since doing an emergency rotation during my medical residency. The only nice thing I could say about working at Emerson's was that the owner hadn't asked for photo identification when I applied, eliminating an awful lot of worry for my undocumented self. Also, I usually dealt with less blood.

Unless, of course, I did bludgeon Gordie with the ham, which would result in a serious amount of cleanup in aisle five.

I only had a few more weeks of checkout duty before I would be moving on, winding my way toward Anchorage. It was just easier that way. Now that I was living in what I called "the gray zone," I knew there was a maximum amount of time people could spend around me before they resented unanswered personal questions. Of course, I'd also learned a few other things, like how to make an emergency bra or patch a pair of shoes with duct tape. And now I was trying to learn the zen art of not bashing an indecisive cornflake lover over the head with preserved pork products.

I glanced back to Gordie, who was now considering his oatmeal options.

I swore loudly enough to attract the attention of my peroxide-blond fellow retail service engineer Belinda. Middle-aged, pear-shaped, and possessing a smoker's voice that put that *Exorcist* kid to shame, Belinda was the assistant manager at Emerson's, the closest thing to a retail mecca in McClusky, a tiny ditchwater town on the easternmost border of Alaska. Because I was still a probationary employee, I wasn't allowed to close up on my own. But Belinda was friendly and seemed eager to make me a "lifer" at Emerson's like herself. I suspected she wasn't allowed to retire until she found a replacement.

"I've known Gordie for almost forty years. He can make a simple decision feel like the end of *Sophie's Choice*," she said, putting a companionable arm around me as I slumped against my counter. It was an accomplishment that I was able to give her a little squeeze in return.

"You're thinking about throwing one of those canned hams at him, aren't you?"

I sighed. "I guess I've made that threat before, huh?"

Belinda snickered at my irritated tone. I glared at her. She assured me, "I'm laughing with you, Anna, not at you."

I offered her a weak but genuine smile. "Feels the same either way."

"Why don't you go on home, hon?" Belinda suggested. "I know you worked a double when that twit Haley called in sick. For the third time this week, I might add. I'll close up. You go get some food in you. You're looking all pale and sickly again."

I sighed again, smiling at her. When I'd first arrived at Emerson's, Belinda had taken one look at my waxy cheeks and insisted on sending me home with a "signing-bonus box" of high-calorie, high-protein foods. I was sucking down protein shakes and Velveeta for a week. Every time I put a pound on my short, thin frame, she considered it a personal victory. I didn't have the heart to tell her that my pallor wasn't from malnutrition but from stress and sleep deprivation. I gave her another squeeze. "I haven't been sleeping well, that's all. Thanks. I owe you."

"Yeah, you do," she said as I whipped my green Emerson's apron over my head and stuffed it into my bag. As I made my way to the employee locker room, I heard her yell, "Damn it, Gordie, it's just Cream of Wheat. It's not like you're pulling somebody's plug!"

Chuckling, I slipped out the back through the employee exit, waiting for the slap of frigid September air to steal my breath. I snuggled deeper into my thick winter jacket, grateful for its insulating warmth. Years before, when I'd first arrived in Alaska, I'd brought only the barest essentials. I'd spent most of my cross-state drive shivering so hard I could barely steer. Eager to help me acclimate, my new neighbors had taken great pains to help me select the most sensible jacket, the most reasonably priced all-weather boots. I missed those neighbors with a bone-deep ache that I couldn't blame on the cold. I missed the people who had become my family. I missed the valley I'd made home. The thought of trying to make a place for myself all over again tipped my exhaustion into full-on despair.

Fumbling with the keys to my powder-blue-and-rust Pinto, I heard someone say, "Just tell Jake I'll get him the money in a week."

A gruffer, calmer voice answered, "Marty, relax. Jake didn't send me. I just stopped in for a burger. I'm not here for you."

I closed my eyes, hoping to block out the shadowy forms in the far corner of the employee lot that Emerson's shared with the Wishy-Washy Laundromat and Flapjack's Saloon. I didn't want to see any of this. I didn't want the liability of witnessing some sort of criminal transaction. I just wanted to go home to my motel room and stand in the shower until I no longer felt the pain of sixteen hours and a jumbo jar of mayonnaise on my feet. I turned my back to the voices, struggling to work the sticky lock on my driver's-side door.

"Don't feed me that bullshit," the reedier, slightly whiny voice countered. "He sent you after me when I owed him ten. You don't think he's going to do it again now that I owe him seventeen?"

"I'm telling you, I'm not here for you. But if you don't put that gun away, I might change my mind."

Gun? Did he say "gun"?

Who the hell has a gunfight in the parking lot behind a Laundromat?

I focused on keeping my hands from shaking as I jiggled the key in the lock. *Stupid circa-1980s tumbler technology!* I gave myself another five seconds to open the door before I would just run back to the Emerson's employee entrance.

That was my plan, until the point when I heard the gunshot . . . and the screech of tires . . . and the roar of an engine coming way too close. I turned just in time to see the back end of a shiny black SUV barreling toward me and my car. I took three steps before throwing myself into the bed of a nearby pickup truck. Even before I peered over the lip of the bed, I knew the loud, tortured metallic squeal was the SUV pulverizing my Pinto.

"Seriously?" I cried, watching as my car disintegrated in front of my very eyes.

The SUV struggled to disengage its back end from the wreckage of my now-inoperable car. As the driver gunned the engine, I followed the beams of the headlights across the lot to a man curled in the fetal position on the ground.

My eyes darted back and forth between the injured man and the growling black vehicle. This was none of my business. I didn't know this guy. I didn't know what he'd done to make Mr. SUV want to run him down like a dog. And despite the fact that every instinct told me to stay put, stay down until this guy was a little man-pancake, I launched myself out of the truck bed and ran across the lot. I dashed toward the hunched form on the ground, sliding on the gravel when I bent to help him. I tamped down my instincts to keep him still while I assessed the damage, assuring myself that any wounds he had would definitely prove fatal if he was run over by a large vehicle.

"Get up!" I shouted as the SUV wrenched free of my erstwhile transportation and lurched toward us.

Mr. Pancake-to-Be struggled to his knees. I tucked my arms under his sleeves and pulled, my arms burning with the effort to lift him off the ground.

"Get your butt off the concrete, *now!*" I grunted, heaving him out of the path of the SUV. I felt a set of car keys dangling out of his jacket pocket. I clicked the fob button until I heard a beep and turned toward the noise.

Just as I got him on his feet, the headlights of the SUV flared. We stumbled forward, falling between his truck and Belinda's hatchback. The hatchback shuddered with a tortured metallic shriek as the SUV sideswiped it. I jerked the passenger door of the truck open, slid across the seat, and dragged him inside. When I pulled it back, my hand was red and slick with blood. He groaned as he tried to fold his long legs into the cab. I reached over him to slam the door.

"Not smart," I mumbled, slipping the key into the ignition. "Like 'and she was never heard from again' not smart."

I watched as the SUV careened off the far corner of the lot into the grass. The ground was soupy and particularly fragrant, thanks to a septic-tank leak. The owner of Flapjack's had warned us not to park anywhere near it, or we'd end up stuck to our axles in substances best not imagined, which is what was happening to the SUV the more it spun its wheels. I glanced between my demolished car and the guy who seemed so hell-bent on killing my passenger. At this point, I didn't know which was more distressing. The SUV driver stepped out, slipping and sliding in the muck that had sucked him in to the ankles. There was a flash of metal in his hand as he strode toward the truck. A gun. He was pointing a gun at us.

Fortunately for me and my barely conscious passenger, the SUV guy wandered a little too close to my Pinto. And my rusted-out baby, being the most temperamentally explosive of all makes and models, had not taken kindly to being squished by the big, mean off-roader. My notoriously delicate gas tank was leaking fuel all over the parking lot, dangerously close to the lard bucket Flapjack's set out back to catch employees' cigarette butts. And because the saloon was staffed by likable though lazy people, there were always a few smoldering butts lying around on the gravel.

WHOOSH.

The fuel ignited, sending my car up like a badly upholstered Roman candle. Mr. SUV was thrown to the ground as a little mushroom cloud exploded over us.

Good. Explosions drew a lot of attention. People would come running out to see what had happened, and Mr. SUV couldn't afford that many witnesses. This guy would get the (fully equipped) medical attention he needed . . . and I would end up answering questions for a lot of cops.

Not good.

I hadn't even realized I'd punched the gas before I felt the gravel give way under the tires and the truck lurch toward the open road.

He slumped against the window as I careened out of the parking lot and onto the highway. The closest medical facility was in Bernard, about seventy miles up the road. As we neared the town limits, I passed the Lucky Traveler Motel, wishing we had time to stop and pick up my clothes and medical bag. But nearly everyone in the bar knew where I lived. The SUV driver would only have to ask a few people in the crowd that gathered to roast marshmallows around my immolated car and he'd find me in about ten minutes. For that matter, he could have been following us at that moment. Somehow, that made my spare contact-lens case and stethoscope seem less significant.

"Mister?" I said, shaking his shoulder, wincing as I noticed the blood seeping through his shirt. Gunshot wounds to the abdomen usually meant perforated major organs and damaged blood vessels, but his blood loss was minimal. I held out hope, though I knew that wasn't necessarily a good sign. There could be some complication or an exit wound I wasn't aware of. I pulled my apron out of my bag and pressed the green canvas against his belly. He groaned, opening his burnt-chocolate eyes and blinking at me, as if he was trying to focus on my face but couldn't quite manage it.

"You," he said, squinting at me. "I know you."

I swallowed, focusing on the situation at hand instead of the instinctual panic those words sent skittering up my spine. "No, I'd remember you, I'm sure. Just hold on, OK? I'm going to get you to the clinic in Bernard. Do you think you could stay awake for me?"

He shook his head. "No doctors."

I supposed this would be a bad time to tell him I *was* a doctor.

"Not that bad. No doctors," he ground out, glaring at me. I scowled right back. His face split into a loopy smirk. "Pretty."

His head *thunk*ed back against the seat rest, which I supposed signaled the end of our facial-expression standoff.

And now that I had time to study said face, I could appreciate the shaggy black hair, eyes so intensely brown they were almost black, and cheekbones carved from granite. His lips were wide and generous and probably pretty tempting when they weren't curled back over his teeth in pain like that.

"Please," he moaned, batting his hand against my shoulder, weakly flexing his fingers around it.

Well, damn, I'd always been a sucker for a man who kept pretty manners intact while bleeding. "Fine," I shot back. "Where do you want to go?"

But he'd already passed out.

"And she was never heard from again," I muttered.

A few miles later, my passenger stopped bleeding, which could mean that he'd started to clot . . . or that he'd gone into shock and died. My optimism had reached its limit for the evening.

Keeping an eye on the road, I pressed my fingers over his carotid and detected a slow but steady pulse. I took a deep breath and tried to focus. I'd been through so much worse. It didn't make sense to panic now. How had I gotten myself into this? I'd worked so hard to avoid this kind of trouble. I'd kept my head down, stayed low profile. And here I was, driving around in a possibly stolen truck with a possibly dead body slumped over in the passenger seat. If I'd had one operating brain cell in my head, I would have run screaming into the bar the minute I heard the men arguing in the parking lot. But no, I had to help the injured stray, because living with the less-than-civic-minded side of humanity over the last few years had apparently taught me nothing.

I saw a sign ahead for Sharpton. Since he didn't want to go to the clinic, I'd turned off the main highway and stuck to the older, less-traveled state routes. I tapped the brakes, afraid I would miss some vital piece of information hidden between the words "Sharpton" and "20 miles." As the truck slowed, the big guy slumped forward and snorted as his head smacked against the dashboard.

Good. Dead people do not snort. That was my qualified medical opinion.

"Hey, big guy?" I said loudly, shaking his shoulder. "Mister?"

He snorted again but did not wake up. I laughed, practically crying with relief. I gently shook my . . . passenger? Patient? Hostage? What was I going to do with him? He didn't want a doctor, he said. But as much as I needed a vehicle, I didn't have it in me to just leave him on the side of the road somewhere and drive off.

Just over the next rise in the road, I saw a sign for the Last Chance Motel, which seemed both ominous and appropriate. I took a deep breath through my nose and let it slowly expand my lungs. By the time I exhaled, I'd already formed my plan. At the faded pink motel sign, I turned into the lot and parked in front of the squat, dilapidated building. There were two cars in the lot, including the one in front of the office, which seemed to double as the manager's quarters.

I reached toward the passenger seat and gently shook the big guy's shoulder. His breathing was deep and even. As carefully as I could, I raised the hem of his bloodied shirt and gasped. The bullet wound, just under his ribs on his left side, seemed too small for such a recent injury. The edges of the wound were a healthy pink. And the bullet seemed to be lodged there in his skin.

I pulled away, scooting across the bench seat. That . . . wasn't normal.

Calm down, I ordered myself. *There's no reason to panic. This is good news.*

Maybe some weird act of physics had kept the bullet from penetrating deeply in the first place, I reasoned. I hadn't gotten a good look at the wound while I was playing action hero in the dark parking lot. In my panic, it must have looked much worse than it was. Either way, the wound looked almost manageable now.

"Just hold on tight," I told him, placing my hand on his shoulder again. He leaned into my touch, trying to nuzzle his cheek against my fingers. "Uh, I'll be right back."

It would appear that I was footing the bill for this little slice of heaven. I couldn't reach his wallet, as it was in his pocket, firmly situated under his butt. I had just enough cash in my purse (a twenty and a few lonely singles) to cover one night. After that, I was dead in the water. The rest of my cash had been stashed behind a dresser in my motel room near Emerson's.

I jumped out of the truck and tried to look calm and normal as I walked into the motel's dingy little office and saw its creepy-as-hell occupant. The hotel seemed to have run a bizarrely specific Internet ad that read, "Wanted: semiskilled applicant with off-putting sex-predator vibe and lax standards in personal hygiene."

And this guy was no exception. It took no less than three refusals of a "room tour" from the night manager before I was permitted to trade a portion of my precious cash supply for a little plastic tag attached to the oldest freaking room key I had ever seen.

"Two beds, right?" I asked, taking the key.

He shook his head, leering at me. "Single rooms only. We like to stay cozy here."

"Is there a pharmacy anywhere around here?" I asked.

"In town, about four miles down the road. Opens in the morning, around eight," he said. "But if you're feeling poorly, I have something in my room that might perk you up."

I turned on my heel and made a mental note to prop a chair against the outside door once I got to the room.

I opened up the passenger-side door and saw that the big guy had managed to sit up and had his head resting on the seat back. He was snoring steadily. I spotted a bulky duffel bag in the backseat of the cab and threw it over my shoulder. I unlocked the room door, tossed the bag inside, and steeled myself for the task of hauling his unconscious ass into the room. Careful to keep his bloodied side away from the manager's window, I hoisted his arm over my shoulder in a sort of ill-advised fireman's carry and took slow, deliberate steps toward the open door. The movement seemed to reopen the wound, and I could feel blood seeping through my shirt. We made it through the door.

I heard a distinct metallic *plink*. I looked down and saw that the bullet had rolled across the filthy carpet and hit the wall.

I meant to set him gently on the bed but ended up flopping him across the bedspread. The rickety bed squealed in protest as he bounced, but he didn't bat an eyelash. I huffed, leaning against the yellowed floral wallpaper to catch my breath. "Sorry. You're heavier than you look."

I locked the door and wedged the desk chair against the knob. The room was so outdated it was almost in style again but the dirt and neglect screamed "dingy," not "kitschy." The carpet was a dank greenish-brown color that could only be described as phlegm. The bedspread, threadbare and nearly transparent in places, matched the shade.

I shook off the Norman Bates flashbacks and told myself it was just like any of the other crappy indigent motels I'd stayed at in any number of cities, and I hadn't been stabbed in the shower yet.

I turned back to the sleeping giant on the bed. The flannel shirt made an unpleasant ripping noise as I peeled it away, the dried blood causing the stiff material to adhere to his skin. The wound seemed even smaller now, the area around it a perfectly normal, healthy color. I pushed back from him, away from the bed, staring at the minuscule hole in his flesh.

This couldn't be right.

Taking a step back, I knocked over his duffel and saw a bottle of Bactine spray sticking out of the partially opened zipper. I arched an eyebrow and pulled the bag open. "What the—?"

Never mind having to run to a pharmacy. The bag was filled to the brim with well-used first-aid supplies— mostly peroxide and heavy-duty tweezers. And several different types of exotic jerky. But not much in the way of clothes.

I glanced from the shrinking bullet hole to the enormous bag of meat treats with its distinct lack of clothes . . . and back to the bullet hole.

Oh, holy hell, this guy was a werewolf.

2

This Is What Happens When You Roughhouse

I dropped my butt on the bed, staring down at the unconscious shape-shifter and feeling very stupid. I'd spent the last few years as the family physician for a large pack of werewolves in the Crescent Valley, several hundred miles away in southwestern Alaska. I'd recently resigned my position, if one could consider sneaking away in the dead of night a resignation.

Yes, werewolves were real. They walked among us humans, living relatively normal lives, working normal jobs, and occasionally shifting into enormous wolves and hunting down defenseless woodland creatures. They weren't alone in the shape-shifting animal kingdom. In my time with the valley pack, I'd met were-horses, were-bears, and even a tragically less cool were-skunk named Harold. If it was a mammal, there was a group of people out there somewhere who could shift into it. (Fish and reptiles were problematic, for some reason.) Presided over by an alpha male—or in the Crescent Valley pack's case, an alpha female— a pack usually lived "packed together" in a limited amount of space, such as a single apartment building or a trailer park, depending on the clan's resources.

All major life decisions had to be approved by the alpha, from mate selection to college enrollment. Everything had to be deemed for the good of the pack.

Accepting that (a) these creatures existed and (b) they were now my patients was a strange adjustment for me. I'd had a complete *Maggie must have slipped me special mushrooms* breakdown the first time she shifted in front of me.

The scientist in me still had problems accepting the paranormal element of werewolves. I tended to think of their abilities as a genetic bonus, which was easier to accept than *magic exists, but you just weren't lucky enough to have any in your life until you stumbled upon a pack full of eccentric shape-shifters in your late twenties*. But after a while, I realized that compared with living with someone whose moods shifted from moment to moment, living with people who had exclusively unstable *physical* forms was practically a vacation.

I flopped back onto the bed, noting with a frown that my weight didn't even jostle the wolf-man. *Of course.* Of course I would walk away from one of the largest werewolf pack settlements in North America, only to end up trapped in a run-down motel room with a wounded one. Only someone with my logic-defying bad luck could possibly defeat the unlikeliness of those odds. I was the ass-backward Red Riding Hood.

Had Maggie Graham, my former boss, sent this guy to search for me? The big guy did have the look of the Graham family—dark, rough-hewn, and handsome, not to mention bigger than a barn door, as my gramma would say. But I'd cared for every single member of that pack, treating everything from swine flu to suspicious puncture wounds brought on by "scuffling" with porcupines. I didn't recognize him, and I certainly would have remembered someone who looked like him.

Not to mention that werewolves rarely strayed this far from their territory. They were genetically programmed to protect their packlands, to crave hunting within their family's territory with an ache that went way beyond homesickness and edged into crippling obsession. The chances of some distant Graham cousin venturing this far from the valley for such an extended period of time that I hadn't met him in the four years I lived there? Not possible.

And frankly, none of this mattered, because I wasn't planning on sticking around long enough for *getting to know you* conversations.

I sighed. Werewolf or not, I couldn't let him sleep with bloody, unclean wounds. I searched through the bag and found bandages, tape, Bactine, and hydrogen peroxide. The bathroom was surprisingly clean, which, sadly, was turning out to be the highlight of my day. I ran a washcloth under a warm tap and used it to wipe away the brownish blood from his skin, noting the wound was now about the size of a dime. Worried that it was too deep to use the Bactine, I irrigated it with the peroxide, catching the runoff with a towel. He hissed, arching off the bed, but he ultimately slumped back into unconsciousness. Just to be safe, I sprayed the wound with Bactine and bandaged him up.

It had taken me some time to get used to werewolf physiology and adjust my medical training to it. While the spontaneous-healing thing made my position as pack doctor easier, it also meant that untreated broken bones could set in bad positions. Wounded skin could heal over foreign matter and dirt, which led to infections.

Beyond wound care, my chief responsibility had been monitoring and faking state-sanctioned paperwork for as many as a dozen pregnancies at a time. Werewolves were ridiculously fertile. Maggie also appointed me the "supervisor" of the pack's seniors, who, although they aged a bit more slowly than the average human, were just as susceptible to the typical blood-pressure and joint problems associated with getting old. But they were far less open to accepting these issues, considering them "human problems." For one thing, werewolf metabolism burned through calories so quickly that it was damn near impossible to monitor their diets, cholesterol, or salt. Try telling a seventy-year-old who can eat three whole fried chickens in one sitting that he needs to watch his triglycerides. The reaction will be swift and hilarious, and then he will go fetch his friends to tell them what the funny new doctor said.

The first time there was an emergency with the pack, I'd panicked. It was just claw marks from an unfriendly interaction between Maggie's lovable idiot cousin Samson and a grizzly. Frankly, he could have healed up on his own within twenty-four hours, but a few stitches moved the process along faster. Samson's back looked as if he'd made out with Freddy Krueger, and the injuries were so extensive I froze. I couldn't seem to pick a location to insert the suture needle in his skin.

And then, of course, Samson was himself.

"Hey, Doc, stop staring at my ass and stitch me up," he'd called over his shoulder.

That had broken the ice and allowed me to relax and make the first stitch.

Being able to practice again was a gift I couldn't quite fathom. Before the valley, medicine had been something I'd had a certain knack for but not something I cared for passionately. I made a healthy salary, which I appreciated. I was good at putting patients at ease and had a talent for sorting through the mysteries of diagnostics. But I didn't wake up in the morning and think, *Oh, what a lucky girl am I!*

In the valley, I rejoiced in the birth of every cub, mourned every death, and felt fortunate to help my patients through every stage in between. Through the pack, I found my purpose. I was able to feel like myself again, without the risk of being discovered. I could feel as if I was putting the very expensive education my parents had helped fund to good use. I had a place of my own making, a community that I'd earned. I built a calm, competent exterior that didn't garner me any close friendships but kept me on good terms with my neighbors. While the people who greeted me so cheerily each morning may not have known the real me, they appreciated the me they did know.

Now that my time in the valley was over, I wondered if I would ever find that again. I would likely spend the rest of my life working at places like Emerson's, where the people were friendly and the work was dull. I supposed I should be grateful for the time I'd had to use my education.

The big guy would be right as rain in a few hours. I, on the other hand, stood a really good chance of pulling a muscle trying to haul his enormous frame into a comfortable position on the bed. It took a couple of tries, but I managed to pull him by the shoulders until his head was near a pillow. Standing there, watching his chest rise and fall, I was suddenly very tired. I looked down and saw the fist-sized rusty-red splotch on the shoulder of my shirt.

Damn it. I only had one clean shirt left in my bag. And since I'd left behind everything I owned, I would probably be wearing that shirt for a while. I went into the bathroom, throwing the bloodied towels into a far corner. I dragged my stained shirt carefully over my head, rinsed it as best I could, and hung it over the shower-curtain rod to dry.

Swiping at my cheeks, I looked in the mirror. My hair had been all of the colors of the Clairol spectrum since I left home, from jet-black to white-blond. But after I reached the valley, I'd let it go back to its original reddish-gold. It was nice to be back to strawberry-blond, even if people did expect me to be wacky and/or zany, which was irritating on so many levels.

I looked as exhausted as I felt. I'd been born with open, happy features: wide eyes, a pert little nose, a determined chin. My skin had been peaches and cream, without dark circles under my eyes. My lips had curved into an easy smile for friends, strangers, anybody. And my eyes had been a clear, untroubled green. Now I didn't even have the energy to offer my reflection an apologetic shrug as I stripped out of my clothes. I locked the bathroom door and took a few deep breaths as I ran the bath tap. I always dreaded motel showers. You never knew what you were getting into. This one had the perfect balance of hot water, just enough burn to bite, but all the pressure of a dime-store water pistol.

Shampooing with the cheap, splintering bar of motel soap, I prayed that one day I would stumble into a motel that stocked Garnier Fructis for its guests. I rinsed out my dirty underclothes, although I knew there was little chance they would dry before morning. Now that I was clean, I faced a dilemma. I had one change of clothes that I always kept in my tote. I had a backup bag, packed with clothes, cash, and spare ID, in my trunk, but that trunk was now a charcoal briquette.

I poked my head out the door to make sure the big guy was still out cold. I crept over to his bag and selected one of the few T-shirts, one that advertised the Suds Bucket in Fairbanks. My short, undernourished frame would swim in it, but it smelled OK, and it covered me, and that was enough. I slipped it on over my last pair of dry, clean panties.

I checked the locks again and surveyed my sleeping options: the bed, the floor, or the wooden chair currently propped against the door. The idea of sleeping on the nasty carpet was too repulsive. Sleeping on the chair would take a contortionist's balance and flexibility. The bed won.

I repacked my bag and placed it on top of my clean jeans, socks, and sneakers, within easy reach of the bed. I pulled back the bedspread, no small task considering that he was lying on top of it.

"Hey, I'm going to get in the bed now. I'd like to point out that assaulting someone who's provided you with medical treatment is tacky." He snored on, a deep, rumbling sound spiraling out from his chest. "OK, I'll take that as a tacit promise to be a gentleman."

I slid under the stiff white sheets and tried not to think about the last time they'd been washed. I punched the flat pillow into shape and lay on my side, facing the door, which also meant being nose-to-nose with my practically comatose roommate.

Blinking at him sleepily, I finally had time to appreciate my bed partner's face. He was definitely attractive in that rough-hewn, competent way. I sort of wanted to nibble on him, all of him. Was that wrong?

I groaned and rolled away, putting my back to him. Yes, it was wrong. These were bad thoughts, bad thoughts that led to bad things. Bad things that would probably feel pretty good but would ultimately bite me on the ass. Of course, with that little overbite of his, being bitten on the ass might not—

I groaned again, pressing my face into the pillow. This was not like me. For the first few months after I ran, I was too scared of my own shadow to let a man within three feet of me, much less see me naked. Sure, I'd been attracted to other men. Hell, the valley had been packed with handsome, eligible fellas who basically threw themselves at anything female and single that they weren't related to. But I'd been able to stay unattached. I hadn't dated. I just couldn't open up to anyone else like that. I didn't want to give anyone else that sort of power over me.

There's no such thing as a one-night stand when you live in such a small community. You see that person over and over, and the awkwardness can be deadly. I hadn't engaged the services of a no-strings-attached "bounce buddy," no matter how dark and lonely the winters got.

And it just felt wrong, starting any sort of relationship when I was still technically married. Lying to someone about my name was one thing. Letting someone think I was a normal, available human being was another.

Clearly, years without sex had disrupted the important responsible-decision-making neurons in my brain.

I scooted across the bed as far as I could. I shoved what would have been his pillow between us. That would provide an impenetrable measure of overnight security, right? I switched off the bedside lamp and pulled the covers up to my chin. I closed my eyes, waiting for sleep to take me.

I was going to be all right, I told myself. It took a while to learn to live without a cushion, with no safety net.

The rush of desire to be still again, to go back to the life I'd made, caught me off-guard. Having friends again, a home, a job I didn't have to settle for, these were dangerously beautiful lures that sent me right back to square one. Square one sucked.

I knew I wasn't exactly happy in this gray zone, but I was safe. And for a long time, before the valley, safety was the only happiness I needed. The idea that it might not be enough anymore made my chest ache with the effort to breathe.

I used to have backup plans and savings accounts, credit cards, and a skin-care regimen. I arrived home from work promptly at 5:25 every night to start dinner. If I arrived after 5:30, Glenn started to worry. And that would mean panicked voice mails on my cell, calls to the state police and the emergency rooms to see if I'd been in an accident, and a lot of fuss and fuming over nothing. I'd learned quickly that it was just easier to leave work ten minutes early every day than to try to convince Glenn that he was being unreasonable.

When we first started dating, I thought that sort of concern meant that I was important to him, that he was afraid of something happening to me. It's what I told myself, even when I was assuring my supervisors at the hospital that my husband was a big practical joker after he left threatening voice mails for the head of cardiology. He spotted the two of us chatting at a colleague's retirement dinner and was convinced we were sleeping together . . . which pretty much guaranteed I would never attend another staff party, just to avoid the potential humiliation. That was, I imagine, the whole point. I lost so many friends, any sort of personal relationships with the people I worked with. I was slowly pared out of their lives, until all I had was Glenn. Just the way he wanted it.

I'd made so many mistakes, so many exceptions to protect my pride, to prevent admitting, even to myself, how bad my situation had become. My road to hell was paved with rationalizations.

"Stop it," I whispered into the dark. "Stop thinking about it."

It was the shock of the parking-lot confrontation, I told myself. The yelling and the flames and then all that adrenaline and blood. That sort of upheaval was bound to bring up unpleasant memories. Tossing under the scratchy sheet, I found myself pressed against my bed-mate. The pillow between us had been nudged down on the mattress, so that his face and shoulders were visible. I curled toward him, toward the heat of his body. He smelled of the woods, earthy and wild. Wasn't that funny? Someone who spent his time in dive bars and honky-tonks smelling like fresh wind and moss? It wasn't a werewolf thing. I'd spent enough time around the species to know that they weren't all "April fresh." He just smelled right, which in itself was a little alarming and prompted me to shove the pillow between us a little higher.

Sniffing lightly, he rolled toward me, his hand sliding over my shoulder and resting near my neck. Somehow, I'd expected it to be uncomfortable, being touched like this again. But while I certainly had some lingering werewolf-gunshot-wound-related questions, it didn't feel wrong to have this man's hand on me. I felt warm, down to the tips of my toes, comfortably, blissfully warm. I leaned closer until my forehead was resting against his arm and just lived in that warmth for a moment. In my head, I was basking in the summer sun on my parents' back porch, knowing my mother would come out any minute to fuss at me about putting on sunscreen. I hadn't heard my mother's voice in such a long time. What I wouldn't give just to hear her fuss at me about wrinkles and sun spots once more. But she was gone.

My eyes fluttered open, and I pulled out of the recollection. I wouldn't think of my mother right now, not in a place like this, with a supernatural creature snoring beside me. She definitely wouldn't have approved of my getting myself into this sort of situation. This was far outside of the realm of problems that could be fixed with sunscreen. I reluctantly moved away. But I found that my head was a lot clearer. I closed my eyes and started playing the "Random Game" in my head, a little brain exercise I'd made up to help me sleep in strange places. I would think of one of my favorite things from my old life—a TV show, a book, an ice cream flavor—and then randomly connect it to something else I liked, and something else, then something else. The pleasant imagery, combined with stream-of-consciousness thinking, lulled me right to sleep. I remembered going to see this terrible movie, *The Chase*, with my best friend, Teri. It was one of the first movies we'd been allowed to go to the theater to see on our own. And we picked a movie starring Charlie Sheen and Kristy Swanson. Oh, the vagaries of youth.

Kristy Swanson also played a fictional version of Anna Nicole Smith on *Law & Order*. I remembered watching some weird clip of Anna Nicole's reality show on *Talk Soup*, where she was riding around in a limousine, whining and eating an obscenely large pickle. They used to serve pickles like that at basketball games at my high school. The booster clubs would serve them in little paper cups. If you ate one in front of my classmates, you could expect a lot of remarks about oral exams at school on Monday.

My brain bounced around like that for a few more minutes, from overrated Sheens to celeb-reality to giant pickles. My limbs were heavy. My eyelids fluttered closed. As I drifted off to sleep, I had no idea what tomorrow would bring. I didn't know how I was going to get out of this little town, where I would go, how I would live. For now, I was clean, and I wasn't sleeping in my car. And I'd managed to help someone who needed it. The rest I could sort out tomorrow.

3

Plastic Handcuffs:
Fun for the Whole Family

I was warm. I was safe. There was a pleasantly heavy weight against my stomach, and someone was rubbing his thumb along my cheek. My hands skimmed over the shape on top of me and threaded through thick, silky hair.

Wait.

My eyes snapped open. The werewolf was on top of me. I bit back a scream when the warm, rough hand clasped the back of my neck. Whiskers scratched my neck, leaving a burning path in their wake. I tapped at his shoulders, unable to push his heavy weight off of me.

"Um, hey, I think you've got the wrong ide—*mmph.*" His mouth closed over mine. It was soft, wet, and hot. My bedmate broke the warm, wet kiss, running the tip of his nose along my throat and making sweet, soft rumbling noises. My hands went from batting at his shoulders to lightly tracing the line of his neck.

It wasn't entirely unpleasant to have someone this close, to have the heat from someone else's skin seeping into mine. I wasn't so startled when he kissed me again, teasing my tongue with his own as I opened to him. His hand cupped the weight of my breast in his palm before lightly pinching the nipple through his Suds Bucket T-shirt. I arched off the bed, and he used the opportunity to slide a hand under my butt, grinding his hips against me.

Blood flowed into my cheeks, and a pulsating coil of tension started building between my legs. My eyes fluttered open. His were shut, and not just in a "busy kissing" way. They were half-shut in that dazed, heavy-lidded expression of someone who's only just woken up and is on the verge of passing out again. But his movements, while languid, had a purpose, and that purpose seemed to be stripping me out of my clothes.

I pulled away slightly, my eyebrows furrowed. *Was* he asleep, or was he faking this?

I'd heard of sleepwalking, but sleep-*snuggling*?

Was this a werewolf thing? Should I wake him up? I'd heard that was dangerous. Of course, letting a stranger have unprotected sleep sex with you couldn't be terribly safe. Frankly, his touching me didn't feel wrong or bad. I traced my fingers along the contours of his face, thumbing the arch of his cheekbones. He leaned into the caress and made that happy purring noise. I smiled into the darkness of the room. I'd gone far too long without any sort of connection to another human being. I missed something as simple as choosing to be touched.

Leaning closer, I let the tip of my nose run along his cheek, inhaling the warm, woodsy fragrance of his skin. I sighed, tangled my fingers into his mass of dark hair, and kissed him greedily. He moaned, a deep, rumbling sound that vibrated from his chest to mine. I expected him to reach for his belt. I was prepared for it. But he just pulled me back to his chest and wrapped his arms around me, holding me close. His lips worried my throat in tight little circles, his teeth nipping lightly at the skin until he reached the spot where my neck met my shoulder. I was relaxing into him, enjoying the alternately soft and sharp sensations, when I felt him scrape his teeth along the line of my throat. He paused, pressing his canines into the soft web of flesh where my shoulder and neck joined, hard enough that he was millimeters from breaking through the skin. I gasped, tensing my back so quickly that the crown of my head caught his chin. He yelped, then licked at the spot he'd injured, nuzzling it, cuddling against me as if trying to apologize. This was so far outside the etiquette of *how to thank someone who has treated your gunshot wound* it wasn't even funny.

I tried to wriggle out of his arms, but I might as well have been wrapped in an iron cage. He was immovable. But instead of trying to bite me again, he simply tucked his face into the crook of my neck and commenced snoring.

Now suddenly wide-awake, I stared into the darkness of the motel room and rubbed at my neck. *And she was never heard from again.*

• • •

I lay there at dawn, blinking into the dark, until the sun rose. After climbing out of bed, I got my bag together and put on my last clean shirt. The mark he'd made on my neck just looked like a bad hickey, the impression of his teeth barely visible. In the light of day, I could not explain what the hell he'd done. Had he meant to hurt me? Was it some weird flashback to an old girlfriend?

I didn't know what it meant. It was probably significant in some way, but I didn't know how. That was what bothered me. Werewolves were born, not turned, so I didn't have to worry about going all furry the next time I got pissed off at the post office. Side note: The fullness of the moon wasn't a factor for werewolves. After their initial postpuberty transition, they could phase whenever they felt like it. Or when they got angry. Or happy. Or bored. Or when they were asleep and had a particularly wolfy dream.

I sighed, rubbing my tired eyes. I was not as familiar with werewolf sexual practices as one might think. It was natural that I overheard ladies-locker-room talk from some of the females, rumors about size and stamina and other subjects that gave the wolf-aunties reason to laugh at my red cheeks. But as pack leader and the alpha female, Maggie was adamant that there were some things I didn't need to know. And considering what her cousin Samson did let slip, that was probably best for the sake of my emotional health.

I knew that a claiming bite was part of the delicate

werewolf mating protocol. But we hadn't been naked, much less had sex, and he hadn't managed to break the skin. So surely my wicked hickey didn't count. Right?

I really didn't want to wait around for this guy to wake up so I could ask whether he'd intentionally bit me and what that meant. But there I sat, at the edge of the bed, watching him, unsure of what else to do. Should I ask him if I could ride with him to the next thing resembling civilization? Did I want to stay with him? I mean, he'd almost bitten me. And he had people shooting at him, which didn't say much for him in terms of character. If I were smart, I would creep quietly out of the room and be on my way.

But I just couldn't. Before I left, I needed to make sure he was going to be OK. I felt responsible for him. Somehow, I'd fallen into pack thinking, without the actual werewolf genes or the cool superpowers. I had gotten the short end of the T-bone on this deal.

And on top of everything else, I was starving. I hadn't eaten since lunch the previous day. Between the cold, my low BMI, and whatever fresh hell the road was going to throw at me that day, I needed calories desperately. I considered the turkey jerky, which was the least weird, compared to the alligator, ostrich, and venison. But I didn't think my roommate would appreciate waking up to find me rifling through his bag, stealing his preserved meat. I considered driving closer to town to see if I could find a diner or something. But he definitely wouldn't appreciate waking up to find that his truck was missing, either. I was still contemplating grand theft auto versus exotic jerky when his eyes fluttered open, slowly taking in the room. With a jerk, he rolled off the bed to his feet. He seemed to be searching the room. And when his eyes settled on me, the searching stopped.

He stared at me, as if trying to jog his memory. His nostrils flared, and he seemed to recognize something. His eyes narrowed.

Damn it.

"Hi. I was there last night when you were, um . . . well, I got you here and cleaned you up." I hitched my bag over my shoulder and made for the door. "Room's paid up till eleven. Good luck."

He was at the door before I could blink. "*Ack!*" I cried, hating the way I cringed against the door, arms curved protectively over my head. With his head cocked to the side, he curled his fingers around my wrists and pulled them down. I nearly yanked them back, but his hands were gentle. He ran the tip of his nose along my hairline.

"L-look, you can check your bag, I didn't take anything," I stammered.

He moved closer, inhaling deeply while his fingers traced over the mark on my neck. And there was that weird purring noise again.

Right, pretend ignorance of werewolves and their near-bite-y tendencies. Avoid explanations of why you know about the existence of werewolves. Those conversations could only lead to bad places.

"If this is about the shooting . . . I won't tell anybody. I don't even know who would believe me."

He nuzzled his cheek against my temple. "Mine. You stay with me."

I arched an eyebrow. "Beg pardon?"

His eyes were all spacey and bleary as he murmured, "You stay with me."

"I don't stay with anybody," I told him. "I'm leaving."

His fingers curled around my arms, and he pulled me close, trailing his nose along my hairline and caressing the spot where he'd tried to bite me. "No."

"Hey!" I pulled at his grip, but damn it, this guy was strong. My hand snaked into my purse for the slapjack I carried, thin layers of leather surrounding a heavy lead ball that hurt like hell when it connected with a sensitive joint. "Let go of me."

"No."

"Stop now!" I said in the most commanding tone I could muster. Shoving him away from my body, I brought the heavy weight of the slapjack down on the wrist that held my arm. And I stomped on his foot, hard.

"Ow!" he yelped. He seemed to come back to himself, his pupils were less constricted. He blinked a few times and cleared his threat. "Ow," he said again, almost absentmindedly, rubbing his wrist. "Who are you?"

"Anne McCaffrey," I blurted out, hoping that he didn't spend a lot of time reading carefully crafted science fiction. His realizing I'd just used my favorite author as an alias would prove . . . awkward. The werewolf frowned at me, as if he could sense the lie, but before he could comment, I added, "I helped you out last night when you were hurt. And now I would like you to back away from me very slowly, so I can open the door and get the hell out of here."

Where was I going? I had no clue. More important, I had no vehicle. But it had to be safer than hanging around werewolf shooting victims with toothy tendencies.

His glance shot down to the slapjack in my hand, and he took a careful, small step back. "That was you?"

"Yes."

"Who are you?"

"I thought we covered this. Did you bump your head?"

"What were you doing in the parking lot last night?" he demanded.

"What does it matter? I bandaged you up, borrowed your shirt. I figure that makes us even. So I'm going to be on my way."

"No," he said, shaking his head and clamping his hand around my arm. "I owe you. You stay with me."

"Well, it's lovely that you've moved on to using definitive sentences, but I think you'll find that you are not, in fact, the boss of me. Now, let go of my arm, or I reintroduce you to Mr. Slappy." I waved the slapjack in his face. A guilty expression slipped across his features, and his fingers loosened their hold.

He scrubbed his hand over the respectable growth of stubble on his cheeks. "Look, I'm sorry. This is all a little too much for first thing in the morning with no coffee and a gunshot wound."

I glanced down to his middle, which he didn't seem to be babying all that much. He'd had a few hours for his tissues to knit themselves back together. But the stupid ingrained medical training had me blowing a long breath from my nose as I asked, "Are you in pain?"

He rubbed his hand over the gauze absently. "It's fine, no big deal."

"Being shot is no big deal?" Before he could stop me, I was peeling the bandage back from his skin, making him yowl as the adhesive caught tiny dark hairs of the little happy trail down his stomach.

"Ow!" he exclaimed as I attempted to examine him. He batted my hands away.

"Oh, don't be such a baby. I just want to make sure you're OK."

"I'm fine," he grumbled, pressing the bandage back into place and angling his wounded side away from me. He didn't want me inspecting his wound, I realized. He didn't want me to see that it was now fully healed, barely distinct from the rest of his skin. Because he wasn't sure how much I knew about the whole werewolf thing, and he didn't want me getting extra clues.

Right. This was my cue to exit, before he could pull me into some other bizarre werewolf bullshit or vice versa. "OK, then, well, if you're feeling all right, I'll just toddle along."

I had just managed to get the door open when he yanked it closed again.

I glared up at him. "This is becoming really annoying."

"Where are you going?" he asked.

I wanted to keep that information to myself, to be able to walk away from this situation feeling some dignity about the way I'd handled myself. Also, he just wasn't entitled to know. So all I said was "South."

He smiled. "Just 'south'?"

"Southern *Alaska*," I added.

"Thank you for clarifying. And what a coincidence. I was heading that way myself."

I deadpanned, "You don't say."

"I do say." He gave me a sharp nod, as if this was exactly according to some crazy, half-naked military plan he had tucked away somewhere. "So . . . Anne, you're staying with me."

My mouth fell open, and I made an indelicate snorting noise. "Why on earth would I do that?"

"Look, you're pretty, you're fun-sized, and you're up here on your own," he said, ticking my offenses off on his long fingers. "It's not safe."

"Really? Not safe? Like I could be minding my own business and then suddenly get pulled into a gunfight and car explosions by a total stranger? I don't think that will happen more than once. And I definitely don't need anyone to take care of me."

He scoffed, that mocking white grin splitting his tanned face. "No, you seem to be fine on your own. Working a shitty job in a grocery store in the middle of nowhere. That's the sweet life, all right."

My cheeks flushed hot. "Screw you, pal."

"It's Caleb."

"Screw you, Caleb." It was a struggle, resisting the urge to kick him in the shins. It really was.

"Do you have a better plan? Or *any* plan?" he demanded. "What's the first thing you're going to do when you walk out that door? Hitchhike, right? You'll be lucky if one or two trucks pass this way, this time of day. And you never know what sort of psycho could be behind the wheel. With me, at least you know what you're getting into."

"Yeah, I'm getting a condescending he-man who sniffs me."

And attempts to bite me while sleep-snuggling.

"Well, you smell nice," he said, shrugging as if that excused the scratch-and-sniffery. When I didn't respond to his "charm" with the expected giggling and swooning, he sighed. "Just let me make sure you're safe, OK? I have to do some driving for work. You might find another town you like, find someplace to stay. Until then, I can keep an eye on you, repay you for saving my life. Do you think you're going to get a better offer from a random trucker?"

I glared up at him and didn't answer.

"Besides, who knows what could happen to me with this nearly mortal wound I've suffered?" he said, gesturing dramatically to his bandage.

I leveled a disbelieving gaze at him through my eyelashes. "The mortal wound that was 'no big deal' just a little while ago?"

"I could lose consciousness or develop an infection, maybe even get shot again without someone watching my back. You don't want that on your conscience, do you?" Caleb's beatific smile was too well rehearsed to be genuine.

I pursed my lips, considering the pros and cons of this insane situation. Maybe I was being unfair to Caleb. Other than their astronomical caloric intake and their propensity for public nudity, werewolves were just regular people. They were nice, for the most part,

with the exception of the psychotic, power-hungry ass-
holes who occasionally staged coups to take over neigh-
boring packs.

Happened more often than you might think.

Caleb didn't strike me as a psychotic asshole. So
far, he hadn't lied to me. He hadn't hurt me, intentionally. And even when he'd invaded my personal
space, I hadn't panicked or felt threatened, and that
was saying something. I had the distinct impression
that if Caleb told me he would keep me safe, I would
be safe. And safety was tempting, too tempting, as
I considered how long it would take me to come up
with a plan to get to Anchorage with no money and
no car.

"OK. But if we're going to do this, you're going to
have to stop that," I told him.

"What?"

"That!" I said, shrugging off his hands, which had
been absently running up and down my arms. "The
touching and the sniffing and the . . . nuzzling. That
stops, right now."

"But what if you want me to nuzzle you?" he asked,
his voice returning to that gruff, husky tenor from the
night before. And I felt my knees sag a little bit.

Damn it. "I won't."

He stepped a little closer. I pressed back against the
door. "What if you ask me to?"

"If I say the words, 'Caleb, please nuzzle me,' you
can do your worst."

"All right, then." He grinned at me again in a way
that can only be described as "happy puppy" and loped

away toward the bathroom. I wandered to the bed and dropped to it, dazed.

What the hell just happened?

Now that I could get a good look at Caleb's truck in the daylight, I could appreciate the serviceable vehicle. While the exterior red paint was pristine, the inside showed the wear and tear of a lot of time on the road. The passenger-side floorboard was littered with meat snack packets and foam coffee cups. And while Caleb had managed not to bleed on the cushy gray upholstery, the dash was covered in gas receipts and dust. I hadn't noticed any of that the night before, but it's amazing what you can overlook when someone has a bleeding gut wound.

After my nuzzle embargo, Caleb gave me a pretty roomy space bubble on the ride into town. The only time he even reached across the center line dividing the front seat was to hand me some peanut butter crackers he had stashed in the console.

"So, no bullshit, what's your real name?"

I frowned at him and repeated myself. "Anne Mc-Caffrey."

"I said no bullshit." My mouth dropped open, and he smirked. "Trust me, I'm familiar with faked names. Besides, you think you're the only person who's stepped inside a bookstore? Now, what's your name?"

I sighed. There was no sense in trying to continue the lie. Frankly, it was embarrassing to be caught. Just my luck to have found the only male werewolf to have read *The Dragonriders of Pern*. It was worth a shot, but I'd gotten used to answering to Anna, anyway. "It *is* Anna."

He pressed a little bit more. "Anna what?"

"All you need to know is that you should call me Anna," I told him.

He frowned, looking more hurt than irritated, but obviously decided to drop the subject. "So you didn't answer my questions before. Where you from?" he asked as I tried hard to refrain from shoving the crackers into my mouth like a carb-lover on her cheat day.

"Around," I said, barely containing the cracker bits from spewing out of my mouth. I was, as Maggie was prone to saying, a delicate flower.

"Where?" he persisted.

"Illinois, Ohio, Kansas, Texas, Nevada, Idaho, Oregon." Let's just say it was a long and winding road from leaving my marriage to arriving in Alaska. "I don't like to be tied down to one place for too long. I like to explore my options."

"As a grocery checker?" He snorted.

I stared up at him. That was the second time he'd referred to my job at Emerson's. How the hell did he know about that? It wasn't as if I'd introduced myself to him as a grocery checker/impromptu medical professional. My hand crept along the door, fingers curling around the handle. Because doing a *Charlie's Angels* roll out of a truck onto the highway was an *awesome* idea. And just then, my bloodied Emerson's Dry Goods apron caught my eye.

Oh. Right. He was capable of picking up visual cues.

Feeling very foolish for my paranoia, I countered,

"Grocery checker, dog shampooer, waitress. You got a problem with that?"

"I have no problem with grocery checkers or waitresses," he assured me, smiling cheekily. "As long as they remember the ketchup. "

"I'm guessing you get your food spit in a lot."

"I guess you were getting off of work last night, and that's why you happened by my, uh, discussion with Marty?"

I nodded and glanced sideways at him. "So what are you?" His brow creased, and he stared at me, as if he was trying to find some hidden meaning in the question. "What do you do for a living? Given the number of jerky wrappers and to-go cups on the floorboards, I'm guessing you spend a lot of time in this truck."

"Have you met any other people like me?" he asked, still eyeing me carefully.

"Is there a reason you're answering my questions with completely unrelated questions?" I asked.

"I'm trying to keep some mystery about me," he said, his tone flat.

I crossed my arms over my chest, harrumphing as we reached the main drag of Sharpton. Caleb's big red truck caught the attention of the handful of shopkeepers opening their doors for the day, making them stop and stare after us as we drove by. Everyone knew everyone in little settlements like these. New people attracted a lot of attention. And longtime locals were n't particularly friendly to "outsiders." But for the most part, they were strong little communities. Neighbors relied on one another for resources and entertainment, particularly during the long winters. Beyond my medical skills, I had been highly valuable to the pack for my ability to make homemade caramel corn. Werewolves loved caramel corn. It was the only way to make the Gilbert boys take their flu shots without biting me.

We pulled into the parking lot of a diner that looked halfway reputable. As the truck slowed, I heard something, probably one of the dozen or so ChapSticks I kept in my bag, roll under the seat into the back of the cab.

"I'll get us a booth," Caleb told me as I shoved the seat forward. Peering under the front seat, I felt along the hard plastic edge for my errant lip balm, but instead, my fingers closed over a strange metallic curved object tucked into a groove under the seat.

"What the—?" I pulled it out into the light. Handcuffs. I felt under the seat again and found plastic zip ties, a collapsible metal police baton, duct tape, and rope, all Velcroed to the bottom of the seat. And now that I looked at the back of the front seat, I realized that there was a collapsible metal grate attached to it, the kind that cops had in their squad cars to keep suspects contained in the back.

I dropped my bag, backing away. This guy had a serial killer's tool kit in the back of his truck.

A strange sense of betrayal bloomed, astringent and bitter, in my chest. For a moment, I'd let myself believe in this guy. I'd wanted to trust in that promise of safety, in the prospect of being able to relax into familiar wolfy territory for just a few days, to feel that I wasn't alone. The fact that I'd wanted it so badly, so quickly, scared me even more than the possible uses for three sets of adjustable bungee cords.

I scanned the front window of the diner. Caleb was already sitting in a booth. If I just slipped away, he probably wouldn't notice for a while that I hadn't followed him in. There was a bar up the main street. Maybe I could hitch a ride with someone there. I hadn't done that in a while, and obviously, my self-preservation skills were pretty rusty. But I guessed the devil you didn't know would likely be safer than the devil you knew had freaking duct tape and cuffs in his truck.

I had to admit the collapsible baton was cool. I supposed it was much more effective than my slapjack, not to mention having a better reach. And I rationalized that if I took it, he wouldn't be using it on unsuspecting hitchhikers. I palmed it and dropped it into my bag.

Slinging that bag over my shoulders, I glanced back at the diner window but didn't see Caleb. I backed away from the truck and—

"*Ack!*" I shouted, jumping out of my skin and cursing myself for not keeping the baton handy. No matter how much time I'd spent around them, it was always shocking to me that big, bulky werewolves could move so quietly.

While his tone was friendly, his posture was tense. He frowned down at me. "Just wanted to see what was taking so long. You OK?"

"I think this is a mistake," I said, my fingers frantically searching through my bag for the slapjack. I stepped away from him, putting the open truck door between us. His brow furrowed, and he took a step toward me. I stepped farther away, onto the sidewalk.

"What's a mistake?" he asked.

"This whole 'riding together' idea. I'll be fine on my own, really. Thanks for getting me this far, though." I turned, taking brisk, long steps up the sidewalk. He stood, staring at me, perplexed. "Good luck . . . with your whole Ted Bundy thing," I muttered softly as I rushed away.

In a blink, Caleb was in front of me, holding my arms against my sides. "What did you mean by that?"

Great, I forgot that my new best friend had an advanced serial-killer kit *and* superhuman hearing. Oh, and healing powers. I was one lucky girl.

"What did you mean?" he demanded. His eyes followed mine back to the open truck door and the cuffs and zip ties lying out on his floorboards.

"What normal person rolls with this sort of thing in his backseat, Caleb?"

"There's a good explanation for this."

"I'm sure there is. I just don't care," I retorted.

"Look, come inside, have some breakfast with me, and I'll explain. If you still think I'm a serial killer afterward, I'll pay the check, and you can stay here at the motel until you figure out what you want to do."

I shrugged. "OK."

"Great, let's go inside," he said.

"I wasn't serious!" I exclaimed. "How stupid do you think I am?"

"Look, what's the harm in having breakfast?" he chided. And he added, "With plenty of witnesses."

I might have objected that I was fine, not hungry in the slightest. But then my traitorous empty stomach growled, as if on cue.

He smirked at me. "I bet this place has great pancakes."

I growled in frustration, my shoulders sagged, and I let him nudge me through the front door of the diner. There was a chubby middle-aged man cooking in the kitchen and a bored-looking teenage girl taking orders. Two burly men in plaid flannel sat at the counter, quietly eating steak and eggs. No one, including the teenager, bothered to look up when we walked in.

I might have been embarrassed by my nervous habit of cataloguing each new room's occupants, but Caleb was equally funny about the seating arrangements. He insisted on a booth by the front window, but he seemed uncomfortable sitting with his back to the door. His safety concerns didn't exactly increase my trust in him. And despite the fact that I needed the restroom with increasing urgency, I didn't want to leave him unattended around my food or drink. He was paying for my French toast, but that didn't entitle him to mickey my OJ.

The food arrived without fanfare from the apathetic teen queen. Caleb's breakfast consisted of six strips of bacon, sausage, a bloody steak, scrambled eggs, and three pancakes, which I watched him devour with a fascination I used to reserve for *Shark Week*.

"OK, we're eating, you're paying, now spill," I said around a mouthful of maple-soaked fried bread. "What's with the hardware?"

He looked a bit sheepish, chewing his pancake thoughtfully while he chose his words. "I'm a sort of bounty hunter," he said. "I track people down, people who don't want to be found. I take them in, collect the reward. Generally, they kick and spit and scream on the long drive home, so I have to restrain them. That's why I have the handcuffs and the bungee cords."

My fork practically clattered to the table as a cold weight settled into my belly. Well, that certainly explained why I hadn't seen him around the valley. He was out wandering the roads, ruining the lives of perfectly nice fugitives. A ripple of alarm skittered up my spine. I clutched the table's edge with my right hand to calm the slight tremor there. I swallowed carefully and wished I could reach for the juice without bobbling the glass. "Show me your ID."

His eyebrows rose. "What?"

"Bail bondsmen are required to carry ID with them when they make 'citizen's arrests.' Show it to me."

He cleared his throat and washed down half a pancake with some coffee. "Well, some of my collars are not quite . . ."

"Legal?" I suggested.

"Yeah," he said, looking embarrassed for a millisecond.

"Do you carry a gun?"

"No, I don't get shot at very often."

"And if that's not an endorsement for a profession, I don't know what is," I said, slowly and deliberately reaching for my juice glass. It was a miracle of concentration that held my hand steady as I sipped. Over the rim of the glass, I kept my eyes trained on his face, as if I didn't have a care in the world. Nothing to fear. Nothing to send me running for the nearest exit.

"Normally, people don't get the drop on me," he said defensively. "I have a certain set of . . . skills, and they help me when I'm tracking a person. The people in my family have always been hunters. I just apply it in a different way."

I snorted. He wasn't kidding. Werewolves had supersensitive noses and ears, not to mention their intuitive ability to track whatever creature was unlucky enough to be targeted by an animal built for hunting.

But again, I was supposed to be playing dumb. Because if I blurted out, *Yeah, I know about the whole werewolf thing that is supposed to be forbidden knowledge for a human such as myself*, there would be a lot of awkward questions. More awkward than the ones currently being bandied across the table, anyway.

"I make a lot of money at something I'm good at. No questions asked, as long as someone is willing to pay me my fee. And sometimes all I have to do is get a little information and pass it along. I like those jobs. Easy money and less time spent rooting around in parking lots."

His conversation with the guy who shot him made so much more sense now. This Marty guy had been afraid that Caleb was taking him in on money he owed, so he freaked out and started shooting. I did not need this. I did not need to hitch myself to any form of law enforcement, no matter how slipshod. Glenn had contacts in more places than I'd ever imagined—old college buddies, online gaming clubbers, and sketchy cousins I hadn't been allowed to speak to at the wedding reception. And all it would take was a couple of opportune Google searches for Caleb to find the online message boards where Glenn had put out feelers for me.

I didn't think Caleb would have any qualms about handing me over to my ex, "no questions asked." Even the way he phrased it gave me chills. He sounded so cold, so calculated, so like—

Never mind! Get out! My brain screamed at me. *Get away!* The ladies' room was to the immediate left of the door, offset by a small hallway. So feigning a bladder issue and sneaking out the front wouldn't work. There was probably another exit in the back, through the kitchen, and a fire exit, but both were in Caleb's line of sight. I willed my face to relax, first my jaw and then my cheeks, so I could speak without looking tense. I took a casual bite of my bacon.

"How do you get your assignments? How do people know how to get ahold of you?" I asked. I leaned forward, resting my chin on my hand as if he had my rapt attention. I glanced behind him. Maybe there was another way out off of the restroom area. These places always had fire exits, but I couldn't risk setting off some alarm.

"A buddy of mine owns a bar about an hour outside Fairbanks. If people want to get ahold of me, they know to call me there. And I have contacts of my own in Anchorage, Portland, Seattle. Mostly PIs who don't want to make the trip up here. They get a finder's fee for hiring me," he said.

"And you just bounce around on the road?" I asked, swiping the last bite of French toast through the golden puddle of syrup on my plate. I savored the crisp edges of the fried bread, unsure when I'd be able to get another nice, hot meal.

"Sometimes I head home to see my family. But I haven't been there in a while. They live in the Crescent Valley near Grundy, very tight-knit."

That explained why I'd never met him. He hadn't been to the valley for years. I'd heard stories about a Caleb from Maggie, strange "stupid criminal" tales from her cousin the bounty hunter, who hadn't come back home since his dad, Artie, had died of stroke complications shortly before I was hired on. The funeral service had been held just after I'd arrived, while I was off restocking the clinic's medications and supplies. I was still so pale and shaky and skittish that Eli, the former pack leader, insisted on sending one of the distant pack cousins with me on the supply run. I only realized later that it was because he was afraid I would take off and not come back. I remembered now that Artie's son left town before I returned two days later, and that had upset some of the older aunties.

Still, I wondered how Caleb managed to stay away from the valley for so long. Maggie's brother, Cooper, had exiled himself for a while after a particularly violent interpack confrontation, and the separation nearly drove him insane. How could Caleb stand it?

Not that I could afford to care about that sort of thing, since I was contemplating escaping from this booth and bursting through the front window of the diner like something out of a *Die Hard* movie. While his being a part of Maggie's pack was a pleasant surprise, that didn't necessarily make Caleb a good person. As evidenced by Eli, the interim alpha who hired me just before going on a hiker-killing spree and framing Maggie's brother, Cooper, for the maulings. Werewolves hit a lot of different points on the spectrum between "awesome guy who is occasionally an apex predator" and "furry Lord Voldemort."

"So how about you?" he asked, forking up another massive bite of steak. "What's a nice girl like you doing bouncing around the Great North?"

I gave him a bland smile. "I wanted to see more of the country."

His being part of Maggie's pack didn't make me trust Caleb any more than I had before. I'd made a clean break with them and couldn't let on that I knew his family. They couldn't know where I was or where I was heading. It was safer for them and for me. Also, I was pretty sure Maggie would kick my ass for leaving the way I did. She was a stickler about policy and procedure.

"And why are you traveling south?" he asked. "Getting too cold for you?"

"I'm meeting up with a friend," I lied smoothly.

Caleb tensed. "What sort of friend?"

"An old roommate, Cindy," I said.

The tension drained out of Caleb's frame, and he scooped up another bite. "Well, that's nice. But you never know what could happen."

I arched an eyebrow. "What do you mean?"

"Well, plans change sometimes," he said vaguely.

What did he mean by that? Was he going to change my plans for me? Under the table, my hand instinctively wrapped around my shoulder bag. I considered the ladies' room again. I couldn't remember seeing bathroom windows on the front of the building. Did that mean they opened at the sides?

He laughed. "So do you believe that I'm not, in fact, a serial killer?"

I kept my face neutral. No, he was something much more dangerous. And I had a sneaking suspicion he was probably quite good at his job.

I smiled blandly. "I'm almost convinced." I stood and hooked my shoulder bag over my arm.

He scowled. "Where are you going?"

"The ladies' room? I've had three glasses of juice."

He gave me an apologetic little shrug, although he eyed my purse with suspicion. I turned on my heel and walked as casually as I could through the dingy restroom door. Swearing mental apologies to any other girls in the dining room, I shoved the rubber wedge stopper under the door until it couldn't be budged.

The bathroom was a pink-tiled one-seater with a crank window just over the toilet. I stood on the seat, trying to gauge whether my shoulders would fit through. Glancing outside at the unkempt little side yard between the diner and the garage next door, I turned the window crank. Given the ungodly squealing noise it made, I guessed that it hadn't been used in a while. Cringing, I glanced over my shoulder, waiting for the sound of Caleb the bounty hunter approaching the door.

I turned the crank again, and it gave a bit, lifting the

window slowly. After a few turns, it was open just wide enough that I could squeeze my head through. After giving it one last rotation for good luck, I zipped my shoulder bag and tossed it through. I carefully stepped on top of the toilet tank, praying it would support my weight while I slithered through the opening.

I told myself it was a game, a claustrophobic version of limbo. How small could I go? Contracting my body into the most aerodynamic shape possible, I slipped my hand into the cool morning air. My head and shoulders slid out easily, but my stomach and hips caught sideways on the ledge, stealing my breath.

"Stupid French toast!" I muttered, wiggling myself free.

I looked down and realized I was a good five feet off the dirt, head down, with no clue how to land safely.

"This was a stupid plan," I told myself, gritting my teeth against the pressure on my middle, debating if taking my chances with Caleb would have been a better option than giving myself a traumatic brain injury involving a toilet.

Suddenly, my hips worked loose, and I free-fell. I shoved my hands over my head as I flailed my legs. My ankle caught against the sill on the way down, slowing my descent, so I was able to flop down on my back instead of face-planting.

"Stupid, stupid plan." I huffed, struggling against gravity and my lackluster upper-body strength. "Stupid gravity."

"Is there a reason you're hanging out of the bathroom window by your feet?" Caleb asked wryly.

"Dang it!" I cried as my feet lost their tenuous hold against the windowsill.

I dropped, rolling my shoulder against the asphalt and landing with an *uhf*. In a few seconds, Caleb was lifting me by my underarms, my feet barely brushing the ground.

"Well, this is embarrassing," I grumbled, twisting out of his grip.

Reluctantly, he dropped me to the asphalt, and I yanked my rumpled clothes back into place. "What were you doing?"

"If you have to ask, you're probably not a very good bounty hunter," I retorted, with far more dignity than I deserved, given the whole hanging-upside-down-from-a-bathroom-window thing.

"Why the hell would you run from me?" he asked, sounding genuinely insulted. "I thought I'd made myself clear that I am not and don't plan to be a serial killer."

"I don't trust you. I thought I'd made *myself* clear about that."

"Why wouldn't you trust me?"

"I don't know you," I shot back.

"Well, you didn't know me last night when you drove me away from a crime scene and doctored me up. What's different this morning? I just want to help you the way you helped me."

"Why is it so important to you to help me? You don't even know me."

"Well, you helped me, didn't you?" he countered. "I mean, I was hurt. It didn't turn out to be as bad as you thought it was, but without you fixing me up, I would have been pretty bad off . . . right?"

His voice sounded strained, as if it was important that I believed him.

Caleb cleared his throat, interrupting my mental telemarketing tangent. "Look, you need a ride south. I am heading in that direction. I need to make a few stops along the way. I just want to know that you get there OK. In the last twenty-four hours, you've dodged a random shooting and slithered through a bathroom window for no reason. You need someone to watch out for you." I arched an eyebrow, prompting him to add, "And maybe you can watch my back, too."

I pursed my lips, considering exactly what watching Caleb's back could entail. I would imagine it involved more than just staring at his jean-clad butt, as tempting as that prospect was. His offer would solve my selling-organs-to-obtain-transportation issue. I liked my organs where they were, so this was a much more attractive option. "What does 'eventually' mean?" I asked.

He shrugged. "Just a few stops."

I brushed the gravel from my jeans, considering. All of the reasons I ran from Caleb at the diner were still very valid. And he clearly knew I didn't trust him, which had weakened that polite façade we had going for that brief morning interlude. But he was part of Maggie's pack. Every story I'd ever heard about "Cousin Caleb" had involved his honesty and all-around good-guy-ness. On the other hand, he could still be just as ruthless and cash-hungry as his job self-description implied . . .

Oh, screw it, it's not like I have a better choice. I was in the middle of nowhere, without transportation, money, or supplies. I was up shit creek without a paddle. I didn't even have a canoe at this point. But I'd be darned if I was going to admit that.

"Fine." I sighed, gesturing toward the parking lot.

"Are you going to be this excited about everything?" Caleb asked as he hitched my bag over his shoulder and we ambled toward the truck.

"I *can* drive, you know," I told him as he climbed in. "Obviously, not when I'm in exhaustion-related hysterics, but we could switch off, to make it easier on you."

He leaned across the seat to open my door, informing me solemnly, "No one drives my truck but me."

"Well, you didn't seem to mind when I was hauling your ass away from explosions and gunfire," I muttered, slamming the passenger door.

"Special circumstances."

I gave him a weak glare while nudging his bag of law-enforcement equipment with my foot. "Do I get to play with your big bag of toys?"

"No, you do not." I crossed my arms over my chest and frowned, so he added, "But you can keep the baton, as a gesture of good faith."

"You noticed I took it, huh?"

I would have described the over-the-sunglasses eye roll he sent me as a "bitch, please" gesture, but so far, he didn't strike me as the type of guy to use that sort of facial-expression language, so . . . I would just stick to being embarrassed at being caught so easily.

Clearly, I needed to brush up on my sleight of hand.

"Someone looking for you?"

"None of your business."

He rolled his eyes, but continued as if I hadn't answered. "Do you want them to find you?"

I stared at him, my expression completely flat, prompting another werewolf eye roll.

"OK, then. Well, before my little detour at Flapjack's, I was on my way to scoop this guy, Jerry Stepanack, up from Flint Creek. That's about two hours from here, so you didn't cost me too much time," he said, ignoring the way I rolled my own eyes at that statement. "Jerry's none too bright, and there's a pretty healthy price on him."

"What did he do?" I asked. "And I am assuming this is not an assignment from legitimate law-enforcement authorities?"

"To answer the first question, you don't want to know, and to answer the second, you *really* don't want to know," he said. "But a word to the wise, sweetheart. If you borrow lots of money from bad people to buy a couple of tow trucks so you can steal cars and sell them for parts, don't default on the loan and sell the *trucks* for parts. It makes those bad people cranky."

I frowned, sliding my oversized sunglasses onto my nose, and settled back into the seat. "I'll try to keep that in mind."

4

All the Best Friendships Start with Lost-and-Found Underwear

It turned out Caleb's job was mostly driving around and talking on his cell phone.

I spent the first fifteen minutes of our "business arrangement" gathering the foam coffee cups and jerky packets from the floorboards and stuffing them into an empty grocery bag. Caleb insisted that I keep the gas receipts, as he needed them for expense reports, so I stacked them in the glove compartment.

Cue the wolfy eye roll.

"I just don't want to spend the next few days sitting around in filth."

The drive reminded me of why I'd fallen in love with living in Alaska in the first place. After spending so many years closing myself up into safe, cramped corners, the wide-open spaces were a welcome remedy to my growing claustrophobia. I loved the crazy patchwork of foliage across the landscape, the expected greens mixed with a riot of purples, golds, and grays. All of this would be buried under a dense blanket of blinding white in a few weeks, but even that would be beautiful and welcome.

I finally got to see some of the country, now that I wasn't always on the run. Some of it looked too beautiful to be real—purple stone mountains and trees that seemed to swallow the road whole and forests so thick no light could break through the evergreens. I loved never knowing when a little town was suddenly going to pop up around a bend in the road. Caleb seemed to know this road like the back of his hand. I had the idea that if he'd driven down a road just once, he would still be able find his way back and tell you in detail what sort of rocks he'd seen by the side of the road.

I would miss this landscape. I didn't know where my new identity would take me. I knew it wasn't likely that I would stay in the Great North. And the southeast was definitely out—too close to Glenn. I could only hope that I wouldn't end up in the desert somewhere. I had come to love the snow. I just couldn't handle one-hundred-plus-degree summer days and scorpions in my living room.

We wound through rolling, low-lying mountains lightly dusted with snow, the landscape laid out before us like an endless Christmas card. I wrestled with the fatigue I'd kept at bay over the last twenty-four hours. But between the warm truck, the full belly, and the late-afternoon sun beating through the window on my face, I fell asleep long before we arrived in Flint Creek.

It had been a long time since I'd simply ridden along in a car, and the exhausting events of the last few, well, years caught up with me. I still slept lightly, waking with every turn Caleb made, checking to make sure he hadn't driven us to Tijuana or taken liberties with my ChapSticks. But he hadn't even changed the radio station. He just glanced in my direction every few minutes, frowned, and then turned his attention back to the road.

Resting my forehead against the warm glass, I wondered if there would be an opportunity to send an e-mail to my Network contact, "Red-burn92@qwickmail.com." I needed to explain that my situation had deteriorated quickly and ask for a rush job on my new identity. Red-burn was pretty good about responding to e-mails within twenty-four hours, so all I had to do was come back the next day to buy more Internet time.

Although I'd never met her, Red-burn had been instrumental in my move to Alaska. She worked as part of the Network, a widespread group of people who helped women escape from abusive domestic situations, particularly when those situations involved stalking. Operating beneath the radar of law enforcement, the group arranged for new, untraceable driver's licenses, social security numbers, and birth certificates in new names, not to mention securing employment and housing. They were discreet, well funded, and frighteningly good at making people disappear.

After leaving Glenn, I'd bounced around the country for nearly a year before I heard about the Network from a fellow waitress. Red-burn was the one to connect me with the Crescent Valley job, informing me that the people in Crescent Valley, Alaska, needed a new physician, as the old Dr. Moder had retired.

I was pretty annoyed with her for failing to mention the whole werewolf issue. Of course, she didn't know about it, but still, I reserved the right to be irritated. A Dr. Moder had treated the valley's residents since before the government started insisting on all of those pesky birth and death records. In addition to dramatically shortened pregnancies and high fertility rates, were-wolves tended to die in violent, somewhat difficult-to-explain ways, such as *disagreement with a large bear while in wolf form*. Eventually, census boards and medical examiners start to pick up on those things. It was easier for the pack to have someone they could trust to file the important papers. The first Dr. Moder took the position in 1913, but when he died, his successor didn't have a strictly legal medical license, so the pack simply passed his credentials along to make it seem as if the original Dr. Moder was still working. My predecessors were like me, medical professionals who'd inadvertently ended up on the wrong side of the legal line. The name "Dr. Moder" stuck and became a tradition. (I suspected that we all shared the same degree from a medical school in the Philippines.) The Dr. Moder just before me had testified against a prescription-pill mill linked to organized crime in Miami. She'd hidden in the valley for ten years before she felt comfortable moving back to the lower forty-eight.

Red-burn was the one to convince me that I was strong enough to move so far away, to a cold, alien place where I would be isolated from anything I knew. She was the one who called me the night before my cross-country drive and told me not to be a wuss. Redburn believed in tough love. She told me about her own past abuse. Although she was happily married to a much nicer guy, she still regretted that she hadn't been brave enough to leave on her own terms. So now she helped other people escape their bad relationships and felt as if she was taking some of her power back, bit by bit. She was funny and sweet, but she brooked no bullshit. She insisted that I do half the work to get myself moving, telling me I wouldn't appreciate my safety without a little effort.

Then again, it was Red-burn who had sent me the e-mail warning me that there had been a not-elaborated-upon but still quite scary "development" with my ex-husband. She said it was time to pull my "escape hatch," my preplanned departure route that we had put in place before I even moved to the valley, while she worked on establishing a new place for me. That did secure some of my loyalty.

And run I did, *tout de suite*. I took my truck, which technically belonged to the village, and drove it as far as Grundy. I left it in the care of Nate Gogan, the town lawyer, whom I could trust to get it back to Maggie, and I tricked him into accepting twenty dollars for his trouble and gas money, which officially earned me attorney-client privilege and kept him from giving Maggie any details. I hitched a ride to Dearly with Evie, who had to make her weekly run for supplies. I gave her some excuse about needing to pick up some prescriptions and then disappeared through a side door of the pharmacy. I walked to the nearest used-car lot and plunked down seven hundred dollars for my poor departed Pinto. Of course, if I'd known I was buying an extremely expensive incendiary device, I might have upgraded to a Camry.

I drove as far as I could trust the Pinto to take me, camping out in McClusky and getting the job at Emerson's while I waited for Red-burn to come up with a new identity for me. I shivered, tucking the collar of my coat closer to my chin. Although it was early autumn, the first hard frost wasn't too far off. And that meant winter, with its rural-road-crippling snows and blood-freezing temperatures, was nipping at my heels. In the valley and the nearby town of Grundy, the first frost meant a big party to celebrate the last opportunity the locals would have to see one another socially before the snows set in and isolated them in their homes. Now it meant I had precious few weeks to get my butt to Anchorage and then haul ass across the state to wherever the Network had established a place for me. There were definitely times I despaired having to travel relatively close to the valley after "pulling my escape hatch" and running all the way east, but Anchorage was my checkpoint and that's where I would go.

I would miss this. I would miss living in my cozy little house on the edge of the valley. I would miss the thrill of first snows of the season and the relief of the spring thaw. I would miss the irreverent, unpretentious humor of the pack members. I would miss the magic of watching people I shared a post office with shifting from two legs to four and back.

No, I thought, practically whacking myself on my nose with an imaginary newspaper. *No reminiscing.* None of this mattered. I'd left the pack to protect them, not so much from Glenn's violence—that hadn't come until the end of our marriage—but from his intrusion.

If he wanted to, Glenn could make life for Maggie's pack very difficult. He could compromise the pack's municipal bank accounts, causing the community considerable hardship. He could go to the authorities and raise all sorts of questions about "Dr. Moder" and how someone with the same credentials had managed to practice in the valley for so many years, essentially preventing the pack from getting medical treatment. He could call attention to discrepancies in the pack's birth and death records. He could point out the number of mysterious disappearances involving drug dealers and other undesirables who wandered too close to the pack's territory. He could put the pack's secret in serious jeopardy. And after everything the pack had done for me, I simply would not allow that to happen. The pack had survived for hundreds of years without exposure to humans. I wouldn't let my crazy ex-husband ruin that streak.

And if I told Maggie what I was going through, she would insist on "opening a werewolf-sized can of whoop-ass" on Glenn, and that would bring up a whole new set of problems for an alpha already stretched pretty damn thin by integrating two packs and a recent marriage. And

I certainly didn't want to complicate the pack's ability to hire a new Dr. Moder, not with so many couples from the newly merged packs expecting cubs. There were plenty of doctors out there who could take my place as Dr. Moder, doctors without my baggage. It was easier for everyone if I just removed myself from the equation.

Caleb gently jostled me awake in the late afternoon and led me stumbling into another dingy room, this time at the Flint Creek Motor Inn. I chose not to comment on the lone queen-sized bed. I was too tired to protest the possibility of spooning with Bitey McWolfPants again. Caleb practically had to tuck me into bed like a toddler, pulling off my shoes as he explained in his gravelly voice that he needed to talk to some local contacts about Jerry. I stayed up long enough to lock the door behind him and promptly fell asleep again in the squeaky little motel bed.

It was the dream of my darling former husband that woke me up, the dream of him breaking down my motel-room door. I was screaming and screaming for help, but no sound was coming out as he dragged me away. I sat up, making a strangled whimper, clawing at the imagined hands at my throat.

I sprang out of bed into the dark, empty room. I blew out a breath and pushed my hands through my short, snaggled hair, then padded to the door to check the lock again. I shook my head and wondered whether I was going to be waking up like that for the rest of my life. But I still double-checked the bolt.

Better safe than sorry.

I crawled back into bed, pulling the covers up to my chin. How had I sunk to trusting my security to a cut-rate dead bolt? I used to be a pretty nice girl, back when I was Tina Campbell-Bishop, M *dramatic pause* D. I had everything. A nice husband. A nice home. A promising career. And I walked—well, ran—away from all of it. All the things I took for granted when I was growing up, such as feeling safe, having an indoor place to sleep and food on the table, people being polite and taking notice of me—I lost them somewhere along the way. I got harder, meaner. Rather than looking at people as human beings whom I might be able to help, I viewed them all with a calculating eye, analyzing how they might help me or hurt me before they could even introduce themselves.

Most people can't pinpoint the exact moment when everything in their life goes to shit. I consider myself lucky to have such a definite timeline, so that if I were ever given the opportunity to travel through time, I could hop into the DeLorean, drive directly to April 10, 2004, walk into the break room at the hospital, and bitch-slap myself before I could meet the new technical-support hire, Glenn Bishop. But we seemed like such a good match! It was such a sensible solution to my dry spell, a string of bad dates that made me want to see someone safe for a while. And Glenn was so accommodating, easygoing. We liked the same kinds of movies, food, and, wouldn't you know it, music. We enjoyed lazy weekends and trips to the lake. He was proud of my medical career and the energy I devoted to my work.

I thought I was lucky to have fallen into a relationship with someone so easily.

I thought that's what relationships were supposed to be. My parents were married for almost forty years before they died, and in all that time, I couldn't remember them fighting. They didn't really argue, because they knew how to talk to each other and how to compromise. I thought that was what I'd found with Glenn. He was sweet and attentive and dependable. He was *that guy*, the guy of substance your mother told you to be on the lookout for, just in case he came along.

Being with Glenn was always the easy part. The hard part was spending time with anyone else. Glenn was slight, bookish, and shy, which I sort of liked. It was a nice switch from the alpha-male types I normally went out with, burly, athletic types with dozens of friends and interests I had to compete with for attention. It was lovely to be able to have a conversation with a man without him eyeing the waitress or spotting someone across the restaurant he wanted to speak to, leaving me to fiddle with breadsticks for ten minutes while he bro-hugged some guy from his intramural basketball league.

The problem was that Glenn's shyness became my issue. He had no trouble spending hours online gaming or chatting with total strangers, but he didn't want to go to my work functions or casual drinks with my coworkers. He spent too much time around my colleagues anyway, he said, and my colleagues got enough of my precious time. Before I realized what was happening, Glenn slowly but surely made it more difficult for me to maintain friendships. He pouted when

I wanted to go out with the girls, saying he never got to spend time with me. He even hid my car keys a few times so I couldn't leave, all the while claiming it was just a "joke" he was forced to play because he loved me so much.

Of course, I couldn't tell my friends, "Glenn doesn't want me to spend time with you," because that made it sound so unseemly and controlling. So when I retreated from those relationships, my friends thought it was my choice. I was one of those women who can't maintain friendships after they get into a relationship. I was a *Cosmo* cautionary tale, in more ways than one.

As time went on, a lot of Glenn's problems became my problems. We'd committed to each other, moved in together. It seemed petty and shortsighted to leave my fiancé because he was a little needy. His demands grew so incrementally that I didn't see how unreasonable they were becoming. If I loved him, I'd dress a bit more feminine, keep my hair long, cook the things he liked, enjoy staying home on the weekends the way he did. If I loved him, I would keep my personal cell phone on me at all times, even though it was against hospital policy. I would ignore the "accidents" I seemed to have whenever Glenn was angry with me, like tripping over his feet after an argument about rent and smacking my head against the coffee table. I would pass up the big white wedding debacle and get married on a beach in the Caribbean, which is what we did, one not-so-special weekend when I came home to find Glenn holding the plane tickets. I was the proverbial frog in the pot of slowly boiling water, dying by degrees.

And then, there were the family "issues." I was an only child, a late-in-life miracle for my lovely, rational parents. We'd shared a close, slightly unorthodox relationship, as my parents tended to treat me more like a small adult colleague than a child. I'd been disappointed that Glenn wasn't interested in spending time with them. My parents didn't like him, he claimed. My father made him feel as if he was being interrogated for the entire visit, and my mother was too clingy with me. He caused huge fights right before we were supposed to go to family events, so that either we would skip them, or I would end up fighting off tears for most of the night, sparking tension and uncomfortable questions from my parents. It ended up being easier to tell my mother that we had other plans or that I was working. While he was mollified by my efforts to "focus on us," he grumbled that he didn't understand why I wanted to go see my parents so often anyway.

I tried to tell myself it would take time for Glenn to warm to my parents. But then Mom was diagnosed with advanced pancreatic cancer about two years after our wedding and passed away within six months. Dad never quite recovered from the shock, passing in his sleep a year later. I would always regret missing those last Christmases and birthdays with them. And while I couldn't blame Glenn for my failure to protect my time with my parents, I could blame him for expecting me to bounce back from their deaths as if they were just an inconvenience.

At first, I stayed because I was afraid to admit, even to myself, that my marriage was such a mistake. I didn't love Glenn. He'd strangled any love I'd felt for him with his insecurities and his manipulations. But I was a successful doctor, on my way up the ladder at a major Nashville medical center. Marriages that lasted less than one presidential term were not supposed to happen to women like me. I was ashamed and embarrassed and every other word that expressed world-shaking regret. When Glenn started talking about having children of our own, instead of going all warm and tender at the idea of starting a family, I panicked. I knew I couldn't be tied to him in that way for the rest of my life. So I made a clean break.

With my parents gone and my friendships damaged, nothing prevented me from moving across the country. I didn't have enough evidence for a restraining order, so I elected just to disappear. I used computers at the public library to find a new job at a hospital in Tampa and used what was left of my inheritance to set up an apartment there. I filed divorce papers and moved out before Glenn could make it home from a late-night department meeting. I used my own name to start my new life but thought I was being smart by listing a post-office box on bills and accounts. I hoped Glenn would just move on, get bored, find someone else.

As usual, I'd underestimated him. He hacked into my e-mail accounts, no matter how many times I changed the address or password. I had to change my credit-card information and post-office box three times after he managed to buy some nice Jet Skis, a flat-screen TV, and a bass boat on my dime. When I complained to police in our hometown, he told them it was simply a predivorce credit spat and that we were working through it in family court. With me in another state, they were all too happy to let me fend for myself.

And still, I didn't realize how bad things could get. I'd made the mistake of staying in contact with old friends. They'd been so convinced by my "perfectly happy wife" act that most of them were shocked by the sudden shift. One well-meaning (read: ill-informed and utterly without boundaries) college friend gave Glenn my address, thinking I'd given up on the marriage too quickly and should give him another chance. Having followed me through the lobby of my building and through my front door, he walked right into my new apartment and broke my jaw.

I didn't know that it was possible to hurt that badly. I could barely crawl to a sitting position as Glenn ranted and raved over me.

After Glenn *let me know how much I had hurt him*, he told me to wait in the bedroom while he went to fix himself a drink. He was so convinced that I would do it, he just walked out of the room, leaving me right next to a phone, and never even considered that I would use it to call for help. That chapped my butt much later, when I was in my *analyze every moment so I can better blame myself* phase. He was so sure of his "shock and awe" campaign. He was so sure I would just cower on the carpet. It never occurred to him to take the phone with him.

It wasn't the first "accident" I'd had around Glenn, but it was the first that I couldn't treat myself afterward. I called 911, and Glenn—to my shock—stuck around.

The paramedics—to Glenn's shock—didn't accept his assertion that a fully dressed woman with dry hair fell getting out of the shower, so he was arrested on assault charges. I was a patient in my own hospital for two days, treated to pitying looks from my coworkers as I recovered from a broken jaw, several broken fingers, and internal injuries.

I knew what would happen when he was released. I'd had him arrested. To Glenn, that was unforgivable. When I went to file a restraining order, I found that he had called some online-gaming friend and given him some sob story to convince him to post bail. Glenn skipped town, without regard for his friend's bail collateral. And when I tried to file the restraining order, I found out that Glenn had been fired from the hospital months before and moved out of our apartment. Other than his birthdate, I had no information with which to file the order, which would make it difficult to serve and enforce. If I wanted to keep this new life I'd started and continue the divorce proceedings, I would have to stay put. Although I couldn't find a trace of where Glenn might have disappeared to, he would know exactly where I was. And he could come back anytime he wanted. And even if I moved somewhere new and started over, if I wanted to practice medicine, it would be impossible to hide. Hospitals and private practices expected their doctors to post profiles on their Web sites, appear in ads, and have some public presence. Trying to make myself invisible would mean the end of my medical career. Walking away from the divorce proceedings would stall them, giving credence to Glenn's claims of my mental instability and "cruelty." But it had to be done.

I'd learned my lesson. I checked myself out of the hospital against doctors' orders and ran. I sold everything I had, which wasn't much after Glenn's playing Russian roulette with my credit rating. I bought fake IDs and a junker car and drove in jagged lines across the country, until anyone Glenn used to find me would be so confused they wouldn't know where I was heading. I figured Alaska was as far as I could go without having to switch citizenships.

Most people try to use abandonment as a reason to dissolve a marriage. Glenn had used it as a reason to stall the divorce decree, stating that I should be present for the decision. He used the fact that I couldn't return home to keep me tied to him.

And now, all these years later, Glenn was looking for me again. And I was running. Again.

How long was I going to live this strange, untethered half life? Would I be an eighty-year-old woman working under an assumed name in a bowling alley in Saskatoon, dreading that day my geriatric ex wobbled up to my door on his walker? Would I ever have a home again? Would I ever have a family? I was lucky to have escaped my marriage without a child. At this point in my life, a child, particularly Glenn's child, would be a liability, a beautiful burden I couldn't protect or move without worry. But the idea of never having one of my own put a cold, insistent pressure on my heart. I'd delivered so many children to the valley werewolves. Then again, having a baby would mean trusting someone enough to let him see me naked, perhaps even telling him my real name. If I had to wait until I was eighty to do that, it was going to be disappointing on several levels.

Shaking off those depressing thoughts, I shuffled into the bathroom, whacking my ankle against the bed frame. I showered in the surprisingly clean bathtub, hoping the hot water would help unwind the muscles in my back and neck.

After stepping out of the shower onto an improvised washcloth bath mat, I mopped the water from my skin with the thinnest towel this side of cheesecloth. I carefully sorted through Caleb's bag, praying I wouldn't find anything else that would set off my weirdo alarm. The gray boxer shorts swamped me, but they kept me from wandering around a strange motel room bottomless.

I shrugged into an old flannel shirt of his, curled back under the covers for warmth, and buried my face in the sleeve of the shirt. I may have looked like I was wearing the latest in refugee chic, but Caleb's mossy, spicy smell made me feel . . . safe. As safe as I'd felt in a long time, which, considering how little I knew of him, was disconcerting at best.

I glanced down at the soft, well-worn plaid I was wearing. *You will not steal this man's shirt and shorts*, I told myself. *There are limits*.

I was totally stealing Caleb's shirt and shorts. I'd never slept more comfortably in my life. No dreams of screaming ex-husbands, confusion, and bruises. No dreams of running down the winding halls of the hospital, looking for coding alarms in a patient room, only to find that battered, flatlining patient was me. I didn't dream at all, and it was lovely.

I woke up hours later to find Caleb reading through a case file from a plastic mobile drawer I'd seen earlier in the back of the truck. Each file was tagged with its own color-coded label and contained newspaper clippings, police reports, and carefully typed notes. Caleb was sitting on the uncomfortable wooden chair, stretching his long legs against the little wood-laminate dinette table. It would have been more comfortable to sit on the bed, but I appreciated that he gave me the space. He'd taken the time to change into a soft blue-and-gray plaid flannel shirt and jeans. I'd seen men in three-thousand-dollar tailored suits who didn't make their clothes look that good. The lamp behind his head gave his black hair a bluish corona, as if some dark paper-pushing angel had fallen to earth.

Stupid good-looking, confusing werewolves.

He'd glanced over at me every few seconds, in a pattern that took me a minute or two to pin down. Review a page, check on me, review a page, check on me. It was as if he thought I would jump out of bed and launch myself out the window if he read two pages at a time.

I sat up, blinking blearily at him. "You have very neat files."

"And you have ink on your back." He grinned at the outraged expression on my face. "I never would have expected that from a girl like you."

My cheeks flushed as I pulled at the hem of his shirt,

covering the dark shapes dancing up my spine. Somewhere in Indiana, I had started getting tattoos, one star for every place I'd lived for more than a few nights. I'd read somewhere that foster kids do that sort of thing, keeping a list of all the families they've lived with. For me, it was a galaxy of tiny stars swirling along the ridges of my spine to remind myself of the number of times I'd managed to start over.

I'm not generally a superstitious person, but all this stuff started happening to me less than a week after I added the thirteenth star for McClusky, Alaska.

"Lucky star, my butt," I muttered, knowing Caleb probably heard me but not really caring.

"I made some calls to Emerson's and the motel where you were staying," he said in a faintly bored tone, without looking up from his files. "Belinda is worried about you, and the state police want you for questioning in connection with the explosion in the parking lot. I told her I was your parole officer. She wasn't surprised, by the way, figured anyone as quiet as you had to have some sort of past. But other than that, she—and the motel clerk—had nice things to say about you. Hard worker, dependable, honest but cagey."

My cheeks flushed hot. I supposed I should have expected him to check out my story. He was a sort of semi-private-investigator with a secret supernatural lifestyle. The man had trust issues. Still, the recovering wife inside of me resented the intrusion. I didn't like people checking up on me. Better not to bring it up. Better to ignore it and distract him with something else, avoid an argument.

"What did Belinda mean by 'cagey'?" I grumbled to myself. "Just because I didn't blab all of my personal problems doesn't mean I'm cagey. I thought we were friends."

Caleb smirked at me.

"I'm discreet," I told him.

"Rabbit, I know cagey. And trust me, you're cagey."

"*Hmph*. Where were you while I was in my coma?" I asked, wiping at my face, because I was pretty sure I could feel dried drool patches on my cheeks. That was unfortunate, because Caleb was staring at me. Really hard.

"A bar down the street," he said. "The owner is a friend of mine, and I thought he might have some information about Jerry. Nothing happens in this town without him knowing about it."

"Your friend is a big gossip?" I asked as he held out a foam cup of lukewarm coffee, with little packets of sugar and creamer stacked carefully on top, which I drank greedily. It was bitter and tasted a little like battery acid, but it was also caffeinated. I would take what I could get.

"Bartenders are like priests armed with truth serum. People tell them everything," he said. "If Len ever decides to start a blog, every marriage in Flint Creek will—*poof*—dissolve, just like that."

I snorted an unladylike amount of coffee up my nose at the thought of a rural Alaskan bartender turning *Gossip Girl*. The coffee splashed down my neck, soaking into the front of his shirt. I blotted at it with a minuscule paper napkin. The intensity of his stare as he watched me dab at my chest made me feel . . . warm, fluttery sensations I had not felt in a very long time.

Get a grip, I chided myself. He was probably just irritated that I'd snorked coffee all over his shirt. "Sorry, I find myself in clothing crisis."

"Looks better on you than it did on me, Rabbit," he said, going back to his paperwork.

I wasn't sure what he meant by that or by calling me Rabbit. But frankly, it was probably better that we couldn't go for a shopping spree at the moment, since, well, I didn't have cash to pay for clothes and didn't want to have to ask Caleb to cover me, literally.

"I suppose it's too late to argue for my own room," I said. "Or my own bed."

The very idea made Caleb's mouth turn downward. He leveled me with those dark eyes and told me, "You stay with me."

"See, that's what you said this morning. But I think it would be better for me to have my own room," I said, feeling small and selfish in my request. But really, sharing a bathroom, a bed, *and* underwear was just a little too much intimacy with someone I'd known for less than two days. "And it still doesn't explain why I have to be your mattress buddy."

"They didn't have any double rooms," he said, clearing his throat. "I don't want to be separated from you . . . you know, for safety reasons."

"The shortage of double rooms in this state is an epidemic," I muttered, padding toward the bathroom. But since I didn't have the cash for my own room, it was hard to argue. And honestly, if he was going to hurt me, he would have done it already. He'd had ample opportunity.

"There's a spare toothbrush in my bag," he called after me.

How had I missed that in my digging through his duffel? Giggling like mad, I scampered back to his bag to search again. I felt ridiculously grateful at the thought of being able to brush my teeth. *This must be how people develop Stockholm syndrome.*

When I emerged from the bathroom, teeth freshly brushed, a bemused Caleb was holding out a leather duffel bag. "What's this?" I asked him.

"I told Len that I knew a young lady who needed some clothes, and he happened to have this in his lost and found."

I breathed a sigh of relief and unzipped the bag quickly, hoping the original owner wasn't particularly tall or busty. My hands swam through neatly folded jeans and a series of progressively smaller tank tops. Whoever this woman was, she had not packed for cold weather.

"It belonged to some biker's old lady. Len said she was pretty short, so I figured it would fit you." When I glared at him, he seemed confused and exclaimed, "You're not tall. This can't be news to you!"

The defensive tone, so different from the voice I'd heard before, martyred and resentful, made me giggle. "There's got to be something in there you can use," he said, clearing his throat.

"I think the jeans and T-shirts might work," I told him, holding up a shirt that read, "The Booby Hatch— The South's Finest Gentleman's Club." I could probably wear the panties, too, I noted, but I wasn't about to tell him that. "I'm going to have to wash it all first. I have my pride and parasite-free status to think of. Thanks, Caleb."

He grinned, although I couldn't tell if it was from pleasure or relief that I was, in fact, parasite-free. "There's a laundry room next to the motel office," he said. "I've got a bunch of quarters in the ashtray in my truck."

"So . . . you spent some time with your friend Len. Now what?" I asked as he plopped back into his chair, replacing his files in their neat little box.

"Well, while you were getting your beauty rest—"

"Necessitated by lifting someone's unconscious ass and dragging him around like a sack of wet concrete the night before," I pointed out.

The corners of Caleb's mouth lifted, and he amended, "While you were getting your much-deserved beauty rest, I visited my friend Len, who said that Jerry has been out of town but should be back tonight. I'm going to go to the bar, explain the situation, tell him he's coming with us or I kick his ass in front of witnesses. He's the kind of guy who won't like that much."

It was so strange that Caleb could sit there, perfectly relaxed, and talk about apprehending someone not quite legally as if he was planning a trip to the park. For that matter, it was rather hilarious that the man whose truck floorboards were covered in a thick layer of jerky wrappers kept such meticulous files. He was vicious when threatened but had been relatively gentle with me. Caleb was a study in contradictions. "And then?" I asked.

He shrugged. "Jerry will let me take him in, or I will actually have to kick his ass in front of witnesses. Either way, he ends up in the backseat of the truck. I arrange a drop-off point with the client."

"Who, again, is not a legitimate law-enforcement authority?" I asked. He snorted but didn't answer. "And what will I be doing during this complicated and delicate negotiation process?"

"You will be here at the motel," he said. "This is my job, not yours. Just hang out, watch some TV, get some rest. You look like you could use a little more sleep."

I scoffed. "It's just a bar. I've worked in plenty of them," I admitted, making Caleb frown and shake his head vehemently.

"Fine," I grumbled. "I'll stay home and do some laundry. Darn some socks. Maybe curl my hair and alphabetize coupons while I'm at it."

He lifted a dark sable brow, all the while looking terribly amused, as if I was a barky little puppy trying to intimidate him with fluff and boot chewing. "You're mocking me."

"No, that's sarcasm. And if we're going to spend time together, you're going to need to learn to recognize and respect it. You'll know when I'm mocking you."

Hours later, my newish clothes had been washed and dried. I was now richer by several T-shirts and pairs of jeans. I'd showered and even shaved my legs, a luxury I hadn't taken time for in more days than I cared to admit. Our respective duffel bags were packed and ready to be thrown into the truck at a moment's notice. I'd read the one magazine I could find in this godforsaken town, a six-month-old copy of *Glamour*, and taken all of the quizzes. It was good to know that Channing Tatum was my celebrity boyfriend. I would definitely bring this up the next time I ran into him. A game show played on the TV as I determined what my "sleep style" said about me (*night terrors + insomnia = insane person*). The low rumble of applause from the TV provided a pleasant enough background while I mulled over glossy, airbrushed vapidity.

In other words, I was bored out of my skull.

This, combined with sudden nervous fidgeting, was hell on my lips, which I chewed mercilessly. I checked the glowing red numbers on the bedside alarm clock. Caleb had been gone for almost three hours. I was getting increasingly uneasy without his warm, gruff presence in the room. What if he didn't come back? What if he decided I wasn't worth the trouble of hauling all over the state? And why was I suddenly so concerned about him not coming back?

Someday, if I ever had my career back, I would write a peer-reviewed journal article on werewolf Stockholm syndrome and its effects on hormones and mental health.

Oh, wait, that would probably get me committed to a long-term-care facility.

I wasn't sure when exactly I'd decided to slip into the most demure of my biker-mama tops, the black V-neck T-shirt that fit like Saran Wrap, and sneak down the street to Len's bar. I'd paced and fretted around the room, the growing unease settling into my chest like an acidic weight, until I suddenly found myself scampering down a dark, mostly abandoned street.

"What are you doing?" I muttered into the collar of my jacket as I braced myself against the wind. "You're running in the dark toward a bar inhabited by at least one criminal and one werewolf. What are you doing?"

OK, I was worried about Caleb. He'd been gone for hours, and I didn't know what he was dealing with in this Jerry character. It certainly wasn't because I was afraid he was off flirting with some cocktail waitress, because that would be insane . . . right? What if he had been hurt? What if he wasn't able to get to help? The more I thought about it, the more the nervous tension constricted my chest, making it harder to breathe. I needed to see Caleb. For reasons no medical training could explain, I knew that once I saw Caleb and heard his voice, I would feel better.

Besides, the bar was just a short walk in a town that was only a few city blocks long. I had been going stir-crazy in the room. Watching Caleb in his environment might give me some insight into who I was traveling with. I worked through a couple more rationalizations before I sneaked into the bar through the employee entrance and edged my way down a dark-paneled corridor, following the noise of the barroom.

My semiprivileged upbringing hadn't acquainted me with dives like this. Despite growing up in Tennessee, home of country music and hard living, I couldn't say I'd walked inside a honky-tonk until I got a job at a place in Texas called Oil Slick's. The waitresses had to wear tiny red tank tops and jeans that were practically painted on. I'd never waitressed, but I still made decent tips, because the customers found my clumsiness endearing and my butt suitably heart-shaped. Gustavo, the enormous boulder-shaped bouncer who watched over the barroom, made me feel safe when the crowd got too loud and the customers got too close. The other girls were nice enough, as long as I put my share in the communal tip jar. Over the first few weeks, I perfected the art of not answering personal questions, which eventually became a vital survival skill.

But the first time a fight broke out at one of my tables, I ran to the bathroom and threw up. Being around violence like that, I just lost it. I realized it was going to be an occupational hazard, and I thought the best way to desensitize myself to it would be self-defense classes. So two stops later, in Topeka, I took a Monday-morning women's defense class at the Y. I followed it with brief stints in karate and tae kwon do. Heck, I even took a month's worth of jiujitsu before I got spooked by a fellow student whose dark hair and unsmiling blue eyes reminded me of Glenn, and I ran for Nevada. I was far from an expert. I knew just enough to defend myself if needed. I would have to enroll in a class once the Network got me settled again. For the moment, I was pretty happy with my misappropriated baton.

The music grew louder as I made my way to the barroom. It was a blend of rock and country and was very, very bad, which was almost a prerequisite in a place like this. Smoke billowed over the room, the neon from the Early American Beer Sign decor turning the fog a faint, improbable pink.

I paired up with a painfully thin woman walking from the ladies' room to the jukebox, so I could get a better look at the bar. Waitressing had taught me how to move unobtrusively through crowds. Between that and my new wardrobe, anyone who didn't know me would think I just wanted to peruse song selections with my skinny gal pal. In the glow of Hank Williams Jr. and Alabama titles, I spotted Caleb at the end of the battered oak bar. A weathered, chubby man in a dingy gray apron stood behind the bar, shaking his head as he chatted with my werewolf traveling companion. At the sight of his dark head bent over a pilsner, I took a deep breath and felt that terrible tension ease from my chest. A faint, warm, pleasant buzz spread out from my belly to my extremities, easing the wind's chill from my cheeks.

Although his back was turned to me, I saw Caleb perk up the minute I walked in. As he turned, I ducked behind a large biker making his way over to the pool table. If the Harley enthusiast noticed a tiny woman suddenly melting into his shadow, he didn't say anything. Caleb's eyes scanned the room before turning back to his beer.

For a few moments, I watched Caleb in conversation with the bartender. He was relaxed, but there was an air of menace in his posture. Whatever had happened before I arrived, he was not happy about it.

I felt something brush against my shoulder as someone moved from the front entrance toward the barroom. The contact surprised me, and I jumped, barely containing the urge to yelp. Caleb's head turned toward me again, and I scrambled into a nearby booth. Just as I sat down, a weaselly little blond man slid into the seat across from me. He seemed just as surprised to see me there as I was to see him.

The man grinned at me. "Well, hey there, sweetie. How are you?"

I blinked rapidly, recognizing that eager, crooked smile, the bulbous little nose. I'd seen those features in the photos from Caleb's files. Somehow, I'd managed to grab a booth with Caleb's quarry. And he seemed to think my rapid blinking was some sort of eyelash-batting gesture.

Fan-freaking-tastic.

5

The Misadventures of Alcoholus Moronicus

If I jumped out of the booth as if my butt was scalded, Caleb would probably notice. If I tried to slink away quietly and offended Jerry, making a scene, Caleb would probably notice. All I had to do was humor this moron for a minute or two and then hightail it before—

Crap. Caleb had noticed.

And from across the room, he did not look happy. He stood, moving swiftly around the tables, approaching Jerry from behind. I shook my head slightly, prompting Jerry to ask, "Everything OK, sweetie?"

Caleb frowned, and I drummed up the ditzy-blonde voice I'd perfected at Oil Slick's. "Hi! Do you mind if I sit here?"

Jerry's dim but perfectly friendly grin was back. "Well, since you already are, I don't mind at all. Can I buy you a drink?"

"I'll have whatever you're having," I said, smiling sweetly.

He hollered, "Beer!" across the barroom, which prompted a rude gesture from the bartender. Jerry turned back to me. "Well, look at you. Here I thought I'd met all the pretty girls in town. You're new around here, huh?"

Right, right, idle chitchat. I can do this, I told myself. I could keep Jerry pleasantly distracted and maybe even get him outside, where Caleb could intercede without causing a loud, violent scene. Jerry didn't seem like a sleaze, which helped considerably. He just seemed like a rather sad, lonely guy who had very bad judgment regarding auto loans and business transactions. Part of me sort of wanted to help him escape out the back door. I smiled, although the expression was a bit shaky, and leaned across the table toward him.

"My boyfriend and I just blew into town a few days ago. But I can't seem to find him. I guess I'll just have to spend my time with you." I slowly walked my fingers up his denim-clad arm.

"Well, his loss is my gain, sweetie. I'll just get us some drinks." Jerry waved his arms in the direction of the bar and frowned. "Len doesn't seem to be cooperatin'," he said, frowning slightly at the bartender, who was pointedly ignoring him. "Why don't I go get you that beer?"

I smiled, all sweetness and light. "Why don't you?"

He sauntered toward the bar, grinning at me the whole time.

Now was probably a good time to run. As nonsleazy

as he seemed, Jerry could try his own luck with Caleb. When he turned his back to me to order, I hopped up from the table, made toward the back exit, and ran right into Caleb.

There's nothing like a face full of pissed-off werewolf to get your adrenal responses going.

"What are you doing here?" Caleb hissed, dark eyes flashing faintly golden as he wrapped his fingers around my wrist and pulled me toward the corridor. Although he clearly wasn't messing around, his grip wasn't tight enough to hurt, and I felt insistently guided rather than dragged against my will.

"I got bored," I whispered, in an effort not to attract Jerry's attention. "And then I got here, and it all just sort of spiraled out of control."

"I told you to stay at the motel."

"I'm starting to grasp why," I told him. "And I'm sorry. I got anxious when you didn't come back."

And I grasped exactly how needy that sounded as the words came out of my mouth. Maybe if I started drinking, I would develop some sort of verbal filter around this man.

A fleeting, pleased look flashed across his face, just before another more lasting look of . . . guilt? That seemed like a strange response to an awkward admission of semifondness. He cleared his throat and pushed me away, against the wall, until there was enough room to make the dance chaperones at my old high school happy.

"Look, Anna, I think we should talk."

And then, of course—

"Uh, hello?" Jerry asked, returning with beers in hand. "Is this your boyfriend?"

I gave a very startled Caleb an uneasy glance and mumbled, "Ummm . . ."

Even I am amazed by my own smoothness sometimes.

Caleb was the first to snap out of whatever bad-decision haze was circling our heads, drawling, "Yeah, this is my girl. And she doesn't need anybody buying her beers but me." He slid his arm around my waist and pushed me behind his broad back.

Resigning myself to being the mewling damsel in this messed-up situation, I dropped my forehead against the back of Caleb's jacket and sighed, before loudly protesting in full-on Southern drawl, "Aw, baby, he didn't meant anything by it!"

Jerry raised his hands, spilling the better part of the beer down his shoulders. "Hey, man, *she* sat down with *me*. I didn't mean any harm."

"You wanna talk about this outside?" Caleb growled as I backed toward the employee exit and calculated my chances of bolting for the motel room and avoiding the inevitable fiasco of fisticuffs. And frankly, my feelings were a little hurt that Jerry had thrown me over so quickly when faced with my pissed-off "boyfriend."

Defensive and agitated, Jerry retorted, "Hey, maybe if you were taking care of her at home, she wouldn't have to go looking for it elsewhere."

"That's it," Caleb barked, grabbing a handful of Jerry's blue-jean jacket and rattling him back and forth. "Now I'm kicking your ass!"

I let out a plaintive wail, as if I couldn't believe our lovely evening on the town was being ruined by such barbarism.

Jerry clawed at Caleb's hands, trying to wriggle loose, like a worm on a hook. "No, she's not even worth it, man." With that, he managed to jerk away from Caleb's massive hands and turned to walk away.

Now, having spent some time around the male barfly, or *Alcoholus moronicus*, I'd learned to recognize the signs when a guy was faking walking away from a bar fight so he could sucker-punch his opponent. I was about to shout a warning, but Caleb apparently recognized those signs, too, because when Jerry turned to whip his beer at Caleb's head, both of us had already stepped out of the way, leaving the bottle hurtling toward the large barback, who had just carried a keg through the employee entrance behind us. Thinking Caleb was the beer tosser, the barback took a swing at him. But instead of hitting Caleb, the punch landed right in the face of an old, grizzled trucker type, whose partial denture plate went flying out of his mouth and behind the bar.

The toothless trucker was none too pleased about this development and dived at Caleb and the barback. Caleb moved to push me out of the way, but I'd already ducked, naturally falling into step with the waitresses. They tended to tuck away into a safe corner until the fists and flying objects stilled. And considering the way the fight seemed to spread throughout the barroom like a virus, those objects would likely remain in motion for some time.

Caleb had ducked the barback's first punch but caught the second on its upward swing at his chin. Although it would have been better to keep moving, I was transfixed by the grace with which Caleb moved that massive, powerful body around; sidestepping and dodging like a matador, all the while tracking Jerry over his shoulder so the little weasel couldn't escape.

The physician in me couldn't help but tally the injuries. Caleb's emergency-room bill would have been considerable if he wasn't going to heal up automatically. His effort to keep watch on Jerry kept getting him punched in the face. I could hear the bridge of his nose crack under the pressure of the barback's fist, not to mention two fractured ribs and a split in the skin over his left cheek. Across the barroom, I saw an old, wizened trucker flip another onto a scarred pine bar table hard enough to break his clavicle. And a fireplug of a waitress brought her tray down on the trucker's head so hard he was going to have at least a minor concussion.

Unfortunately, Jerry was picking his way across the room, around the flying fists, and seemed to be ducking toward the front door. And Caleb was too distracted by the painfully thin jukebox woman biting his arm to notice.

I scrambled across the room with all the grace of a drunken gazelle and cut Jerry off before he reached his escape route. *OK, brain, what are you doing? You don't approve of Caleb's job, and you don't know Jerry, so why are you trying to come up with a distraction to keep him from getting away?*

"If you wait a minute, I'll show you my boobs." I blurted out the words, stopping Jerry in his tracks.

What?

Jerry had the exact same reaction, blinking rapidly at me as he spluttered. "Wh-what?"

This was the brilliant distraction you came up with? I seethed at my cerebral cortex. *How did you get me through medical school?* I could only blame the bad influence of the biker-babe clothes.

"D-did you say you'd show me your boobs?" Jerry spluttered nervously, as if he was on the verge of giggling.

I scanned the room for Caleb, who was now being detained by the headlock the three-hundred-pound barback was putting on him. And now I was on the edge of panic, because there was no way I was flashing this guy. I did not spend four almost homeless years avoiding a pole—despite several potentially lucrative offers—to start publicly baring skin now. I had backed myself into a corner, in terms of negotiations. I would have to keep this in mind for future bar fights. "Maybe just one."

Behind Jerry, there was a flash of familiar plaid. At some point during my mammary-related musings, Caleb must have shaken off the angry barback, because he was now creeping up behind Jerry, holding a finger to his lips, and brandishing a purloined pool cue. I grimaced, as if in heavy consideration.

Jerry was about to protest this bargain when Caleb crept up behind him and whacked him over the head. If Jerry had any friends who might have objected to him being whacked over the head and then packed out of the bar like baggage, they were too caught up in the fight to notice.

Caleb wasn't even winded by the brisk walk back to the truck under the added burden of hauling a grown man. While I leaned against the passenger door, trying to catch my breath, Jerry was tucked into the truck as meticulously as a newborn babe. Caleb raised the metal gate between the front and back seats of his truck and carefully cuffed Jerry's arms to the ceiling handle, zip-tied his feet, and gagged him with a bandanna. It was disturbing how quickly Caleb accomplished this, as if he was the feature act in some sort of criminal rodeo. But he seemed pretty angry, so angry that he didn't even speak when he stopped at the motel to let me grab our bags and check out. Apparently, leaving me in the truck with a wanted man wasn't something he was willing to do, even if the man was unconscious.

I packed up in record time, although I stared long-ingly at the bed as I marched our bags out of the room. I'd really been looking forward to sleeping in the same room two days in a row.

Story of my life.

Caleb was resting his forehead on the steering wheel when I opened the truck door. I climbed into my seat, and there was a long, awkward silence after I buckled my seatbelt. I could only look around the newly neat interior. Who knew that the floorboards were maroon? I was contemplating whether I could get away with buying one of those little plug-in air fresheners at the next rest stop when Caleb finally raised his dark head, his features completely wooden as he deadpanned, "'If you wait a minute, I'll show you my boobs'?"

I shrugged. "It worked."

The tiniest hint of a smile quirked his lips, but he schooled his features into a more serious expression. He pulled the truck out of the mostly deserted motel parking lot and onto the quiet street. He grumbled, "I told you to stay at the motel."

"Funny thing. It turns out that I have free will and won't just stay put when you tell me to heel," I said, throwing my hands into an exaggerated helpless posture.

He frowned at me and slid his phone out of his pocket to make arrangements for Jerry's transfer.

Jerry was silent for most of the ride, because, well, he was unconscious.

As we drove, Caleb called his clients and made arrangements to drop Jerry at a small bush-pilot operation about three hundred miles away. Caleb's clients, who remained unnamed for reasons I didn't question, would be waiting at the hangar there for us. I chose not to think about what would happen to Jerry once they had him. But given what I'd read in his file—which I had filched from Caleb and read with a pen light while we waited—Jerry wasn't a terribly nice person, with a history of petty and not-so-petty larceny, grand theft auto, and assault. Torn by my strange connection to Caleb and my feelings of solidarity for another "runner," I didn't feel good about the part I'd played in Jerry's capture. I'd acted out of instinct, wanting to help Caleb, to stay in his good graces. But now, the farther we drove, the more I wanted to yell for Caleb to stop the truck and let Jerry out. Or maybe just let me out.

When he finally woke up, Jerry wailed and cursed and grunted for the rest of the drive. I thought Caleb would do the *Dog the Bounty Hunter* thing and lecture Jerry about the bad choices that had led him here. But all he said was "You do something this stupid again, you know they're going to have me right back at your door."

Note to self: Stop making comparisons between Dog the Bounty Hunter *and Caleb.* He wouldn't find them amusing, and I couldn't stop picturing Caleb with a libido-killing haircut. Also, I liked to think I was above calling him Wolf the Bounty Hunter—even behind his back.

"Inspiring," I told him, and we engaged in a battle of dueling body language.

I jerked my head toward Jerry. Caleb shrugged his shoulders. I tilted my head and poked out my bottom lip in the prettiest pout I could muster. Caleb sighed, glanced over his shoulder, and added, "Eat your vegetables. Say your prayers before bedtime. And give a hoot, don't pollute."

I shook my head. "Really?"

Caleb shrugged. "What?"

Unimpressed by Caleb's life coaching, Jerry seemed to exhaust himself thrashing and growling muffled insults at us and fell asleep. It seemed impossible to sleep in that position, but given his steady snores, he was apparently comfortable enough. I napped off and on, only feeling slightly guilty that I'd had more sleep than Caleb in the last twenty-four hours and he was the one who was driving. Since he'd sort of banned me from driving, he could just deal with it. Funny, I'd had intermittent insomnia ever since I'd filed divorce papers, but I was able to nod off in a moving vehicle with a werewolf and a fugitive.

Sometime around midnight, Caleb stopped for coffee at a run-down all-night diner halfway to our destination. I woke up enough to check on Jerry, who was still unconscious, and reassemble my hair into something like a ponytail. I offered Caleb a grateful smile when he handed me a large orange juice. At that point, I wasn't sure if I could handle caffeine or coffee breath.

"It occurs to me that other than your upsetting fondness for plastic restraints and preserved meat, I don't know much about you," I said, sipping the juice and welcoming the rush of blood sugar.

"I'm an open book," he said, and gave me a sunny smile that was just obscene at that hour.

And by the way, werewolves were anything but open and honest. The CIA could take lessons in discretion and misdirection from a werewolf pack. They tended to live in insular communities, separating themselves from the outside world. If humans noticed something "off" about a werewolf, the wolf was a master at redirecting the questioning until those humans were so confused they were no longer sure what they saw. For every odd behavior, they had a dozen plausible explanations. They shared their secrets with a few select, trusted humans, usually the ones they mated with. And for a misguided human who betrayed a werewolf clan . . . well, I don't know what happened to them. I never saw one twice. The problem with dealing with large predators is that they usually know how to hide a body from other large predators—even if those large predators include state troopers.

"And what do you do in your spare time?" I asked.

"Hunting," he said. "Hiking."

"An outdoorsy type, huh?" I asked, having just a little too much fun with the *I know something you don't know* game.

"You could say that," he said. "And what about you? Any hobbies I should know about? Taxidermy? Exotic piercings?"

"How did you go from taxidermy to body piercings?" I asked. "Also, FYI, piercings are not a hobby."

"I never know with you wild tattooed women," he said. I shot him a dirty look. He grinned. "So what do you do for fun?"

I pursed my lips and resolved to do penance for my teasing with a healthy dollop of truth. "Dye my hair. Obtain illegal identification. Forge government paperwork."

Caleb's expression waffled between *uh-oh* and *wow*. I didn't know whether he believed me or not. I wasn't sure whether he wanted to believe me or not. Finally, he cleared his throat and said, "Well, you are an interesting girl, aren't you?" I shrugged my shoulders, all innocent eyes and fluttering lashes. "What are you running from?"

That put a damper on the fluttering lashes. "Columbia House Music Club," I said, recovering my snarkiness quickly. "Oh, sure, they say they'll sell you six CDs for a penny, but they'll hunt you down like the hounds of hell if you miss the payments."

"Stop kidding around."

"I'm not. A Wilson Phillips CD ruined my life."

I was treated to yet another Caleb expression to add to the catalogue, the halfhearted *I'm getting really tired of your shit, woman* glower. Normally, a glare like that would have me retreating a bit, at least leaning back in my seat. But there was no heat in Caleb's stare, just frustration and a touch of irritation. Somewhere in my chest, a little pressure valve opened up, and I was able to release a breath I didn't even know I'd been holding.

Contrite, I told him something real. "I'm not ready to talk about it yet. All you need to know is that I need to get to Anchorage to pick something up. It's nothing illegal. I don't have any warrants. After that, I don't know where I will be going."

Caleb muttered something I couldn't make out, frowning into the distance. Well, if there was any way to kill a fun, flirtatious conversation, that was it. We rode along in silence for a mile or two.

Desperate to recover the previous mood, I said, "OK, lightning round. Siblings or only?"

"Only," he answered. Of course, I knew that. Only children were such a rarity in the hyperproductive pack that the wolf-aunties were sure to *tsk* over "poor Caleb," all alone, the last of his line, handling the details of his father's death by himself.

Caleb's mother, a human, had abandoned him and his father when Caleb was just a little boy, I remembered now, which had been quite the scandal in the little valley community. Did the lack of brothers and sisters make it easier for Caleb to leave the packlands and wander by himself? As a cub, he would have had plenty of kids to run around with, cousins upon cousins to keep from being lonely. But still, after his father died, I could imagine Caleb feeling his connections to his fellow wolves fading.

I couldn't help but feel a little sorry for him. Running with other wolves was supposed to be one of the best parts of being a werewolf. How often was he able to shift out here on his own? How did he avoid hunters and game wardens or running afoul of locals? Shifting alone was considered a big no-no in the valley. The more time a wolf spends with the pack, the clearer his memories during the phasing. There was a sort of collective memory among the wolves, which could be unfortunate, given some of the stupid stuff some of them were known to pull while on four legs. Shifting solo could lead to a werewolf waking up in human form, naked, in a grocery store parking lot two hundred miles from home. (It had happened to Maggie.) Or suspected of eating hikers. (It had happened to Cooper.)

I cast a sidelong glance at Caleb. How long had it been since he'd been able to run? Werewolves had to shift every once in a while just to get the "wolf wiggles" out. Maggie told me once that her kind tended to get pretty cranky if they went too long without phase. It would explain Caleb's occasionally less-than-sunny demeanor.

It seemed my little mental vacation had taken longer than I thought, because Caleb was looking at me expectantly. Oh, right, I was supposed to be participating in car games, not pondering werewolf PMS. Cheeks flushing, I cleared my throat and asked, "College?"

"No."

"Past felonies?" I asked.

"Is public nudity a felony?"

Wrinkling my nose, I asked, "Biggest phobia?"

"Russian nesting dolls. I've always hated those."

"Because you think the tiny baby doll inside could be made of pure evil?" I suggested.

"Yes, I do." He managed to say it without a hint of irony.

"*Rambo* or *Rocky*?"

He scoffed. "*Terminator*."

"Sorry, the correct answer was John McClane," I told him, shaking my head. "Always."

"I feel this quiz is unfairly skewed toward Bruce Willis fans."

"Don't feel bad. I stopped speaking to a friend for a month when she suggested *Love, Actually* was a better Christmas movie than *Die Hard*," I told him. It was true. My relationship with Mo was very strained until she brought me chocolate chess squares as a peace offering.

"Springsteen or Def Leppard?"

He fist-pumped in mock triumph. "Neither. The correct answer is Garth Brooks."

"I don't think we can be friends anymore," I told him.

That obscenely sunny smile made another appearance. "Well, at least you admit that we're friends in the first place."

I rolled my eyes. "Football or basketball?"

"Curling," he insisted, and when I burst out laughing, he added, "I can't help it! It's weirdly compelling. Those poor guys out there on the ice with their little brooms."

"I have no problem with that," I promised him. "Chunky or creamy?"

He raised an eyebrow. "Wow, I hope you're talking about peanut butter."

And so it continued for almost an hour, with Caleb attempting to ask me reciprocal questions. I dodged all but the most trivial, giving him bits and pieces of information that couldn't come back to bite me. Bruce Willis. Florence and the Machine. Born in Kansas. (A lie.) Chicago Cubs fan. (Also a lie. Go, Cardinals.) Chunky over creamy. (True. It was the only way to keep my chunk-phobic father out of my Jiffy stash.) I avoided questions about schooling, employment, past relationships, even the places I'd traveled.

"I don't have much time for vacations," I told him.

"Not even when you were a kid?"

I shook my head. "My family didn't travel much." Another lie. My relatively well-off parents had taken me on wonderful trips to Disney, the Grand Canyon, Mexico. We'd even spent a Christmas in New York City to satisfy my mother's fascination with oversized Christmas trees. But I hadn't talked about my parents in years. And it hurt too much to talk about it casually.

"Still not much of a sharer, huh, Rabbit?" he asked, when I'd sidestepped a question about my birthday. "See? Cagey."

I had opened my mouth to make some excuse, when an indignant squeal sounded from the backseat. Saved by the bell . . . or the tied-up felon, as it were. Muffled by the gag, Jerry's pleas for us to let him go plucked at my heartstrings, and I rolled around in my head the many alternatives to giving him to Caleb's clients. Until Jerry called me a not-very-nice four-letter word beginning with C, which came across loud and clear even with the gag. And while my sympathies cooled considerably, Caleb got angry enough that he pulled over, got a black cotton bag from his serial-killer tool kit, and pulled it over Jerry's head.

"You are really good at that," I told him. "Truly, disturbingly efficient."

"I briefly considered a career as a preschool teacher," he said, chuckling when my eyes went wide.

"Try not to be too angry with him," I told Caleb, patting his arm gently. The gesture seemed to settle him, relaxing his shoulders and smoothing the firm set of his jaw. "I would probably call me names, too, if I was in the same situation."

"I wouldn't let you get into this sort of situation," he retorted. And when I gave him an amused look, he added grudgingly, "I would try."

I snorted. He really seemed to think he could control the universe, but I found it reassuring that he didn't seem to think he could control me. As much as he might want to lead me in one direction or the other, he seemed to have accepted that it was futile. I liked that feeling, knowing that I'd shown some backbone in this bizarre situation, that I hadn't backslid to the faulty instincts that got Tina Campbell into trouble.

I decided to enjoy this small victory and keep quiet for the rest of the drive to the airstrip. Caleb had turned up a Tim McGraw CD to cover Jerry's muffled curses anyway, so further conversation wasn't necessary. I would have to list Caleb's taste in music as the chief of his personality flaws. I could forgive the overprotectiveness and the questionable job, but I drew the line at boot-scootin' music.

As our headlights flashed over the faded red Quonset-style hangar, Caleb motioned for me to slide low in my seat and slipped a baseball cap over my head, covering my face. He unbuckled and turned to me as Jerry noticed we had come to a stop and began thrashing violently.

"I know you don't like being told, but trust me when I say the less these people see of you, the better. Just act like you're taking a nap or something."

I nodded, pulling my collapsible weapon of choice from my bag, but I kept it low and out of sight of the trio of burly men standing near the faded red metal building marked "Bird in the Bush Piloting Service." Considering the sheer size of Caleb's clients and the flash of what looked remarkably like a Russian mob tattoo on the tallest one's hand, I decided that just this once, I wouldn't be contrary. I slouched down and yawned widely, pulling the cap lower over my eyes. I would keep an ear out for any sign of trouble, but a "waking nap" didn't sound too bad, either.

Jerry was deeply unhappy to be unloaded from the truck and marched across the frosted grass, if his colorful, anatomically unlikely insults were any indication. Even after his use of the unforgivable C-word, his whimpers and whining still struck a guilty chord within me. How could Caleb just go through the transaction as if he was dropping off a bag of laundry? And he was delivering it to people who would beat the absolute crap out of that laundry—and that was being optimistic.

While I kept low and still in the truck, I found myself getting more agitated by the minute. What if that was me? What if some bounty hunter came and packed me up like so much luggage and dropped me at some nondescript location to return me to Glenn? Would Caleb help me? Or leave me to the bounty hunter out of professional courtesy? What would become of me if the price of selling me out went higher than the price of keeping me at Caleb's side?

I was pondering these cheerful issues when Caleb yanked the truck door open, beaming from ear to ear, and clapped an envelope into my hand. I stared down at the plain white paper, marveling at its weight. How much had he been paid for Jerry's head? How much would Glenn be willing to pay for information about me? The thought made my stomach pitch, but Caleb seemed oblivious to my queasy distress.

"I don't know about you, but I feel like eating a steak the size of a placemat," he crowed, pulling out of the parking lot with all due haste. "And you, you are getting twenty percent. As much as I hate to admit it, we never would have caught up to him without your boob-showing offer."

I frowned at that and didn't reply, which caught his attention.

"What's wrong?"

"How many of these jobs do you do a month?" I asked hesitantly.

"Depends on how big the payday is. Some catches are worth more than others. There are some months I only have to do one job. Why do you have that look on your face?" he asked.

Without realizing it, I'd been giving him a pretty healthy dose of stink-eye. I sniffed and schooled my features into a more neutral expression. I hated the timidity in my voice as I said, "I don't feel good about what we just did."

I expected him to get defensive or angry. In fact, his lack of reaction was unnerving.

"Other than his penchant for gender-offensive four-letter words, Jerry didn't seem like such a bad guy. And he sounded so scared. I hate to think what those goons are going to do to him."

"Honestly? They're probably going to do something permanent to his kneecaps. But he'll be able to walk away from it." When he saw the doubtful expression on my face, he amended, "Limp away. He'll be able to limp away. The people I look for, they're not squeaky-clean, innocent souls. There's a reason they end up on my radar. It's not because they jaywalk or take more than one penny from that dish by the gas-station cash register. They've done something serious, and that leads me right to them."

"You don't know that," I insisted. "You don't know that the information some of your less-than-reputable clients are giving you is legit. And you don't know what reasons these people may have had to do whatever it was they did to cross your path."

"Reasons?" he asked, looking mildly amused, which just pissed me off.

"Yes, reasons. Life isn't black-and-white. Sometimes decent people do the wrong thing for the right reason."

"Like stealing a loaf of bread to feed starving orphans?"

"Yes, thank you for taking me seriously." I narrowed my eyes so dramatically I actually felt the strain on my ocular muscles. "I'm just saying that you never know what you're capable of until you're in dire straits."

"I think I'm pretty familiar with what desperate people will do." He frowned at me, but his tone was still gentle, which was confusing.

I was questioning him, openly, so why was he being so damn nice about it? How was I supposed to predict his actions if he didn't respond the way I expected him to?

He reached across the seat to jostle my shoulder, drawing his hand away when he saw how I tensed up. "Is there a reason that you're taking this so personally?"

I stared out the window. There were plenty of reasons I could give him. I was taking it personally because there was someone out there looking for me. And I would want someone to take it personally if I was gagged and tagged like a freshly caught deer. Because I knew what it was like to wake up afraid. I knew what it was like to want to ask friends, family, the police—anybody—for help but being too scared.

But that was a heck of a hand to tip toward someone I barely knew.

"I just don't like to see people hurt, that's all," I offered weakly.

He shifted in his seat and seemed to be choosing his words carefully as we sped toward a town called Smithville. "Well, that's an admirable trait . . ."

I sensed an impending *but*.

"But get the hell over it," he told me.

I crossed my arms over my chest with a harrumph. *Nice.*

"Yes, thank you, my moral quandary is completely resolved," I retorted in a saccharine-sweet voice that had him laughing.

"Well, I know what *will* make you feel better," he said. When I arched my eyebrows, he waved "our" pay envelope. "Fresh underwear."

"Jerry's captors gave you fresh underwear that fits in an envelope?"

Feminine-Hygiene Products: The Ultimate in Werewolf Repellent

To celebrate our big win, Caleb took me to the exotic destination of Wall-Mart.

Please note that was *Wall-Mart*, with two Ls.

Given the faded sign lettering still evident on the storefront, I assumed the building had been an actual licensed Wal-Mart at some point, back before they changed their official name to Walmart. When the store closed, it appeared, some enterprising souls had just added an extra L to the sign and opened up their own discount megagrocery. The color scheme, façade, and layout were the same, but all of the employees seemed careful to emphasize the extra L when they said, "Welcome to Wallllllll-Mart." I assumed this was done on the advice of legal counsel.

Caleb seemed nearly giddy about this shopping spree, cart-surfing toward the ladies' clothing section. The selection wasn't exactly diverse, but I was able to find several long-sleeved T-shirts, thermals, and hoodies that I could use. I didn't want to swerve into mom-jeans territory, so I picked some yoga pants. I tossed some plain white cotton undies into the cart without comment from my werewolf shopping partner, for which I was grateful.

I hoped that the identity Red-burn created would involve living in an area with more retail opportunities. I was sincerely looking forward to wearing clothes that were not purchased in a store where you could also buy motor oil and bagged salad. As shallow as it was, I missed open-toed shoes. I missed designer labels. Heck, I missed clothes I could wear just because they were cute, not because they would protect me from frigid winds. I wanted to wear makeup again and not worry that I was attracting too much attention.

As we passed the men's section, I saw a triple-extra-large black T-shirt featuring a *Field & Stream*–style illustration of a wolf howling at the moon. I briefly considered buying it to sleep in, but I figured Caleb might find it suspiciously coincidental.

"You don't seem to be getting a lot," he noted, as we wandered toward the health and beauty section. He nodded toward the cartload of blues, grays, and blacks.

"I don't like someone else paying my way," I told him.

"Well, you helped me snag Jerry, so part of the fee is yours, OK?"

As gratifying as that was, it didn't lessen the humiliation of buying tampons in front of him. I wouldn't have to worry about it for a while, but I definitely didn't want to be unprepared when it happened, particularly if it happened far from civilization. As I stood, considering the various absorbencies, Caleb seemed torn between some need to stay close to me and his excruciating embarrassment.

He cleared his throat. "I'm just going to wait at the end of the aisle."

"I think that would be best," I said as he moved toward the end display.

His eyes widened when he realized that display happened to contain a decorative array of Summer's Eve products. "Maybe even in the sporting-goods section."

"Even better."

He practically left one of those little cartoon puffs of dust in his wake as he ran away. Apparently, protective instincts only extended so far when feminine-hygiene products were involved.

When he was far out of sight, I pondered my options. This was my opportunity to escape. I could walk right out of the store and find a ride with some willing trucker, taking the risk of being assaulted or worse. Kindly, beer-hauling, grandfatherly types willing to give favors, no questions or reciprocity required, were a rarity in the transportation community. But walking any distance in the dark, even in this relatively mild cold, was lunacy.

OK, so Caleb's job was a little—a lot—disturbing. And he had some strange werewolfy instincts when it came to boundaries between relative strangers. But there was something so inherently *good* in the way he interacted with me. He was so calm and patient and seemed to delight in even my more irritating qualities. I could handle spending time with someone who treated me like that. I doubted I would get better offers.

Right, no more getting blown around by the belches of fate. No more decisions based on panic and circumstance. I was choosing to stay with Caleb until I could make it to Anchorage.

I took a deliberate step out of the lady-maintenance aisle and toward the snack section. Caleb had snagged another cart and was filling it with pretzels, nacho chips, and, of course, venison jerky.

"So your arteries are pretty much fossilized under the weight of salt and preservatives at this point, huh?" I said, eyeing the "Around the World Jerky" megavariety pack he dropped into the cart.

"I have a strong metabolism," he said.

"That really doesn't affect the probability of a stroke," I told him.

He rolled his eyes. "Well, you're just a big pot of sunshine, aren't ya?"

"Humor me," I said as I added granola bars to the pile and swapped the nacho chips for pita chips. Caleb bent his mouth into a disdainful frown while making a gagging sound. "Just wait until we get to the produce section."

Caleb slowly but surely integrated me into his life on the road. Although I disliked how he made his living, I could see why he enjoyed it. He got all the fun of being a detective, without the pesky paperwork and professional accountability. He got to see new places, meet new people . . . and handcuff them. It was like an Easter-egg hunt for people, trying to trace their routes and figure out where they were stashed. But his job was scary, too. He was all alone out here. I was his only backup, which, given my pitiful upper-body strength, was a terrifying thought. If he got hurt, there might not be someone to help him. And while he could heal himself from most injuries, the thought of him lying alone and bleeding in a parking lot made me a little ill.

We drove for what felt like days, stopping in saloons and motels along the way, talking to Caleb's contacts, and picking up information—all while I needled him to drive a little faster, to move along so we could get to Anchorage.

Caleb's ability to use his werewolf nature to pick up on his targets' scents made him seem like a human bloodhound. Knowing about his heightened senses helped me figure out how they helped him to see the minute details that the average person would miss, from trash left behind in a motel room to the depth and age of tire and shoe prints outside a target's house. And when he was interviewing people, I knew he could smell changes in their body chemistry, hormonal shifts that indicated stress or deception; he could see their eyes dilate and hear changes in their heart rates. He was a walking lie detector, which made me nervous as hell.

But he had just as many secrets to protect as I did. Caleb did his best to cover his otherworldly traits. He found reasons to be out on full-moon nights, when the urge to shift—while not obligatory for werewolves—

was strong. He occasionally came back to the motel with dried blood on his clothes or a few feathers in his hair. I pretended not to notice, because there was no possible explanation for the feathers that wouldn't send a reasonable girl running.

He might have fooled a newbie with an untrained eye. But to someone who had lived with a pack for four years, he might as well have worn a big blinking neon sign: "I'm a werewolf, ask me how."

Mealtimes with Caleb were an adventure. Like any werewolf, he ate as if it was his job. Bacon, eggs, bacon, steak, more bacon. But he seemed anxious unless he saw that I was eating, too. Clearly, I could never put away as many calories as he was taking in, but unless he saw me consuming a steady stream of nutritious foods, he would nudge them onto my plate. He stopped short of doing airplane noises and trying to feed me, for which I was grateful. As much as I appreciated his concern, my jeans were getting tight, and I was running out of Tums.

Beyond the food issues, he was protective to the extreme, keeping an eye on me at all times. And while it made me uncomfortable—especially when he attempted to follow me into a ladies' room—part of me was reassured that he cared. He wasn't trying to keep me from leaving or keep me from meeting someone who might replace him. He was honestly concerned that there might be someone lurking around a corner, which turned out to be a reasonable anxiety at a rest stop in Layton. OK, so it was a porcupine trying to take a nap, but I doubted I could have fought it off on my own.

We drove and drove through the ever-changing landscape, through mountains and valleys, rolling flatlands. Radio stations were a matter of contention. He preferred country (*country!*), while I stuck to the classic-rock side of the dial. We finally found a Crosby, Stills, and Nash greatest-hits CD at a truck stop in Hanover, which satisfied us both for a while.

We would wake up reasonably early, pack up the truck, and drive to a location where Caleb would either check us into a motel or I would wait in the nearest diner while Caleb met with contacts or snooped around. In the afternoons, we would hit the road again for whatever new trail we were following. At night, we shared a bed. There seemed to be a terrible rash of motels with (a) no double rooms and (b) only one available room, meaning we had to share. I found this highly suspicious, but since Caleb never tried anything untoward, I stopped worrying about it. It got to the point where I doubted I could sleep without the warmth and weight of his body on the bed with me. The Glenn nightmares tapered off to nothing, and for the first time in years, I slept deeply and dreamlessly.

I endeavored to make myself as useful as possible, without actually helping him on those ethical-gray-area cases. I kept a bag of oranges and apples in the truck, which Caleb was happy to munch on. When I couldn't get fresh fruit, we took megadoses of vitamins C and D. Getting scurvy is not all it's cracked up to be.

I became Caleb's personal-assistant-slash-Bluetooth, searching through files as he drove and preventing him from making phone calls that could endanger both of us. I managed to drag him kicking and screaming into the current century by finding a reasonably functional laptop and the world's smallest printer in a pawn shop near our motel in Denali. Being married to a boastful computer genius did have its advantages. I'd managed to pick up a few tricks through the years, especially knowing of Web sites where you could obtain not-quite-legal information about citizens at large. So, with the portable wireless hot spot I persuaded him to buy from the cell-phone store, I was able to (a) help with Internet research and (b) avoid the Alaskan version of hipsters who frequented Internet cafés.

They were like regular hipsters, with more flannel.

And if I happened to find lots of information about those who committed violent felonies but none about people who just owed money to the wrong people, well, that was just too darn bad.

My new "apprenticeship" put me in frequent contact with Caleb's "home base," a bar in Fairbanks owned by Caleb's improbably named friend Suds. A former Alaska State Police trooper, Suds served as a central communications hub between Caleb and the investigators (and other less reputable entities) who hired him, passing along assignments and information. Before I showed up, they communicated primarily through phone and fax. I didn't know if Suds appreciated my "interference," but I did manage to form some sort of bond with him when I spent the better part of three hours explaining how to scan and attach documents to e-mails. I earned his respect when I tolerated the F-word three times in one sentence without getting all delicate about his language.

Since I'd been "promoted," Caleb got me my own prepaid cell phone at a general store in Donwell. He said he didn't want me to have to come looking for him if he was working. But I got the idea that boredom played a factor in the purchase, particularly after he started texting me while he was "in the field" to keep himself entertained.

You know your life has taken a turn for the bizarre when a werewolf is sending you winky emoticons.

In consideration of his lack of computer skills, Caleb let me take over e-mail communications with his clients. I spent most of my nights in the motel rooms, alone, working on the laptop or reading, a simple pleasure I hadn't had time for until recently. I wrote up progress reports, submitted invoices, and even set up a PayPal account so Caleb could collect payments immediately from investigators working in other states. This was a purely selfish gesture. More money in Caleb's account meant a nicer class of motel room (read: motels with cable channels besides porn, but still, mysteriously, no available double rooms).

Unfortunately, Caleb took notice of my primary motive when he came back one night to find six expense reports and even more invoices ready for his signature.

"You seem to be zipping through the paperwork at an alarming rate," he said, blinking at the sheer number of documents I had prepared.

"I just like to be efficient," I said, all big eyes and innocence.

"And it has nothing to do with your wanting me to

work toward your destination just a little bit quicker?" he asked.

"I have no idea what you're talking about."

He slid out of his heavy jacket and kicked off his boots. "We'll get there when we get there, Rabbit, no sooner, no later."

"I have business I've got to take care of in Anchorage. I'm anxious to get to it."

"What kind of business?"

"Personal business, the kind that comes with a deadline," I retorted.

"But you're not rushing through *my* business so we can get to yours faster, right?"

Now was so not the time to tell him that I was punting certain files to let the lesser offenders run free and clear the road to Anchorage. "I'm not rushing," I told him, sounding just a little more prim than I deserved to at the moment. "I'm *streamlining*."

"And I appreciate that," he said. "Just don't streamline me out of a job."

"I couldn't possibly. I would hate to see what you would do with your handcuffing skills as a civilian."

He stared at me, eyebrows raised. "I could think of a couple of things, just off the top of my head."

I groaned. "Walked right into that one, huh?"

He nodded, chuckling to himself as he removed my phone from the charger and plugged his in. He didn't even glance at my screen while he removed the cord. He'd never asked to see the phone. He never checked my messages or the most recent calls. He trusted me with it. Even when it was in his hands, he guarded my privacy.

And that was the moment—regardless of his weird job and supernatural status—when I fell just a little bit in love with Caleb Graham.

My reasons for getting Caleb a laptop had a third, even less altruistic layer of motivation. The private server allowed me to check in discreetly with Red-burn. When I went more than two weeks without an e-mail, I violated protocols and sent her an e-mail requesting a phone conference. She sent back a reply: "Just this once. ☺" Which was why I loved her so much. She gave me a late-night appointment time that coincided with Caleb's meeting with one of his bar contacts.

Not knowing Red-burn's first name bothered me from time to time. This was someone who had saved and changed my life. And I wasn't allowed to know anything about her, not even the state where she was living. She could be sitting in the next building, for all I knew.

Even with Caleb safely ensconced in a bowling alley/dry goods store down the street, I felt the need to close the curtains while I waited for her call. Hearing that voice was a balm for my frazzled nerves, and for the first time in weeks, I felt that maybe everything would work out after all.

"Well, aren't you a voice for sore ears, or something like that," she said, giving a throaty giggle. "How are you doing?"

"Pretty well, considering. I'm just getting jumpy without updates," I said quietly.

"No news is good news sometimes."

"I know." I sighed, hoping I didn't sound too petu-lant. "Can you at least tell me what happened? Why'd you pull the escape hatch? Why now?"

Red-burn seemed to consider this for a long while before finally saying, "You're famous."

My mouth went dry. The last time someone had said that to me, it was after Glenn posted clandestine shower footage of me on YouTube. "What do you mean?"

"When we arranged your transportation to the Great Frozen North, we did it through one of our contacts who works at the Bellingham port terminal," she said. "He's able to hide 'special passengers' on the manifest as unbooked rooms on the ferry."

I frowned. I already knew this. I had met "Captain Anonymous," another Network operative, at the port terminal just before boarding the ferry from Washing-ton. He was a sweet, baby-faced blond in his twenties who gave me a bag of snacks and a Nicole Peeler paper-back along with my tickets and Anna Moder informa-tion packet. I'd gone straight into the ladies' room, dyed my hair dark brown over the sink, and walked out as Anna.

The five-day ride on the *Northern Sea Star* from Washington State to Chenega Bay had been one of the more pleasant experiences on the run—clean sea air, the occasional whale sighting. Once I assured myself that Glenn was not, in fact, the guy selling hot dogs at the concession stand, it was practically a luxury cruise.

"Well, the captain didn't realize that the ferry line's marketing department would be shooting photos for the company Web site during your excursion. There's a media release agreement built right into the ticket's terms of use, which most people don't read, so they don't realize that when they board the boat, they're giving permission for the company to use their image in advertising . . ."

"Oh, no," I groaned.

"Your picture is smack dab in the banner on their home page. It's an adorable little boy and his daddy waving bye-bye to the Washington coast as their adventure begins. You're not front and center or anything, just sort of lurking in the background, looking like one of those Old World malevolent spirits that foreshadow sea disasters."

"That seems sort of harsh," I told her.

"Two words for you, sweetie: undereye concealer."

I snorted. It was such a normal, bitchy, girlfriend thing to say. Red-burn was caustic on occasion, but her dark humor always made me feel better somehow, as if my situation wasn't all that insane if someone could crack a joke about it.

"Anyway, with the dark dye job and the haunting undereye circles, you looked so different from your picture that the captain didn't even recognize you at first, and he's on that Web site every day. So when he did realize what had happened, he went to the company's IT guy to ask about changing the photo on the Web to some other shot. The IT guy told him, 'You're the second person to ask about that photo this week.' He said some online image vendor inquired about that very same photo, hoping to acquire the rights to distrib-

ute it, then got downright hateful when the IT guy refused to give him information about when it was taken.
Just that morning, the company Web site had shown
signs of being hacked, but the only areas of the site that
were improperly accessed were the image files and the
ticketing information logged from the date of your departure. Security footage stored in a completely different server had also been tampered with."

My stomach rolled with the only possibility. Glenn.
Glenn would have the skill necessary to get into any
Web site he wanted.

"But his stumbling across a ferry company's Web
site is just so random," I said. "How would he even
know to look at the port terminal Web site?"

"We're not sure, honey. Maybe he ran a facial-
recognition program set to scan cached images. It's
possible he's figured out where our information is
stored and he got in that way. He's a persistent little
bastard. Next time, try to marry someone who can't
turn on a laptop on his own."

My fickle brain immediately went to Caleb. And I
told my brain to mind its own business.

"Anyway, the good news is that you're nowhere near
that area now, and looking for you in a state that big is
like looking for a needle in a . . . really large haystack
with very few needles."

I snickered. "Didn't think that metaphor through,
huh?"

"Nope."

Red-burn assured me that the Network was using
every resource it had to get me reestablished. We ended

the call with promises that she would send me e-mails regardless of new developments. I just had to stay safe and be patient.

I felt I had staying safe covered, particularly after Caleb sewed a special pocket in the lining of my coat so I would have "my baton" on hand anytime I needed it. (A werewolf with seamstress skills—who knew?) But patience was a little more complicated. I knew I was falling too easily into this routine. I got used to sharing motel rooms. I got used to sharing tiny, dingy bathrooms with a man so tall he could brush his teeth behind me and still see himself in the mirror over my head. I got used to sharing greasy meals over sticky diner tables and rickety in-room dinette sets. I got used to sleeping in a bed warmed by a large body, a definite bonus considering the daily drop in temperature as we rounded the corner into October.

I learned little things, some that endeared me to Caleb, others that made me want to throw all of his Garth Brooks CDs out of the truck window. I learned that Caleb liked having his back rubbed as we fell asleep. I learned that violin music made him edgy. Like most men, he insisted that he didn't need directions, but I insisted even more forcefully that we keep track of our progress on a map.

Without mentioning them, he obviously was learning little things about me, too. He noticed the titles I liked to read and would pick up a mystery or romance paperback for me whenever he found a store that sold books. He would take the tomatoes off of my sandwiches without my having to say how much I hated them. He knew how to adjust the heat vents in the truck so that I stayed warm but not too hot.

I knew it would only last until I relocated, but it started to feel something like a normal existence. What could life be like if we were staying in one place? Would we become bored with each other? Would he realize that there were much more attractive, less emotionally damaged girls out there with whom he could make beautiful wolf-babies?

I wasn't happy that it was taking so long to reach my destination, but there wasn't much I could do about it. For now, I tried to enjoy traveling with Caleb.

Of course, there were nights when I would wake up with a warm, firm body curled around mine, and I would flinch, flipping onto my back and scooting across the bed. Caleb's arm would wrap around my waist, his grip unrelenting despite my mattress gymnastics.

Once my sleep-sluggish brain realized I was with Caleb, I would settle down almost immediately. Caleb's physical presence was like a magnet, constantly drawing me. No matter where he was in the room, I could feel the warmth of his skin radiating out and reaching for me.

He was deliberately giving me space, which I appreciated. I knew it was probably difficult for him. Were-creatures were demonstrative folk, reveling in public displays of affection where maybe only a handshake was called for. They maintained intimacy, from friendship to epic soul-mate romance, through touch. It was as though skin-to-skin contact confirmed the connection, a sort of unwritten, unspoken, *I still love you enough to tolerate your questionable hand-washing practices* memo.

It was diametrically opposed to his nature to avoid touching me, particularly, I suspect, after getting so cozy with me that first night. I appreciated his efforts, but at the same time, I felt more than a little frustrated by the situation. I was trusting Caleb more each day, growing more attracted to him, and he now seemed content to be snuggle-buddies.

And it was slowly driving me insane.

Sex was serious business for werewolves. I knew that in most cases, it meant lifelong commitment and off-spring and all that. Part of me hoped that Caleb was the rare exception who could slip on a steel-belted-radial condom and have his way with a girl he just liked a lot.

It was a long shot.

Then again, did the committed-werewolf-sex issue mean that Caleb had never had sex?

Werewolves were basically breeding themselves out of existence with their mated-for-life policies. Once a male impregnated a female, his DNA wouldn't mix with any other's. The same went for were-females— once they had children with a male, there were no other connections to be made. It was why divorce was almost nonexistent, and widows rarely remarried within the pack. Most males didn't want to give up their chance of having children. Maggie's cousin Samson was a fantastic exception to this rule. He had adopted his wife Alicia's children as his own and was in the process of turning them into miniature knuckle-headed versions of himself.

Generally, werewolves tried to marry other were-wolves, so they would be able to pass on their genes and produce little werewolves. But because of geography and the limited population, more and more wolves were marrying humans, and that resulted in more "dead-liners," humans who shared all the same genes as werewolves but had none of the wolf magic. They couldn't phase and lacked the werewolves' special senses. They weren't included in pack business. Some packs considered them a source of shame, as if the diluted werewolf genes were a sign of weakness, but the Graham pack loved their dead-liners as much as they loved any relative.

Most females wouldn't risk premating sex, because they didn't want to risk being tied to someone they didn't want to spend the rest of their lives with. Some males did play "sex roulette," as Maggie called it, and sometimes they lost, meaning they impregnated unsuitable females and were stuck with them for life. Maggie's stance on this unfortunate practice was "If you don't want to pay, don't play."

Maggie was terribly pragmatic about this sort of thing.

It was difficult to imagine someone like Caleb as a thirty-something-year-old virgin. But I didn't know if I was ready for that responsibility, to initiate someone into sex. Not because I was nervous about sex. I used to be not really wild but on the more adventurous side of the spectrum. I went out with my girlfriends, enjoyed the occasional protected one-night stand. But that was then. Now I was no one's idea of an ideal first time.

Unless, of course, he came out of the bathroom wearing *only* a towel again—then all bets were off.

7

Ethical Organ Thievery

We had been driving for hours. The last time I could remember feeling my own butt was sometime before lunch. Even Caleb was starting to show some wear, hunching over the wheel and occasionally rolling his neck back and forth to hear the snap of realigning vertebrae. I reached across the seat, pleased that I could touch him so casually, rubbing the thick hair at the crown of his head, down to the nape of his neck. He leaned into the caress, a pleased chuffing noise emanating from his chest.

"Sore?"

He nodded.

I rubbed the back of his neck, pressing my fingers deeper into the muscle tissue, feeling for knots. Tracing his hairline with my fingertips, massaging his scalp, rubbing my fingers along the tips of his ears, which I'd heard was an acupressure point for dogs. He turned his head to rub his cheek against my knuckles. I scooted a little closer, rubbing those knuckles along the line of *his cheekbone. He turned his head slightly, pulling one of my fingertips into his mouth. He nipped at it with his blunter front teeth before wrapping his tongue around it, running his tongue along the ridges of my fingerprints. A hot flash ran from my chest to my belly and settled between my thighs. Old, lovely, familiar sensations—lust, excitement, giddy teenage zeal—had me squirming in my seat. My eyes widened at the strength and dexterity of his tongue as he moved it over my skin. If he could do that to a fingertip, what could he do to my—*

I was jolted out of this rather indecent speculation by Caleb's suddenly veering off the road and throwing the truck into park. My seatbelt seemed to melt away, and Caleb was climbing across the seat.

His mouth. My God, his mouth was hot and so very wet against mine. He wrapped my legs around his waist, pressing me back against the seat and grinding his thick, solid, denim-covered erection against me.

I moaned into his mouth, threading my fingers through his hair with one hand and clinging to his neck with the other. His hands spanned the width of my waist, sliding down the front of my jeans and yanking them open. The dark depth of his eyes melted away and gave way to predatory gold. Pressing his mouth to my palm, he untangled my arms from his neck and had me lie back as he pulled my jeans and panties down. His warm, thick fingers slid smoothly inside me. He moved in and out, teasing me with an achingly slow rhythm as his thumb rubbed at my sensitive folds.

He grinned when I made a desperate whimper and crooked his fingers—

• • •

I bolted up in my truck seat, disoriented and dizzy as I watched the scenery speed by. Caleb was driving, of course, and watching me with a little smirk on his face.

"Hey there, Rabbit," he said, jostling my shoulder gently. "You having another nightmare? You were moaning in your sleep."

"I'm fine," I mumbled, shifting in my seat to alleviate the full, tingling sensation of my damp jeans pressing against me.

Why was he smirking at me? Had I said anything in my sleep? I'd never been much of a sleep-talker. I squirmed in my seat, trying subtly to move my uncomfortably wet panties—

Oh, hell.

With a cringe, I realized that he could probably smell that I was definitely not having a *bad* dream. He was teasing me. Stupid werewolf supersenses.

My face went warm, and I nudged his hand away. I grabbed a bottle of water from my cupholder and took a very long, very cold drink.

We'd been driving for three days and had already managed to collect on two relatively minor cases: a guy who passed bad checks in Healy and a woman who was a serial identity thief. I was amazed at how much Caleb managed to accomplish, tracking down about a dozen cases in the few weeks I traveled with him. He worked multiple cases at once, trying to track down several geographically convenient ne'er-do-wells, whether they were wanted by the authorities or . . . other people with less actual authority but more money.

Occasionally, it was as easy as calling the target's

mom and telling her to drag her son to the nearest sheriff's office, where Caleb was waiting. (It actually worked twice.) Others put up more of a fight, which was why—given the Jerry debacle—Caleb tried to keep me as far from actual clients as possible.

At least, he did until Suds called him about the Mort Johanssen case sometime in our second week together. According to the e-mail, Mort Johanssen was a match to his twin brother, a seafood magnate who needed a kidney. Merl Johanssen was getting increasingly desperate and offered Caleb an obscene amount of money to track down his wayward brother, a Delta Junction resident who hadn't spoken to his twin in years because of a dispute over their mother's will.

We sat at a sticky diner table, munching on waffles. Caleb handed me the paperwork Suds had passed on from an investigator in Kodiak. "Merl's got a huge fleet of crab boats and owns shares in most of the fleets in Alaska. If you've had crabs, it's more than likely Merl's had his hand in it." He pulled an uncomfortable face. "That sounded better in my head."

I snorted into my orange juice. "I sure hope so."

I read over the medical report and saw that Merl's renal failure was attributed to damage from a bad reaction to an antibiotic called streptomycin. Generally, when a patient had kidney problems, treating the cause could alleviate the symptoms. But it was difficult to restore damaged tissue. Merl wasn't responding to treatment, and his creatinine levels and glomerular filtration rates were getting progressively worse.

I looked up to see that Caleb was watching me read

the doctor's notes. I smiled and flipped over to the mug shot of Mort, a stubby, round-cheeked man with thinning red hair. He looked like a hungover Cupid. "Do they both look like this?"

Caleb nodded. "Identical. Mort took a test showing him to be a match just before their mom died. Merl was executor of her will and took some family hunting property that Mort thought should go to him. Angry words were exchanged. Mort declared he was keeping his blankety-blank kidney and stopped taking Merl's calls. But Merl's condition is getting worse, and he would like someone to find Mort and persuade him to come back. See, it's almost humanitarian. We're helping to save a life."

"Wait, so we're tracking someone down so he can have a kidney removed by force? Why don't we just get a Coleman cooler and yank the sucker out ourselves?"

"I've never been that good with anatomy." When Caleb saw my distressed expression, he added, "I'm just kidding!"

"No, you're not."

"Fifty-fifty," he admitted, waggling his hand. "Look, all we have to do is walk in there, talk him into the car, and drive him to the airfield."

"Where twenty-four hours from now, he'll wake up in a tub full of ice with a mysterious pain in his side."

"No," Caleb said, indignant. "He'll be flown to Portland for the procedure. As long as he's in reasonably good health, he'll be in and out in no time."

"OK, I've been a little wishy-washy in voicing my disapproval for your job in the past couple of weeks, but let me spell it out for you. We can't do this. We cannot use another human being for spare parts," I told him, lowering my voice when I realized the waitress was staring at me. "It's ghoulish."

"Don't you think Merl should have a shot at living?" he asked.

"I just think Mort should be able to make the decision for himself." I sighed.

"Come on, Rabbit," he said, jostling my shoulder. I glowered at him. "If it makes you feel any better, Merl promised that if Mort donates his kidney, he'll pay about twenty thousand dollars in back child support to Mort's ex. See? It's a win-win."

"I still think it's pretty messed-up," I grumbled, sneaking a piece of bacon from his plate. The fact that he let me get away with it was a testament to his either liking me or feeling guilty for being a kidney snatcher.

Mort proved to be a wilier target than we anticipated. It took more than a week to track him from his snowmobile dealership in Delta Junction. Caleb grew more and more focused. He would disappear from our motel room for the night, coming back smelling of the woods. He wandered the town, searching for any hint of Mort's scent. No one in town would give up information about Mort, either out of solidarity or because they honestly didn't know. His live-in girlfriend, Monica, told me in no uncertain terms to kiss her ass and then slammed the door in my face. None of his employees would say anything besides telling us Mort was ice-fishing "somewhere." Frankly, I was cheering Mort's wily ass on. As far as I was concerned, I'd be happy if we never tracked the ginger escape artist down.

Caleb decided to move on to the nearest lake to scout ice-fishing camps, getting as far as a gas station ten miles outside of Delta Junction. The moment we stopped in the gas-station parking lot, his whole posture changed. His neck craned forward, and his nostrils flared. He jammed the truck into park, throwing me against the seatbelt. Caleb threw his arm across me in the classic "mom brake" maneuver, which I thought was gentlemanly until I looked down to where his hand was clasping my left breast. I cleared my throat. He glanced down, and his eyes went wide.

"What's going on with you?" I asked as he moved his hand.

"Thought I saw something," he said.

"The opportunity to cop a feel?"

"I would say I was sorry, but it would be a lie," he said.

"OK, well, while you search the parking lot for 'something,' I'm going to go get some more jerky. We're down to one bag, and I know that makes you nervous."

I hopped out of the truck and walked into the station. It was a mom-and-pop operation in a two-story building called Mo-Mo's Gas-n-Go. Given the porch structure on the second story, I guessed that the owner lived in the apartment over the store.

After visiting one of the cleaner—if overly bright— gas-station stalls in the Greater Northwest, I visited the jerky display to determine whether I could sneak a similarly packaged, low-sodium version under Caleb's radar. I picked over the cellophane-wrapped tubes of meat, wrinkling my nose at the very idea of jalapeño-nacho-cheese beef jerky.

"Oh, don't even think about it," an amused voice sounded behind me. "If they have to spend that much time doctoring it up to make you want to eat it, you should just stick with corn chips."

"It's not for me, trust me." I turned to share a chuckle with my helpful jerky Samaritan . . . and came face-to-face with the elusive Mort Johanssen. Jowly, bedraggled Mort Johanssen, in a green hunter's jacket, was offering me a friendly smile and advice on meat snacks.

"Oh, nooo," I groaned, dropping my jerky to the gas-station floor. "It's you."

Mort frowned. "Well, that's not very nice."

I pushed him none too gently away from the front window toward the little alcove where the restrooms were, so Caleb couldn't see him. There was a fire exit beyond the restrooms, half-hidden behind giant stacks of milk crates. Unfortunately, Mort was a little too much man for me to move all the way into the alcove, and we stopped just in front of the potato chip display. "You have to get out of here, preferably out that fire exit."

"Wh-who the hell are you, lady?" he spluttered, batting my hands away.

"Look, I know this is going to sound weird and suspicious. But I happen to be traveling with someone who was sent by your brother—"

Mort actually shoved me away from him, paling even more under his decidedly wintry skin tone. "Merl's still after my damn kidney?"

I nodded. "It would seem so."

"And you're with that big guy who's been sniffing around town for me?"

I blanched at the use of the word *sniffing*. But I continued, using my firm bedside-manner voice. "I don't want to tell you your business, but your brother is sick. Really sick. I understand that can make people desperate, but I still don't think that's an excuse to shanghai somebody into nonconsensual surgery."

"What's your point?" Mort huffed.

I snagged a Sharpie out of my jacket pocket and grabbed the first item I saw from the shelves, which happened to be a bag of peanut butter Combos. I scribbled the name of the airfield where Merl had kept a private jet waiting for the last week, just in case we tracked Mort down. "There is a plane waiting for you here. They can be ready to take off within an hour if you show up."

"You have to buy those," he told me, nodding toward the Combos.

"I will, I will." I shook my head at him.

"It's just that I own the station, and every little bit counts."

"OK, I will throw in the jerky *and* one of those little car air-freshener trees if you will pay attention to what I'm saying." I put the bag in his hand and placed my palms on either side of his face so I knew he was looking me right in the eye. "Merl needs your help. The chances of him lasting more than a few months without a transplant aren't good. You need to decide whether you can live with that or if you can find it in your heart to forgive your brother and give him what he needs to survive. Personally, I think you should be given the chance to make that decision on your own terms. So what I'm telling you is that you need to haul ass out of that back door and run for it, so you have *time* to make that decision on your own terms before my friend sees you and makes this whole situation a lot more . . . intense. Now, do you have your car keys on you?"

"He's really sick?" Mort asked.

I nodded. "He's got very little time left."

Mort's watery blue eyes narrowed at me. "Is this a trick?"

"Yes, I'm trying to trick you into escaping," I deadpanned.

"I need some time to think this over."

"Which is what I'm trying to give you!" I threw my hands up. "It's like we're not even having the same conversation."

Behind me, I heard the station's front door swing open. Mort's eyes went wide, and I turned to see Caleb walking in with an anxious expression. That expression shifted from anxious to shocked and then even more confused in just a few seconds.

Shit.

"Go!" I grunted, shoving Mort toward the back door. Of course, Mort left his Combos bag behind, so I had to chase after him and throw the marked snack bag at his head while he ducked out the door. Caleb charged after him. Against all bounds of logic, I hooked my arm through his and dug my heels into the slick tile floor. This, of course, did not work, because he had about seventy pounds and a whole lot of werewolf strength on his side.

"Good Lord, you're strong," I groaned as he dragged me across the floor to the exit.

Just then, I heard the roar of an engine. Caleb turned, taking me with him as we watched a beat-up Chevy four-by-four peel out of the station parking lot and onto the road.

"What did you do?" Caleb exclaimed as I climbed off of him and settled on unsteady feet.

I winced. "I let him go."

"Why would you do that?" he cried, throwing his arms up and making me flinch, which pissed me off.

"Don't you yell at me!" I shouted, catching the attention of the irritable clerk behind the counter.

"You need to clear out if you're going to carry on like that," she said, pointing at the door.

And now I was getting kicked out of a gas station. *Classy.*

Caleb caught my arm and pulled me out the front door. He wasn't hurting me, but the trapped, panicked feeling the sensation evoked had me clawing at his hands. He caught sight of my face and dropped his hands from my arms. But the momentum had me skidding toward the truck, bumping into the side panel with an *ooof*.

"We've spent the better part of a week looking for this guy, and you helped him escape? What the hell is wrong with you? Have I not explained to you how my job works?" Caleb was towering over me, his face livid.

"I wanted him to make the decision for himself!" I exclaimed. "If nothing else, it helps us avoid pesky kidnapping charges. I gave him all of the information for the airfield. He has time to think about it, and I truly, truly believe that he's going to do the right thing and show up for that flight. Everybody wins. His brother gets a kidney. Mort's kids get the back child support. And maybe, Mort and Merl can be closer."

"You don't get to make those decisions!" he exclaimed. "You don't get to just *decide* which cases are OK to pursue and which ones aren't. You don't get to interfere with how I make my living, which is how I support the both of us, by the way."

"I do have an issue with how you make your living. And I never *asked* you to support me. You just scooped me up and put me in your pocket. You didn't ask me what I wanted. You just insisted that you knew what was best for me."

"Because you're incapable of using common sense! You just throw yourself into these stupid situations because you refuse to listen to anybody else!" Caleb shouted. I could feel cold fear winding through my belly, crawling up my spine. My jaw clenched tight. It was better that way, to keep myself from saying something stupid, from making it worse. "Somebody has to look out for you."

I held my hands up defensively, my back pressed against the truck as Caleb yelled.

"And all the while, you sneak around behind my back, doing God knows what, because you decided that you know better. Who do you think you are?"

I nodded, my face practically buried in my own shoulder. I was folding in on myself, trying to make myself smaller. I could feel all of those old instincts creeping back.

And that pissed me off.

And for once, instead of flinching away, I lunged. "What makes you think you can talk to me like that?" I shouted, advancing and shoving my finger into his face. The loud, raging voice coming out of me didn't even sound like my own. Caleb seemed just as shocked, considering the way he backed up. "Don't you talk to me like I'm some stupid child. You don't stand over me and scream at me until I agree with you. Just who the hell do you think *you* are?"

"I'm someone who cares about you," Caleb said, his voice considerably calmer.

"So that gives you the right to make any sort of decision for me? Do you think this is what I wanted? Do you think I would have spent one minute with you if I knew how 'protective' you would be?"

Hurt and guilt flashed simultaneously across his features as his body relaxed from its confrontational stance. "OK, OK. You're right," he conceded. "I shouldn't have raised my voice. Or dragged you around like that. That was wrong."

But I was long past hearing what he had to say. "How dare you!" I yelled, advancing on Caleb until he backed into another truck with a *thunk*. "How dare you tell me what to do, where to go, what to wear, who to talk to?"

Caleb frowned and shook his head. "I never said anything about what you're wearing. I just gave you a bag of clothes."

"I am a person, damn it. I'm an *adult*! I was smart enough to get through school. Why wasn't I smart enough to see you for what you are? Why couldn't I see the stupid excuses I was making for you? Why?"

Caleb stood there, dumbfounded, as I ranted at him and cried. I got angry enough to swing at him, something that would shame me later. He ducked the blow easily and caught my arms to prevent a second round. So I kicked him in the shins, which he clearly didn't expect. The sight of him yelping and grabbing at his leg was enough to snap me out of my conniption fit.

My arms dropped to my sides as Caleb stared at me in horror. We were lucky the clerk hadn't called the cops on us.

I'd hurt him—not much, but the expression on his face was enough to make my stomach roll all over again. I dashed behind the truck and tossed my lunch all over the gravel of the parking lot. And I felt like a first-prize idiot.

Yes, Caleb was occasionally annoying and consistently overprotective, but he'd never done anything remotely hurtful to me. He'd never called me names, never made me feel inadequate or small. Heck, if the bruises currently healing on his shins were any indication, I'd done more physical damage to him than he'd done to me. Over and over, Caleb had shown me that he was not Glenn. He deserved a lot of things, but being my emotional punching bag by proxy was not one of them.

I rinsed my mouth with the water Caleb pressed into my hand. He helped me climb into the truck, and I tucked my arms around my folded legs. I glanced through the front window of the station and saw the clerk watching us warily. Caleb pulled out of the parking lot and drove silently back to the motel. He didn't talk during the drive or while we walked into the motel or even while I stripped down and showered, trying to fight off the chills with lukewarm water.

I shuffled out of the bathroom, wearing Caleb's T-shirt and a pair of sweats, and sat on the bed next to Caleb. He had his hands folded in his lap, staring straight ahead with a completely blank expression. There was a long, awkward silence, in which I speculated that he would finally decide I was too much trouble to deal with and send me on my way. And part of me thought maybe it would be better that way. Maybe it would hurt less in the long run.

Maybe I should take the choice away from him. Maybe I should get up and just start packing. I'd spent too much time procrastinating. I needed to stop this madness and get to Anchorage, start over, and Caleb . . . Caleb was still staring straight ahead, which was starting to worry me.

"So back at the station, you weren't really talking to me, huh?" he finally asked.

I shook my head.

"You were talking to *him*? The guy who gives you nightmares?"

I nodded, not able to look up at him. "I never got around to counseling. I read all of the right self-help books, worked through them as instructed. I was offered anonymous talk therapy over the phone with a specialized counselor, but I just couldn't bring myself to do it. Somehow, admitting what happened to me, making it real, seemed to make all of the progress I'd made unreal."

"I know you have some stuff in your past that you don't want to tell me about. And I've tried not to pry. But eventually, Rabbit, you're going to have to talk to me about it."

"Do you really want a blow-by-blow account?" I asked. "Do you want to look at my journal? There's an entertaining read, or at least it was before I realized he was reading it. Giving me even that tiny bit of privacy was just too much for him. Do you want me to tell you I was some sweet, naive girl who never suspected a thing? Because I did suspect—a lot—but I just couldn't figure a way out of it."

"No. I'm not asking you to share anything with me you don't want to," he insisted. "For now, you should know that I'm not whoever you were yelling at. I wouldn't ever lay a hand on you in anger. I may bluster and fuss, but I wouldn't try to take your choices away. I kind of like that you're always trying to get around me to do what you want. It's what makes you interesting and frustrating and, well, you. I wouldn't want it any other way."

I nodded, resenting him for being so damned under-standing. I didn't know how to respond to this. I knew what to do when someone was yelling or threatening. I didn't know what to do in the face of respectful bound-aries. God, that was sad.

I slipped an arm around him. He tucked my head under his chin and kissed my hair. "Also, you have to stop kicking me in the shin. It's emasculating."

A snort rippled up from my lungs, and I covered it with a cough. "I'm sorry. There's no excuse for it."

"I know."

He ruffled my hair, his hand lingering on top of my head. I leaned into it, tucking my face against his chest. He wrapped the other arm around me and secured me there.

"I'm sorry I raised my voice," he said. "I should have known better. You showed all those skittish signs. I knew you wouldn't tolerate that."

"So I'm a walking advertisement for post-traumatic stress. Awesome," I muttered.

"No, the signs are pretty subtle, but I watch you closely."

"That doesn't make me feel any better."

"Sorry."

I looked up at him. "Can we just go to bed and pre-tend you're not still crazy angry with me?"

"I'm not 'crazy' angry with you. I'm 'sane person' angry with you. And we're going to have to talk about your bleeding-heart tendencies at some point," he told me.

"I know." I sighed, flopping down on the threadbare pillows. "But not tonight."

He scooted up on the bed, under the blankets, and curled his body around mine. He rested his chin on my shoulder and draped an arm around my middle. I closed my eyes and sighed as the heat from his skin seeped into mine.

"My name's not Anna."

He gave me a squeeze. "I figured that out a while ago."

There was another long, silent pause. He wasn't going to ask me. He was waiting for me to tell him myself, to make the choice to share that part of me.

"It's Tina," I told him. "Christina, if you want to be technical about it. But I was named after my mother, and we couldn't have two Christinas in the house. And I refused to be called Chrissie. Since then, I've been called Anna, Melissa, Brandy, Lisa, and Tess. I was Anna the longest."

"What do you want me to call you?"

"When you're not calling me Rabbit, you mean?"

He laughed into my skin, a canine whickering noise that was more wolf than man.

"Tina." I sighed. "I would really like to be Tina again."

He kissed the nape of my neck, sending a pleasant warm tingle down my spine. "I like Tina, too."

I woke up to the sound of Caleb whispering, "You're kidding me!"

I rolled over to see his bare back as he hunched over the edge of the bed. He was talking into his cell phone, muttering furiously under his breath.

"You're *kidding* me," he said again.

I sat up in bed, swiping at my face. I padded toward the bathroom to brush my teeth as Caleb continued muttering into his phone. He wrapped up the phone call by sighing and saying, "She's going to be hell to live with after this."

I arched an eyebrow and spat out the excess toothpaste. He ended the connection and flopped back on the bed, pinching the bridge of his nose.

"What?"

Caleb sat up, rolling his eyes. "That was Merl's office. Mort showed up at the airfield last night, just like you said he would. He checked in to the hospital this morning for presurgery testing. Merl is expressing his gratitude with a rather large check."

My lips wanted to twitch into a grin, but I tamped it down. "Gloating would be an ugly thing to do even when I was insanely right, wouldn't it?"

"Yes, yes, it would," he said, giving me an exasperated look.

He hauled himself out of bed and helped me gather up our bags. We completed our various packing-up chores side-by-side, organizing the files, securing the equipment, checking under the bed and in the bathroom for forgotten items. Caleb was sulking, but it was a quiet *kicking my own ass* sort of self-flagellation to which I was not accustomed. He wasn't throwing things around the room, breaking my stuff, or sending me wounded-baby-deer looks because I was so very cruel. He just silently worked through the moving-out checklist with his mouth clenched shut. As we walked out of the motel room, I bumped him with my hip. His lips quirked, but he actively suppressed the smile. Walking toward the truck, I bumped him again. He laughed, throwing his arm around my shoulders.

"We did the right thing, Caleb. We let Mort make the choice for himself. I'm sorry I went about it in a dishonest way, trying to sneak him out of the gas station. But it all worked out in the end."

"But what if it hadn't?" he asked.

I smiled in what I hoped was a winsome, nonobnoxious manner. "Well, then, I would owe *you* a rather large apology."

"I know you don't agree with what I do."

"Not in all cases," I protested. "But I think that you should check into backgrounds and circumstances a little more before you agree to look for someone. There are people out there who deserve to be left alone."

He nodded. "I'll think about it."

It was probably the maximum amount of progress I was going to make, so I would take it and run. "Who was right?" I asked, preening just the tiniest bit.

"You were right," he said, standing up.

I fairly skipped to stand in front of him, bouncing on the balls of my feet. "Who is smarter than you?"

He crossed his arms over his chest and sighed. "You're smarter than me."

I kissed his chin, because that was as high as I could reach. "Don't you forget it."

"Was that last bit really necessary?" he grumbled.

"Hey, I had a whole 'I Told You So' dance choreographed. You're lucky I'm sparing you that," I told him. He harrumphed as he helped me climb up into the truck. "It was set to the tune of 'Single Ladies.'"

Caleb narrowed his eyes at me. "You are evil. Pure evil wrapped up in a tiny pixie package."

"But I was a *correct* evil pixie package," I said.

8

From Some Senders, All E-mails Are Red-Flagged

I celebrated the arrival of Merl's very large check by finding the world's only Laundromat-slash-Internet café and checked my e-mail while our delicates spun dry. Caleb was meeting with someone about a case that was "too preliminary" to discuss with me. He'd asked me to stick close to the motel, but I needed to check my private e-mail address, and we were running low on clean socks. I was more comfortable with using the café's computers to check the secure server I used for Red-burn's e-mails. I hoped that she'd sent some update on my paperwork.

When I typed my information into the log-in fields, my in-box had sprouted new messages like acne on a One Direction fan. Thirty-eight new messages starting weeks before, right around the time I ran out of Emerson's and saved a werewolf. The subject lines were all the same: "FOUND YOU, BITCH."

I knocked my foam coffee cup from the table, splashing scalding liquid across my thighs and barely noticing the burn. My stomach pitched, and the floor seemed to tilt underneath me. Hands shaking, I clicked on the first one. It was short and to the point: "I found you, bitch. Did you really think you could run from me? Do you think living in the ass end of nowhere will keep me from finding you? Don't you worry, I'm on my way. We'll be seeing each other real soon."

Glenn was smart enough not to sign it, and the e-mail address was listed as gotchubitch23@qwickmail .com. I knew he would be smart enough not to send the message from his home computer. If by some insane chance I went to the cops, they wouldn't be able to trace it back to his IP address.

Also, I found it a little distressing that there were so many people using *gotchubitch* as an e-mail user name that Glenn had to add numerals to it.

I highly doubted that this was some unfortunate cyber-coincidence, a misdirected message, or a prank. I was able to fight through the initial wave of panic, the cold flush that spread from my heart to my limbs, making it impossible to move my fingers the way I should. I knew this was coming, I reminded myself. Red-burn had warned me that he was getting closer. This e-mail campaign was most likely a bluff. He was probably thousands of miles away. Because if he'd really found me, he would be here, right now, telling me what an ungrateful cow I was as he dragged me back to Tennessee.

I took a long, lung-stretching breath and forced

it out through my nostrils, then clicked on the other messages. The next few e-mails were more conciliatory. He missed me. His life just didn't work without me. He didn't know why I'd run away, but he would do anything he could to make our relationship work. Wouldn't I please contact him so he would stop worrying about me? The messages ran in cycles—angry, demanding, pitiful, lonely, and then back to vicious and threatening.

He couldn't scare me, I told myself, hoping that eventually, I would believe it. I could fight him now. I could escape before he even realized we were in the same room. I wasn't the same naive, trusting girl he'd married. He didn't even know me anymore. I wasn't that same person. And there was Caleb to consider.

Oh, God, what if he hurt Caleb? I knew it wasn't likely, what with the whole turns-into-a-giant-apex-predator issue. But even werewolves had to yield to bullets, and Glenn wasn't above bringing a gun to a werewolf fistfight.

Still in a bit of a daze, I gathered our clean clothes together, folded them on automatic pilot, and shuffled back to the motel. In an unexpected turn of fortune, I was able to walk a city block in a rural small town without being attacked or harassed by hooligan lumberjacks. I tried to appear as calm as possible as I walked back to the motel. It wouldn't do to let Caleb see me freaked out. He would ask all kinds of questions, and I would give him answers, because my verbal filters were shaky enough that I'd tell him everything. And then . . . I didn't know what would happen then.

I stopped at the tiny general store and found turkey jerky and some coffee, because Caleb hated the brand that the motel kept on hand. I took several deep breaths outside of our motel-room door and pushed it open with a pleasant smile fixed on my face.

I found Caleb tossing our clothes into our bags. The laptop and the rest of the equipment were already packed and sitting by the door.

"What's going on?" I asked, dropping the grocery bags by my laptop.

"We're going home," he said.

For a terrifying moment, I thought he meant the valley. How was I supposed to explain that? How was I going to casually drop, *Oh, by the way, I know your family. And that you're a supernatural creature. Surprise!*

"H-home?" I asked.

"Well, home base. Suds's bar in Fairbanks, the Suds Bucket. I've had a couple of urgent e-mails from him about a few cases, so I need to go check in."

"Can't you just call him?" I asked, thinking about this new development. Fairbanks would bring me closer to Anchorage but not close enough. It was still a six-hour drive in good weather.

"Suds is getting anxious about a couple of guys we're looking for, big payouts and no developments. So I need to go talk shop with him for a while. We'll leave at first light, stay there with him in a non-motel room, which will be awfully nice. It'll only take a few days, and then we'll be on the road to Anchorage, just like I promised."

"OK," I said, nodding, suddenly distracted by the

neatly folded pile of fresh laundry. One of Glenn's biggest gripes about my housekeeping was my sloppy, haphazard laundry methods. Clean clothes had to be precisely folded or they would end up thrown in a big messy pile in the closet for me to fold all over again. So when I left, my first act of rebellion was to throw my socks into the drawer in a massive sock ball. But now my socks were matched and folded with military precision.

"No arguments, no negotiations, just 'OK'?"

"Uh-huh," I said, nodding again, chewing my lip. E-mails. All it took was a few pissy e-mails from my ex-husband, and I had retreated right back into "life with Glenn" coping mechanisms. What did that say about my progress so far? What did it say about my ability to survive on my own?

I could send Caleb after Glenn.

The thought took root as quickly and stealthily as a poisonous weed. I had a big bad werewolf on my side. He could make my Glenn problem disappear with a snap of his claws. No more running. No more hiding. No more fear. All I had to do was ask. It was on the tip of my tongue.

"Hey." Caleb squeezed my arm gently. My eyes snapped up to his face and its expression of concern. "Are you all right?

I gave him a weak smile. I couldn't ask that of him. I couldn't ask Caleb to kill for me. I wouldn't put blood on his hands, or mine. I would have to handle this myself.

"You spaced out a little bit on me," Caleb said.

"I'm fine, just not looking forward to another couple of hours in the truck. That's all."

He grinned, plopping down on the bed and pulling me into his lap. "Well, that's because I haven't introduced you to the wonders of my Conway Twitty CD collection."

What little smile I was able to produce disappeared, even as he nuzzled my neck. "If there is any good in this world, you are kidding."

Later that night, while Caleb slept, I sat up, thinking over the e-mail issue. How had Glenn found my e-mail address? Before I'd stumbled out of the Internet café, I'd checked the log-in history and didn't see any suspicious account activity. Had he figured out the password? How much longer would it be before he tried to take over the account?

In those few moments before my brain had completely melted down, I'd deleted every e-mail Red-burn had ever sent me and then sent her a quick message telling her it was possible the account had been compromised and asking if she could call my phone. I'd changed the e-mail password and increased the security settings, arranging it so that any changes would be tracked through my cell phone.

Glenn thought he could find me. He had no idea how good I'd gotten at hiding.

With a decisiveness that seemed cold and alien, I swung my feet out from under the covers. I scrawled a short note to Caleb on one of his Post-its and stuck it to the lampshade. I concentrated on keeping my feet silent on the nubby motel carpet. My bags were already packed for the early-morning departure. All I had to do was slip on some jeans and shoes and somehow manage to open the door without waking up Caleb, who had superhearing. No problem.

Dressing quietly, I watched him as he slept, the weak light filtering through the curtains giving his skin a faint yellow glow. Just like the light that would spread over his skin before the change. I was more than a little disappointed that I would never get to see Caleb shift. I would have liked to see what he looked like in wolf form. Of course, his human form wasn't too bad, either.

My fingers fumbled with the button of my jeans, and I shook them out. What was I doing? Why couldn't I just wake him and tell him that I was freaking out and needed his help? Why couldn't I give up my need to run as soon as things got tough? Why couldn't I just tell him I knew about wolfiness?

Caleb let out a whuffling sound and turned onto his side, burying his face in his pillow.

The distinctly canine movement made my lips curve into a fond smile. I couldn't do that to Caleb. I couldn't drag him down with me, into my big bag of crazy. He belonged to the valley, with his pack, not running my ex-husband down like the proverbial dog. He deserved to go back home and find some nice wolf-girl and have furry little babies. He deserved someone who could share her whole life with him, not just carefully edited sound bites.

Just walk out, my brain commanded. *Put on your coat and get the hell out before you manage to talk yourself out of this. Move your feet.*

So that's what I did. I slung my bag over my shoulder and made it all the way to the door. I looked back.

Damn it, why did I look back?

Caleb's hair was all mussed around his face, his relaxed, nearly boyish face. His lips were parted as he breathed deeply. I was going to miss that. I wanted nothing more than to crawl back into bed, where it was warm and safe and smelled like him.

I moved closer to the bed, even as my brain lectured me about mocking the laws of common sense. I stretched out my arm, stopping just short of running my fingers along his cheek.

"Be happy." I pressed the barest whisper of a kiss against his cheek, inhaling his spicy, woodsy scent one last time, and ran out of the motel room as if he was hot on my heels.

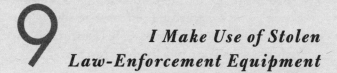

9

I Make Use of Stolen
Law-Enforcement Equipment

I, for lack of a more flowery term, hauled ass up the street to a bar called Slippery Sam's. It had been a while since I'd done any kind of running, and I ended up pulling a hamstring. But it was worth it to be able to close myself up in the dark, smoky room and hide in a booth lit only by a neon blue St. Pauli Girl sign.

The waitress wasn't thrilled to have a nonordering freeloader taking up her booth. So when I mentioned I was looking for a ride, she was quick to point out the bar's beer distributor, Bart, who would be departing for parts unknown within the next thirty minutes. Parts unknown sounded pretty good to me. And the rotund, grandfatherly driver's rig was parked out back, which was even better.

Bart was willing to take me as far as a saloon about four hours away, where he happened to know of a Coca-Cola distributor who ran a regular route to Rooklin, about a hundred miles east. He vouched for Carl, the Coca-Cola man, as a noncrazy non–serial killer and promised to arrange for my transportation to Rooklin, for which I was very grateful. Even when he insisted on showing me a few dozen pictures of his kids, grandkids, and various salmon he'd caught in the past year.

Bart dutifully handed me off to Carl, who turned out to be a skinny, pimply twenty-one-year-old who couldn't see over the steering wheel without the aid of a phone book. But he was very sweet and offered me some insights into *Battlestar Galactica* that I'd never considered. Despite his willingness to share his thermos of coffee, I was pretty much dead on my feet by the time we rolled into my latest destination.

Rooklin was like so many of the small Alaskan towns I'd traveled through, a tiny oasis of civilization carved out of a gap between mountains, surrounded by endless evergreen trees. Main Street consisted of a dozen wooden storefronts crammed close together, as much to save on construction materials as on the cost of heating during those long winters. There were no chain stores or fast-food restaurants, just locally owned essential businesses: a grocer's, a bar, a medical clinic, and a combination pawn shop and office-supply store called Dudley's Duplicates.

Carl sent me off with a plastic bag full of Oreos and a bold pat on the arm, wishing me luck as I wandered down Rooklin's main street to Dudley's Duplicates. It was downright painful to sell the little emerald ring my late grandmother had given me for my sweet sixteen. I'd managed to hold on to it all this time, only to sell it for a whopping eighty-five dollars to a pawn broker. But in a choice between sentiment and a roof over my head, I figured Gramma would understand. She'd been a practical woman.

I supposed this was my official rock bottom.

I had just enough money to rent a room at Rooklin Right-Price Rooms for two nights and buy a loaf of bread and a jar of peanut butter from the market. If I was really lucky, Red-burn might be able to arrange a ride to Anchorage for me before I ran through my meager cash stash. If not, I was going to have to make a choice between buying supplies and keeping all of my minor organs. Maybe I could contact Merl about getting a good price.

Tucked as safe as I could be in the luxurious accommodations at the Right-Price, I sat at the foot of the lumpy bed and stared at the beige-yellow walls. In danger of slipping into crippling despair, I needed to find the bright side. I was alive. I was—for the most part—unharmed. For the moment, life was pretty good. If I could get some sleep, I could face the next day.

I spent two days burning through time slots at Dudley's Duplicates' Internet "café," also known as two wobbly folding chairs and a card table in the corner of the store. I contacted Red-burn through a newly established qwickmail address, using our safe word, *caduceus*, to verify that it was me, not Glenn posing as me. I updated her on my situation and asked for any details on my new identity, which she couldn't provide yet. She did, however, wire me a few hundred dollars so my minor organs could remain unpawned. And because it was a better nervous habit than smoking or knuckle cracking, I reread the restraining-order laws in Alaska. While the state troopers would be willing to assist authorities close to Glenn, I still had no idea where he was. He was smart enough to cover his tracks through a fake IP address, so that wouldn't be any help. I didn't know if he was really getting closer to me or if he was just playing a mind game. I wasn't willing to take the risk, either way.

While I had much better evidence of Glenn's harassment this time, I wouldn't be able to get any sort of legal revenge on him. And my unwillingness to dirty the pack's collective paws cut me off from my avenues to bloody, though clearly justified, illegal revenge. My best hope now was simple escape, even if that meant long-term residence at Rooklin Right-Price Rooms.

Please, good and merciful God, don't let it mean long-term residence at Rooklin Right-Price Rooms.

Constructed in one of those old-fashioned "open courtyard plans," the motel had seen considerably better days. Of course, so had I. I just wanted to get out of the cold and get some sleep. I had trouble sleeping here, and it didn't have anything to do with the cracker-thin mattress or the scratchy sheets. I'd had nightmares about Glenn every night since I'd arrived in Rooklin. The nightmare was always the same: Glenn breaking down my door and dragging me out of bed by the hair, screaming about taking me home where I belonged. But the beds changed in every dream. One night, it was in my bedroom in my cozy little house in the valley; the next, it was my motel room in McClusky; and the next, it was the first room I shared with Caleb.

The guilt, the worry, and the lack of sleep had combined into a strange buzzing sensation that settled between my eyes like a half-formed headache. It had been a mistake, leaving Caleb the way I did. It was cowardly, and Caleb deserved more than that. He deserved more than a stupid Post-it note on a lampshade. And what really sucked was that I would never be able to apologize for it, because I would never see him again. I wasn't sure he'd want me to.

I missed Caleb. I missed his warmth and weight on the other side of the mattress. I missed the weird wolfy whuffling sounds he made in his sleep. I missed his terrible taste in road music and the faint smell of strange jerky in his truck. I missed feeling safe.

I scrubbed my hands over my face. It wasn't like me to be so distracted, wandering around outside like this, but I was just so damn tired. I shuffled down the cracked cement patio in front of the motel-room doors, toying with the plastic key fob as I made my way to my room. There were only twelve of them, and I had rented unit eleven, at the far end of the complex.

Across the lot, two Carhartt-clad men stood hunched over an open truck hood, poking at the engine with tools while they slugged back beer. I gave it no thought when they looked up. I smiled wearily at them.

Both men straightened, two predators scenting the wind for prey. Both smiles stretched just a bit wider in an insincere parody of friendly politeness. But I'd lived with apex predators for four years. I knew that look, the overeager, hungry excitement just before the killing lunge. I had just a few seconds before—

"Hey there," the younger of the two said with a wink. He was tall and broad, with a flat nose and muddy brown eyes.

Damn it.

His voice, with its cruel, teasing tone, had my stomach dropping, a cold, dead weight in the pit of my belly. Without thinking, I closed in on myself. I sank into survival mode, eyes to the ground, face set, ears attuned. I didn't respond, didn't acknowledge that I'd heard one of them speak. I prayed that I was wrong, that these were just a couple of guys passing their time in the parking lot, content with some harmless flirtation with a pretty girl. An available girl, at least.

Could I dash back to the motel office and stall long enough that they wouldn't see which room I was in? Why did I smile? What was I thinking? I'd gotten soft, living with the pack, believing I was safe. I'd gotten cocky. I'd barely had any problems since moving up here. And the minute stupidity and exhaustion made me drop my guard, I landed in a big pile of slimeball.

I wished Caleb was there. It was as if my brain blurted out his name. Caleb said he would keep me safe, and suddenly, I felt like an idiot for taking that for granted. Disturbing law-enforcement-grade equipment collection or no, I felt a lot more comfortable with the way he smiled at me than with these two.

Wait, law-enforcement equipment.

I shoved my hand into my coat and slipped my fingers around the collapsible metal baton. If the parking-lot predators could see the wicked way my lips curved as my hand wound around my trusty weapon, they would have been very afraid. They certainly wouldn't have been circling closer, making nasty comments to each other that they thought I couldn't hear.

I didn't have a burly werewolf to watch over me. I had this big metal stick. And Caleb wasn't my husband or my big, strong protector. He wasn't even my boyfriend. He was a guy who had picked me up like a stray and tucked me into his pocket. And none of this changed the fact that these guys were now standing between me and my room and the office, one on each side. So friendly parking-lot loiterers was out, it seemed.

"Hey, slow down, now, slow down, we just want to talk to you," the younger one said as they moved behind me, toward my door. The elder had a bulky, athlete-gone-soft build and thick salt-and-pepper hair, while his counterpart was tall with wicked-looking tattoos crawling up his neck.

Without replying, I just kept moving. My hands were shaking so hard I was afraid I was going to drop my key. And it wasn't exactly intimidating to see a woman quaking so badly it looked as if she was conducting an orchestra instead of waving a weapon in your face.

Hold it together, I told myself. *Steady hands.*

"Here, let us help you with that," the older one offered solicitously, holding out his oil-stained hands as I struggled to fit my key into the lock. Was it a bad idea to open my door? Would they push me into the room and close the door before I could scream? Maybe I would be better off dodging my way to the office. I shoved the key back into my pocket and backed away

I kept my tone coolly polite. "No, thanks."

"Hey, don't be like that," the older one chided through his yellowed, crooked teeth. "Don't be rude, honey."

"Yeah, you're not being very friendly," the younger one agreed, as if I owed him my time or attention, just because he decided he wanted a conversation.

I hated these guys. I hated these "nice guys" who just waited for some woman to reject their attentions, so they could act the wounded party and avenge their injured pride with slurs and swipes. I'd met far too many of them in my travels, and they never ceased to piss me off.

The younger one—Grabby Hands—tried to yank at my elbow, but I ducked out of the way and put my back to the wall.

"I don't want any trouble. Leave me alone." *Shaky, too shaky. Damn it.* Why couldn't I get my voice to work right? The very air around me seemed to be closing in on me, the edges of my vision darkening and blurring as the men moved closer.

"Want a beer, sweetheart?" Yellow Teeth asked. "We got plenty."

"No, thanks. Have a nice night," I said as I gripped the handle of the baton and backed away from them.

Grabby Hands frowned. "Hey, where do you think you're going? We're not done talking to you."

"Just leave me alone." The good news was that righteous indignation gave my voice some weight, even as Grabby Hands reached up to drag his hand along my arm.

"Don't touch me," I said, growling now.

Grabby Hands lived up to the name I'd mentally tagged him with, poking at my side, as if he was going to tickle me. I dodged again, hissing at him like an angry cat. Yellow Teeth was no longer amused. He clamped his hand around my wrist, dragging me close enough to smell his rank, smoke-tainted breath. I whipped the baton out of my pocket with a loud *zing*.

Grabby Hands reacted faster and stumbled back a step. Yellow Teeth didn't seem impressed with my little metal stick . . . until I cracked his wrist with it, aiming right for the sensitive ulnar nerve. He yowled, snatching his hand away. I went after his knees as if he was a particularly icky piñata. Grabby Hands had his arm around me from behind, lifting me and trying to drag the baton out of my hand. Yanking my arm down, I crashed my head back into his face. He yelped, and I felt the warm spurt of blood from his nose oozing down my back.

"Bitch! You broke my nose!" he screamed.

I swung at him again, the baton make a high whipping noise as it crashed down on his thigh. I thought I heard the bone buckle as another hand closed around the wrist holding the baton. The hand jerked away suddenly, and I focused my attention on Grabby Hands, hunched in front of me. He leaned over, oblivious to me now as he tried to reset his nose. I slammed his head into the concrete-block wall, knocking him unconscious.

A hand wrapped around the back of my neck, the fingers digging viciously into my skin, making me yelp. Yellow Teeth shoved me against the wall, my head whacking against the rough wooden plank. The pain had my arms dropping limp and useless at my sides when Yellow Teeth pinned me to the wall with his hips. I barely kept hold of the baton as his belt buckle dug into my stomach. His stained, nasty smile glinted in the low sunlight. "Oh, sweetheart, you just made this more fun for us."

And that's when I heard a low growl behind us.

I knew that growl. I'd heard more than enough of it during my time in the valley. That wasn't some stray dog or a cranky, city-dwelling bear. That was the growl of a pissed-off werewolf. And I'd never been so happy to hear it in my entire life.

Yellow Teeth kept his hand at my throat as he turned. I'd expected to see fur and four paws over my assailant's shoulder. But Caleb was in human form, eyes glowing an eerie gold, lips pulled back from teeth growing longer and sharper.

"Mind your own business," Yellow Teeth grunted as he threw his weight against my squirming body. "Just walk away."

Caleb didn't like that, if his sharper growls were any indication. A strange, warm calm spread from my chest outward to my arms and legs. My fingers relaxed and held their grip on the baton. The pain in my head didn't matter anymore. Yellow Teeth's grip on my throat didn't matter. I was safe.

And while I was ridiculously happy to see him, I knew that seeing him shift would be very bad. The last thing I needed to deal with was explaining to the state police why two guys I'd beaten up in a parking lot seemed to think my traveling companion could morph into a giant wolf. That was the sort of thing that got attention.

"Caleb, don't," I said in a firm, calm tone.

"What the hell's wrong with his face?" Yellow Teeth wheezed, his grip on my neck slackening.

"Caleb, calm down," I told him, but Caleb was beyond listening.

A ripple of golden light spread from his chest. He was about to shift. In broad daylight. In front of humans. I was wrong before. *This* was the definition of screwed.

"What's wrong with this guy?" Yellow Teeth's fingers slipped off of my neck, and he stared at Caleb.

Caleb advanced, hunching over as his limbs stretched into inhuman shapes.

"Stop," I told him, but Caleb seemed intent on ripping Yellow Teeth's throat out. "Shit."

I grabbed Yellow Teeth's head, as if I was about to give him a big, wet kiss, only to yank hard as I turned and rammed it against the wall behind me with just enough force *not* to fracture his skull. He yelped and went limp. I dropped his leaden, unconscious body next to his equally knocked-out friend.

Caleb snarled and lunged toward them, body in half-phase. I could see the bones shifting under his skin, cheekbones bulging and exaggerated as they moved into their canine shape. His teeth stretched and sharpened into fangs to match the claws growing from his fingertips. And for some stupid reason I could not explain, I stepped between the insta-wolf and my attacker, hooking my arms under Caleb's and throwing my weight against his chest. I could feel fur brushing against my face and had this bizarre urge to bury my face in it.

But that would be insane, right? Right?

Right. Defuse public werewolf transformation now. Evaluate need for heavy doses of antipsychotic meds later.

The fur disappeared and gave way to warm, human(ish) skin. Strong arms swung around my middle with the force of stalled forward momentum. I glanced up to see Caleb's human features twisted into an expression of vicious rage. His eyes darkened from that predatory yellow back to their smooth bitter-coffee color.

I couldn't help but gape up at him, even as he manhandled me. It wasn't just that he was quite the sight to behold. He'd changed back mid-phase. I didn't know that was possible, especially when the werewolf in question was this pissed off. Maggie was one of the most in-control wolves I'd ever met, and it could take her an hour to come back to herself when she was angry.

Caleb's arm curled around my waist, pressing me to his side as he struggled toward Grabby Hands and

Yellow Teeth. I wedged my foot in front of his, pushing him back with all of my might, but it was like trying to change the direction of a tank. He just dragged me along for the ride, my feet scrabbling for purchase against the rough concrete.

"Stop," I told him firmly. "Caleb, you come back to me, or Lord help me, I will find a giant newspaper and whack you on the nose!"

Angry, punctuated breaths puffed through his nostrils as his black eyes stared down at me. Letting out one last angry chuff, he pulled me to his chest, nuzzling my neck. I could add *snuffling* to the list of interesting angry sounds Caleb made as he rubbed his face into my hair. The growls died down to a rumbling purr. I sank against him, my arms suddenly stone-heavy. I dropped the baton to the asphalt with a *clang* as I wrapped my arms around his neck to stay upright. Caleb's breathing evened out, and his hands relaxed against the small of my back, rubbing wide circles. He reluctantly pulled away, cupping my face between his hands as he came back to himself.

He stared down at me, letting his eyes roam over my face, as if he was checking that all of my parts were still intact. He looked a little dazed, and then his pupils snapped back into focus.

And he did not look happy.

"What the hell were you thinking?" he demanded, shaking my arms. "I told you to stay with me. I told you I would keep you safe. And you run off the minute my head is turned? Do you realize what could have just happened to you?"

Right, we were not going to discuss the fact that he'd nearly phased in front of me. Then again, from what I'd seen of pack behavior, he might not have realized he was doing it. The more time werewolves spent alone, away from their pack, the less aware they were of their "wolf time." Cooper Graham had been so out of touch with his phasing cycle that he believed it when Eli made it look as if he'd committed the aforementioned series of hiker maulings.

I wouldn't ask how Caleb was able to find me. It was probably better that I just ignore it in favor of being irritated about the whole shaking-me-like-a-naughty-child thing. Right?

I shoved my hands against Caleb's seemingly immobile chest until he relinquished his hold on my waist. I huffed. "I left because I could. Because I am an adult, and I control my own decisions. You were making me nervous with all your bullet wounds and plastic handcuffs. I decided I was better off on my own."

"Oh, yeah." He glanced down at the unconscious men at our feet. "You have everything under control."

"I was doing just fine," I muttered, shifting my shoulder bag and ignoring his quote-unquote compliment. "I am still upright and conscious. So I think that means I win. And frankly, I did it without much help from you. You just distracted them and made scary faces."

"Scary faces?" he asked, his cheeks paling considerably.

"Yeah, you gave them full-on first-day-of-prison crazy eyes," I said, my laughter just a bit forced. "If I didn't know better, I'd swear they changed color for a second there."

He gave the world's most awkward chuckle. "Yeah, that would be weird, huh?"

Really? I'd just given him the perfect opportunity to talk about his other nature, and nothing? Really?

With a disappointed sigh, I gave his shin a little kick, making him smirk at me and ruffle my hair. He grumbled but grudgingly admitted, "I want to rip them limb from limb, but what you did was probably better." He gestured to the crumpled forms on the ground.

Oddly pleased by his praise, I preened a bit. "Never underestimate the short."

Caleb snorted. "I think we need to clear out of here before they wake up. I'm amazed the manager hasn't come out to yell at us for messing up his nice empty parking lot."

I stared up at him. If he was willing to follow me this far, he wasn't going to let me just walk away and plot my own course to Anchorage. And he was handy to have around when one was under attack by parking-lot perverts. Still, I had to give him a little grief. "But I'm paid up for two more nights!" I protested, although I will admit there wasn't much heat in it.

He cast a derisive look at the peeling green motel-room door. "Well, that just goes to show that your judgment has been off in a lot of different areas."

I gave him my unamused dead-eyed stare. "I'm not above kicking you again."

"Frankly, I'm thinking about kicking you back. You left me a two-word good-bye note on a lampshade."

He growled, as if he suddenly remembered that he was angry with me. "Two words: 'I'm sorry.' What is wrong with you?"

"I don't know!"

"That's not an answer!"

"I know that!" I cried, throwing my hands up in the air.

"Why are you yelling at me?"

"I don't know!" I yelled. I frowned, looking down at Yellow Teeth and Grabby Hands. "Should we stash them in my room?"

He nodded toward Yellow Teeth. "Get his feet."

"I don't think so." I gestured at Caleb's thick upper arms. "You came after me to 'protect' me, you might as well do the heavy lifting."

"I didn't come for you, I came for the baton," he said, scooping it up from where I'd dropped it on the ground. "You're just an amusing fringe benefit. So," he asked in a tone far too casual to be sincere, "is there a reason you ran from me?"

He was pretending to be looking down at Yellow Teeth and Grabby Hands, all the while staring sidelong at me. Could he be mulling over my lack of questions about his finding me? Or why I hadn't mentioned the strange yellow glow-y trick of light over his skin? Maybe the little peculiarities had built up to the point where a "normal" girl couldn't have ignored them. Had it been a mistake to put that one last barrier between our real lives and what we were trying to show each other? Would I have too much to explain now if I told him I knew about were-creatures?

I opened my mouth to say, *My ex-husband's determined stalking and your connections to my former employers, not to mention your werewolf issues, are freaking me out.* But I lost my nerve and suggested, "Generalized anxiety. So how far are we going today?"

"I don't know," he said, apparently caught off-guard by my sudden change of topic. He peered around the abandoned parking lot. "Where are we?"

For some reason, that struck me as funny. I started laughing. And I kept laughing, even as Caleb chucked the unconscious guys into my motel room and locked the door, then led me toward the truck. He kept an arm around my waist, as if he was afraid I was going to collapse from shock or crippling hyena laughs. Instead of shrugging off his protective grip, I held on to his arm like a lifeline.

"Come on, Rabbit," he said, gently lifting me into the truck while I wiped at my eyes.

"I'm sorry. It's been a long night—day—whatever." I sighed as he tucked my legs into the cab. I grabbed his arm before he could close the door. "Caleb, thanks."

He gave me one curt nod and slammed the truck door.

We drove for the better part of two hours, my head leaning against the cool glass of the window. The strange white buzzing in my head had faded away, and I could feel my muscles unwind from the unbearable tension I'd been under for the last few days. Caleb didn't say a word for the entire drive. He barely looked at me, keeping his eyes glued to the road, as if he wasn't driving on highways he'd wandered on routinely for the better part of five years. I closed my eyes, grateful just to be able to rest them for a few moments.

My eyes snapped open as Caleb turned into a motel parking lot. The Burly Bear Inn was no Ritz-Carlton, but it was certainly in better shape than the Right-Price. All of the rooms in the newly painted three-story building had exterior doors, at least, which couldn't be said of my last "residence." Caleb hopped out of the truck and walked into the motel office, presumably to get a room. He even left the keys in the ignition. It was either a sign that he trusted me enough to leave me unsupervised in his truck or a test to see if I would run off again.

I bunched my hands into fists to avoid the temptation. Because this was not a conversation I wanted to have with Caleb. It wasn't a conversation I wanted to have with anyone. The only person I'd ever discussed my marital "difficulties" with was Red-burn, and that was over the phone. Talking about it face-to-face with Caleb would be considerably more painful.

Caleb emerged from the office after a few minutes, shoving a plastic key fob into his pocket. He opened my door, grabbed his duffel, and hooked my bag around his arm, nodding toward the first floor of rooms. I followed him, wondering where I would even start with my sad, sordid history.

Caleb unlocked the door, and I stepped inside the room, fidgeting and twisting my hands. He dropped the bags, his relentless stare pinning me to my spot on the questionable motel carpet. I took a deep breath. "Caleb, I—*mrpgh*."

Before I could make another sound, Caleb was across the room and kissing the absolute hell out of me. His arms snaked under my own and lifted me off the ground, the sheer force of the impact throwing my legs around his waist. My mouth dropped open in surprise, and his tongue slipped between my lips.

Breathing. Breathing would be good. But I couldn't seem to draw air. His mouth was everywhere, nibbling my lips, trailing along my jaw, nipping at my throat, stealing all of my oxygen and rational thought. There were no muffled voices from the other rooms. There was no questionable carpet. Only warm lips, clashing teeth, and strong fingers digging into my hips.

I was so focused on the hot, insistent pressure against my mouth that I didn't notice that somewhere between the door and the bed, my shirt came off. I yanked at his jacket, pushing it from his shoulders as he stumbled back and landed against the mattress with a squeak. Our descent had just enough bounce to send me tumbling toward the edge of the bed, but Caleb caught me and rolled me back over him.

I barely resisted the urge to laugh into his bare chest, biting down gently on his Adam's apple. He moaned softly, threading his fingers through my short hair and pulling me closer. His hands stroked and petted, slowly peeling away my jeans and bra. My pulse jumped every time his hands brushed my breasts, and my hips jerked.

I lost track of time, getting acquainted with the body that, well, let's face it, I had been ogling for weeks. His skin was so smooth. I couldn't resist reciting the muscle-group names as I traced my fingertips along his arms, down his stomach and thighs. Deltoid, pectoralis major, external oblique, quadriceps femoris—all connected and fairly shaking as I ran my hands over them.

He flipped me onto my back, growling low as he worried my collarbone with his teeth. Lips open and wet, he ran his mouth in one smooth line from my breasts to my belly button, pressing one last kiss to the little bow on the waistline of my panties. I giggled, until he nudged the panties aside and plunged two fingers inside me. Then I gasped, grinding my hips against the palm of his hand. I came with embarrassing speed, but it had been a very long time since someone had touched me. I threw my head back, panting as I felt that first spasm of my climax. I rode it out, wave after wave, until I was sweaty and still beneath him.

I heard the crinkle of foil as he settled between my thighs, peppering my breasts with kisses as he aligned our bodies. I hissed as parts of me long left ignored stretched and flexed around him. He stopped, hovering over me, watching me.

I felt overwhelmed by his size, the searing heat of his skin. I'd never felt so small, so breakable, in a positive way. As his hands ghosted over my skin, I knew that I could trust him to be careful with me.

"Move," I begged him. "Please move."

He obliged, thrusting his hips and driving me back into the mattress. I felt his teeth, worrying at the same spot on my neck he'd attempted to bite before. Was this it? Was he going to claim me? He nuzzled my throat, scraping his sharp teeth over my skin. Just when I felt them digging in, I tensed, wincing away from the pain.

The silence of the room, punctuated only by the sound of our breathing, rang in my ears as he balanced his forehead against mine. He stroked a hand down my cheek and kissed me, long and hard. He grinned down at me and clutched at my ass, rolling against me until he hit a spot inside me that had me shuddering. Heat seared from my navel to my thighs, rippling up my body. The fluttering waves of release made me scream so loudly that our neighbors banged on the wall and told us in very colorful language that they did not appreciate my enthusiasm. Or volume. Or Caleb's long howl when he followed me over the edge.

Caleb rolled onto his back, wrapped his arms around me, and pulled me close. I clapped my hands over my mouth and muffled a giggle, because I figured laughing at our neighbors' protests would not improve their mood. Caleb did laugh, pressing his face against the crown of my head. He looked indecently pleased with himself. "Been a while, huh?"

"Four years, two months, two weeks, and three days. Not counting the sex I've been having with myself, which was actually better than the two-party . . . never mind. So why weren't we doing this weeks ago?"

"Oh, trust me, if I'd had my way, we would have christened every motel between here and Canada," he told me. "But you were so jumpy before. You let me touch you, but you tensed up so much I was afraid that you would run off if I tried to get closer." He nipped at my earlobe. I turned my head, admiring the way the moonlight played on his features, making him look like the sullen canine he was. "Please don't run from me again," he whispered into my hair, winding his legs with mine. "When I woke up and you were gone, Rabbit, I can't tell you how that made me feel. I didn't know where you'd gone. I didn't know if you were OK, if I was ever going to see you again. I almost lost it."

His whole frame tensed up just talking about it. His eyes bled gold into dark brown and glowed against the dark backdrop of the room.

I wondered if *almost losing it* meant he'd wolfed out and destroyed our motel room. What was the cleaning fee for something like that? Did he have a credit card devoted specifically to tacky-motel-room damage? I trailed my fingers along his cheek, stroking it in what I hoped was a soothing, non-werewolf-freak-out-inducing manner.

"Look, Caleb, I know you're upset with me."

"That would be a massive understatement, yeah."

"But can we skip talking about it for right now?" He opened his mouth to protest, so I added, "You have every right to be pissed, especially with the whole lampshade thing, and we have a lot of things we need to talk about. And we can yell and scream as much as you want later. But for right now, for the next few hours, can we just not?"

He bit his lip and then bit mine. "There will be talking," he told me sternly. "And possibly some yelling, but definitely a lot of talking, because there are things we need to talk about. Because you scared me. I'm angry. But I'm not going to do anything to make you run away again, because I missed you. Also because your running away again would just start the whole losing-it, pissed-off, scared cycle all over again."

"I missed you, too." I craned my neck to press my lips to his and let my head drop to the pillow.

10

A Furry, Friendly Wake-Up Call

Even if I did know about the existence of were-wolves, it was still shocking as hell to wake up spooning with one.

I was still mostly asleep when I registered the feeling of a wide, warm tongue rasping down the length of my cheek.

"Morning. That's different." I chuckled, pressing my face into the pillow. I squinted into the semidarkness of early dawn, running my fingers through Caleb's hair. It seemed coarser and thicker . . . and there was a lot more of it. In fact, it seemed to cover his entire body.

"What the—?" I opened my eyes and found myself staring into the brown eyes of a huge gray wolf.

I scrambled out of bed, falling to the floor, scuttling back over the carpet into the wall. "Caleb!"

Our sonar-sensitive neighbor pounded on the bedroom wall, and I heard his muffled voice call, "Too damn early for that! Decent people are trying to sleep!"

Whining, the wolf shook his way up onto his haunches and stretched. He looked over the edge of the bed at me, head tilted to the side, as if he was trying to figure out why I was acting all weird. OK, OK, this wasn't a big deal. I'd seen werewolves before. Unless they phased out of anger or fear, they were usually pretty calm. And Caleb wouldn't hurt me. It was just a shock to see him in his natural state. The Caleb wolf shook his head, and that golden light spread over the gray fur, slowly fading away to skin.

"Don't be scared," he said, scrambling toward me.

I flopped back against the wall, holding my hand up like a crossing guard. I looked up at my werewolf paramour, all panicked and wide-eyed. I looked down at the stray gray hairs on the sheets. And I burst out laughing. It was just so ridiculous, him crouching naked on the bedroom floor while asking me not to freak out over his wolf body. I laughed and laughed until I fell over. Until I realized I was touching nasty motel carpet and sat back up. I wiped at my eyes.

"Werewolf."

Caleb's mouth flapped open like a guppy's as he stammered, "Uh-uh, no, you must be having a bad dream. Uh, yeah, that's it, there was no wolf here."

I smirked at him. "Are you trying to Jedi-mind-trick me right now? 'Cause you kind of suck at it."

He cleared his throat and followed with a weak "Maybe you hit your head?" His tone was uncertain and quiet, as if he didn't want our neighbors to overhear. He pulled my arms gently and led me to the bed. "You're not running away and screaming. Why are you not running away and screaming?"

I winced, biting my lip. *Right, how to explain this . . .* "I kind of knew already."

"How?" he exclaimed. I shushed him. "How did you know?" He sat heavily on the bed, stared at me for a long moment, and then groaned. "The night I was shot. Did I say something?"

I shook my head, but my continued silence seemed to make him chatty. "I just, uh, put some things together. You're not the first werewolf I've met."

"It's not a big deal, really. I don't hurt anybody. I don't freak out under the light of the full moon. It's just a genetic condition, you know, like color blindness or being born with an extra toe. Just, you know, furrier."

I stared at him, suddenly blank-faced. That was the saddest description of werewolf-dom I'd ever heard.

"So how do you know about us?"

I sighed. "Promise you won't get mad."

"I can't actually promise that," he said, crossing his arms over his chest. "But I won't phase or yell or anything."

I leveled a doubtful look at him.

He nodded and walked to a corner, the farthest point in the room away from me. "OK, hit me."

"I've been working with werewolves for years. I was the pack doctor for your family in the valley for the past four years. I worked under the name Anna Moder." The words ran out of my mouth so quickly I was surprised he managed to pick up on what I'd said. But I could tell it had registered by the shocked expression on his face.

"The cute little pack doctor Maggie was always going on about?"

I nodded.

He sighed and then burst out laughing. "Do you have any idea what I've been going through trying to cover for my little *issue*? Do you know how hard it is for one of us to go *this long* without phasing regularly?"

"I'm sorry," I said, pressing my lips together to keep from laughing. Because antagonizing a naked werewolf seemed counterintuitive. "I didn't want to freak you out, and I didn't know if I could trust you at first. And after that, it seemed a little late to tell you the truth, and I panicked, and here we are. Also, it was sort of funny to see how far you would go to try to conceal your wolfy tendencies."

"So you know about everything?" he asked, incredulous.

"Not everything but most things. I treated Samson for a lot of different bramble- and bear-related injuries."

He shuddered. "But you know my whole family?"

I nodded.

"And you've probably heard a few stories."

I nodded again.

"You know about the incident with the moose, huh?"

My eyebrows arched. "Uh, no."

"Never mind."

I pushed myself to my feet and gestured to the bed.

"Can we get off the floor now that all our cards are on the table?"

He practically dived across the room and under the covers, fluffing them into a strange, nestlike configuration around him. He lifted the corner to let me crawl in next to him. Leaning against the headboard, he pulled me against his chest. He pushed my tangled hair back from my face. "So you're a doctor?"

"Mostly emergency medicine, but then I transferred to more of a family practice a few years ago. I had to leave that job for, uh, personal reasons."

"I know," he muttered. When I shot him a confused look, he added, "It's just a surprise, that's all. I thought we were on a more even playing field."

"I'm still the same person. I just have a couple extra pieces of paper you didn't know about."

"But you must have made a lot of money before, been comfortable. Why are you living in cheap motels and working in grocery stores?" he asked.

"I did make decent money early on in my medical career. I was very comfortable. And I can honestly tell you I have never been so miserable in my life. Living up here works better for me."

"Why?" he asked, and we both laughed a little.

"Because Glenn can't take it all away again. I had just enough time to start thinking of Tampa as home before he showed up and broke my face. And that was after he harassed me 'anonymously' at work until my new coworkers were scared to be seen with me or go out with me, because they didn't know what my crazy ex-husband would do. I made the people around me tense and nervous. It felt like I was taking everybody around me down with me."

Caleb seemed to grasp the fact that he needed to ignore the unusual number of details I'd just let slip in favor of mocking me in some way. "What was your plan? Just bounce around the country forever?"

"Not forever, just a couple of years!" I exclaimed.

"That's a crappy plan."

"As opposed to your plan of waiting until you phased next to me in my sleep to tell me that you're a supernatural creature?"

"I was going to tell you!" he protested. "It's a difficult thing to fit into conversation, that's all. Do you realize how much easier this would have been for me if you'd just told me you knew I was a werewolf?"

"So you keeping secrets from me was *my* fault?"

"No. That's . . . wrong. But people who live in lampshade-note-shaped houses shouldn't throw stones." He tapped me on the nose with his fingertip for emphasis.

"Any other little secrets I should know about?"

He pursed his lips. "No."

"You hesitated."

He made an alarmingly human helpless-man face, complete with flailing outstretched hands. "Any guy would hesitate in response to that question!"

"So no more surprises."

He raised his hand in a mockery of the Boy Scout salute. "Not so much as a surprise birthday party. If you ever decide to tell me your real birthdate. I'm assuming the one I found on your ID is fake."

I gasped. "You looked through my wallet?"

"While you were asleep that night at the motel, when we went after Jerry," he said, wincing when I smacked him. "You didn't think I was going to do some checking up on the woman riding in my truck and sleeping in my bed?"

"I'm not the one who's cagey," I muttered into his skin.

He tucked my head under his chin and hugged me tight. "Glenn—that was his name?"

I blinked, tensing up against him. Caleb rubbed circles on the small of my back to try to get me back into a relaxed state. Glenn was such an enormous part of my head space. Avoiding him was the motivation for so many aspects of my life, and I hadn't shared anything about him with Caleb, someone who had so recently taken up another considerable chunk of my thoughts. While I didn't want them to meet under any circumstances, it seemed unfair to shut such a big part of my life away from Caleb—especially when Glenn could be the reason I eventually left.

I took a deep breath, closed my eyes, and resolved to tell Caleb everything.

"Have you ever had one of those moments in your life where you wish you had a time-traveling De-Lorean?" I asked Caleb as he settled against my side to listen to my tale.

11

Foxy Boxing Is Way More Difficult Than It Looks on Those Questionable Cable Channels

Caleb listened to every word, stopping me to ask a question here or there but never judging, never demanding answers. I poured out the whole sorry story and felt better for getting it off my chest. I explained about the e-mails and how Glenn claimed to have found me. And while he still wasn't happy with me for sneaking away instead of telling him, he dropped the subject. Exhausted by relating the sad story of my marriage, I fell asleep balanced on Caleb's chest and woke up just before noon. Caleb had left a note by the door (as far away from the lampshade as possible) stating that he'd gone for a "run."

I felt very sorry for the woodland creatures that might have crossed his path.

Unfortunately, this honesty seemed to have put another space bubble between us. Caleb suddenly seemed worried about rushing me physically or crowding me.

He didn't sniff me or touch me casually as much as he did before. I had to initiate kissing or any other fun-time activities. I made it a point to become even more affectionate with him, to try to snap him out of it. But the stubborn wolf was going all noble on me.

Caleb managed to get Glenn's basic information out of me: name, last known address, birthdate. He seemed determined to find some solution for my situation, which was sort of sweet and at the same time a little in-sulting, as if he was going to magically find some easy fix I hadn't thought of yet. A nearly impossible-to-file restraining order, restarting my stalled divorce proceed-ings, even a legal name change—all of that paperwork could be tracked and could lead Glenn right to my door. Living a little less legitimately was inconvenient, but it kept me off of Glenn's radar. It was my choice, and it made me feel safer. So I rebuffed these sugges-tions—and any attempts to get personal information about Glenn—with indifference and subject changes, making Caleb restless and snappish.

We didn't talk about my running away because we had new subjects to discuss, namely Glenn and my his-tory with the werewolf pack. Caleb did, however, spend a lot of time talking to Suds, taking several calls out on the porch of the motel, despite temperatures dipping near the single digits. He was worried and agitated, and part of me wished I hadn't told him about my past. He knew everything now. He knew how damaged I was, and I couldn't be that quirky, mysterious girl who had saved him from a half-assed bullet wound.

One morning, he strode into our room and tossed

me a case file. "We're going to Goose Creek. You have twenty minutes to pack."

"Now?"

"Yes," he said. "Or at least, in twenty minutes."

I harrumphed at this sudden change in demeanor, as if he hadn't spent the last week in a state of grumpy old werewolf-ness. Phasing issues or no, I didn't appreciate mood swings that left me feeling gaslighted. I flipped through the file, reading the summary. "We're looking for a stripper named Trixie?"

Caleb cast me another smirk. "I think they prefer 'exotic dancer.'"

"Why are we looking for a stripper named Trixie?"

"See, that's a question a man would never ask."

I gave him my best stink-eye, but he only grinned impishly at me. Holding his gator jerky over the garbage can got his attention.

"Hey!" he howled. "Trixie is the errant girlfriend of Lolo Kardakian, medium-sized hood out of Anchorage. They've had a disagreement."

I inadvertently dropped the bag of jerky, more out of surprise than revenge. "We're chasing down a woman to drag her back to her angry criminal boyfriend?"

"Do you know how hard it is to find that brand of gator jerky?" he asked, peering into the garbage can to see if the bag was salvageable.

"You have a jerky problem. Suds and I are going to have an intervention."

"I had to order it over the Internet!" he exclaimed.

I dug a fingertip into his side, making him wince. "Caleb!"

"We're not exactly dragging her back. Look, I know both of them pretty well. He isn't going to hurt her, he just wants a valuable item she took with her when he and she had their last, um—"

I raised my hand to cut him off. "Let's go with 'date.'"

"OK, then. On their last date, Lolo informed Trixie that he wasn't planning on leaving his wife. And while he was in the shower, she took his wedding ring from the nightstand."

"Why doesn't he just have the ring replaced?"

"Well, it's Lolo's father-in-law's ring. It's an antique and apparently pretty distinctive. Plus, Lolo's sort of superstitious. He wants *his* wedding ring back. He's afraid that without it, his marriage will be doomed."

"Yeah, his carrying on with a stripper named Trixie won't have any effect on it at all."

"All we have to do is get the ring back to Lolo in Anchorage. I thought you'd be excited to finally get there."

"I object to this job on moral grounds . . . on several levels. Quests for evil rings rarely turn out well. Too many potential Gollum issues. Also, I don't like the idea of working for a guy whose name could belong to a *Star Trek* villain."

"Them's the breaks, sweetheart," he said, shrugging as I pouted. "We aren't actually taking custody of anyone, so your argument isn't valid. And you've objected to most of the jobs we've done together on some grounds. If it was up to you, we would let everybody go with a sternly worded warning."

"Fine," I grumbled. "How do we find this girl?"

"My buddy Abe owns a bar down in Goose Creek—"

"Yet another member of the League of Caleb's Barkeep Super Friends," I interjected.

"Please don't mix Marvel and DC references. You're better than that," he said, shaking his head disdainfully. "As I was saying before I was so rudely interrupted, Abe's on Trixie's circuit. Most of these places can't keep girls on full-time. You don't find a lot of pretty girls willing to strip in a small town year-round. So these girls travel a sort of circuit a few months each year. The bar pays a flat fee, the girls keep all the tips. The male patrons see a little boob. Everybody walks away happy."

"Except for feminists. And health inspectors."

"Is this going to be your attitude for the entire job? Because that will make it real difficult for me to enjoy working on this with you."

I frowned, although relief at seeing the old Caleb return was gradually setting in. "Am I supposed to try to help you enjoy a job involving strippers?"

"I honestly don't know how to answer that without getting poked in the ribs again."

Abe's bar, which was just called Abe's, was more respectable than most of the places we'd visited so far. It was an old, shopworn sports bar, but it was clean. And nobody propositioned me as I walked through the front door, which I considered a much higher recommendation than any Zagat rating.

Of course, the lack of propositions could have had something to do with Caleb's arm being firmly wrapped around my waist, but why split hairs? The interior reminded me a lot of the Blue Glacier in Grundy: scarred pine bar, worn pine floorboards, neon beer signs, and taxidermically preserved fish specimens decorating the walls. Two obviously well-loved pool tables occupied the far corner of the room. Since one of them was marked with a little green "reserved" sign, I assumed that one would serve as Trixie's stage for the evening.

There were plenty of perfectly respectable teetotalers in the Great North. But in some smaller towns out "in the bush," bars and saloons served as the social hubs, sources of gossip and entertainment to break up the monotony of living in a place where a snowfall could mean being cut off from your neighbors for months. People didn't come for the booze so much as the conversation. The problem was that some bars were "less nice" than others and attracted people who were similarly less nice than the average citizen. It all depended on what the ownership was willing to let the patrons get away with.

My opinion of the caliber of the bar changed when a tall bottled redhead with an ass you could bounce a quarter off of sidled up to us, calling out to Caleb. My werewolf paled a little and pulled at the collar of his jacket.

"Mary Ann, hi," he said, clearly uncomfortable, which in some perverse way amused me immensely. "How are you?"

"Lonely." She scowled at me. "This your old lady now?"

Caleb looked from her to me and back to her. And then back to me. "Uh . . ."

Part of me enjoyed watching Caleb twitch a little bit. But a much more influential part of my brain wanted this woman away from us, away from my man, before I started some Maury Povich catfight, rolling around on the floor, pulling at her hair. So I decided to step in.

"Oh, come on, Caleb, don't try to hide our love," I cooed, stretching my arms around him. I beamed at her, all silly and cow-eyed. "We just got matching tattoos."

Mary Ann's eyes widened. "Really? Can I see?"

I winked at her. "Not where we put them, no, ma'am."

"I thought you said you didn't want big commitments," she said to Caleb.

And the ever-erudite werewolf responded, "Uh . . ."

She gave me one long, disdainful look. "When you figure out what you're missing, you give me a call," she said, turning her back on me.

"It was really nice to meet you, Mary Ann!" I chirped.

She sashayed away, her butt swishing back and forth. Caleb closed his eyes as if he was wishing the whole situation would go away. "Never going to live this down, am I?"

I shook my head. "No."

Before he could come up with some explanation, a tall blond man came barreling up to Caleb, pulled back his fist, and punched my werewolf square in the stomach.

Seriously, I couldn't take him anywhere.

Caleb grunted, doubling over and propping his hands against his knees to get his breath back. I hissed out a growl and yanked my trusty baton out of my bag. I flicked it to full extension, but Caleb pulled himself upright and grabbed my wrist before I could swing. "No! This is my old friend, Abe Clarkson."

Caleb took time off from reassuring me to swing up at Abe's gut, doubling him over. Abe gave a wheezing laugh right before using his lowered center of gravity to fly-tackle Caleb and send him toppling against a booth.

"Do any of your old friends like you?" I asked him as both men roared with laughter. None of the bar patrons seemed to notice the exchange, as if it was a regular occurrence for Abe to brawl with customers.

Caleb brought an elbow down between Abe's shoulder blades. "No, that's just how he says hi."

With Abe's grasp around Caleb's waist weakened, Caleb shoved his alleged friend halfway across the barroom. I assumed that the abusive greeting ritual had concluded, because Abe approached me, gave me a once-over, and waggled his eyebrows. "Who is this sweet little thing, Caleb? You know, Mary Ann's been missing you—"

Caleb interrupted him with a loud clearing of the throat. "Abe, this is my Tina. Behave yourself."

Abe instantly straightened up, his expression more friendly than flirty now. I guessed Caleb's calling me his held some sort of special significance. In a second, I'd gone from hanger-on to lady of significance. I felt

I deserved nonflirty respect either way, but given the eager, open smile on Caleb's face, I wasn't going to be churlish about it.

"Well, it's very nice to meet you, Tina," Abe said, shaking my hand. "I was afraid he was going to end up as the male version of a crazy old cat lady."

"That's still a possibility," I told him, making Abe frown at Caleb.

"She's a kidder," Caleb assured him. "She's crazy about me."

I snorted. "'Crazy' is a good word for it."

Abe shot Caleb a sly look. "Oh, I like her. You deserve her, buddy. I'm looking forward to watching how this plays out. You in a relationship? That's like one of those shows about guys who wrestle with wild gators. I don't know how it's going to turn out, but it will be bloody, and I'm pretty sure I'm going to laugh."

"Is Trixie here yet?" Caleb asked, ignoring Abe's jab. "I would like to snap her up before these guys figure out I'm taking away their entertainment. That could get ugly."

"She's not due for another thirty minutes or so," Abe told him. "You got a minute, man. And I need a favor." Abe jerked his head toward his office. Caleb gave me a skeptical look, as if he didn't want to leave me alone, but I waved him off.

"Go have fun," I told him. "I'll be fine."

"The last time you said that, you ended up offering to show Jerry your boobs," he said.

Abe's mouth popped open to comment, but instead, he asked, "You hungry?" The blond man laughed at himself. "What am I saying? You're with Caleb 'Jerky Hog' Graham. Of course you are."

Before I could respond, Caleb protested. "That was one time! And you left the bag in the truck. What was I supposed to do? Starve?"

Abe shook his head, giving me a knowing look, and flagged down his bartender, a pretty brunette. "A beer and a crab special for the lady. Anything she wants is on the house."

I started to protest, but Caleb lifted me up and deposited me on a bar stool.

"Eat," he told me. "Sit here. Stay in one place. Please try to stay out of trouble."

"You're not the boss of me," I informed him.

"You're right, but as someone who cares about you, I am only asking that you eat a good meal and try not to jump directly into harm's way, waving a sign that says, 'Here I Am!' in big red letters."

I hated it when he made sense. "I don't have a sign," I grumbled.

"It's invisible to everything but trouble," he told me, making me laugh.

"*Augh*," Abe groaned. "I was wrong. This isn't funny. It's adorable. I wasn't expecting adorable. I *hate* adorable." He grabbed the scruff of Caleb's neck and dragged him toward a door marked "Office."

"I will never understand men," I told the brunette behind the bar. The airbrushing on her shirt identified her as Pam.

Pam shook her head. "We're not supposed to, honey."

"Well, that's comforting."

In a few minutes, I was served a surprisingly delicious sandwich consisting of a whole-wheat roll stuffed to the brim with a spicy, fresh King crab salad. Not exactly the greasy fried bar food I'd come to expect. I dived into that sandwich as if seafood was about to be declared illegal. The cold, delicately seasoned crab was perfectly complemented by a peppery citrus dressing. It was the perfect accompaniment to the creamy wild-rice soup and beer. I hadn't eaten this well since the valley. I savored the dish and the opportunity to eat in a little island of silence in the crowded, conversation-filled room.

And it gave me an opportunity to consider the implications of our conversation with Mary Ann. Caleb *was* one of those werewolves who played sex roulette with tavern wenches. How was I supposed to feel about that? But I wasn't sure I wanted to follow Mary Ann's act. She looked like the kind of girl who knew tricks. Or turned them.

"Don't pay what Mary Ann said any mind," Pam said, sliding a fresh beer in front of me. "She's been after him for the better part of a year. Never could take a hint."

"So they never . . ." I left that question hanging in the air, along with several vague hand gestures.

"Oh, no, they probably did," Pam said. "But Caleb never made any promises or anything."

I *thunk*ed my head against the bar and groaned.

He'd never made me any promises, either. He clearly liked me. But he'd never said he loved me. And although I'd tried to skirt around those feelings for a good while, I knew they were there. I still believed in love. It was impossible not to when you were surrounded by a bunch of people who mated for life. I saw how fiercely werewolves could love, with everything they had. But Caleb never mentioned anything about love, just safety and protection. And he certainly didn't say anything about the long term, just that I should stay with him. He never said how long he wanted me beside him.

"But I'm sure that you two . . ." Pam continued. I looked up at her, eyebrows furrowed. She pursed her lips. "I'm going to stop talking now."

"Probably for the best." I nodded.

Pam busied herself behind the bar, leaving me to pick at the remains of my sandwich.

This was such an inconvenient moment to figure out that I was in love with Caleb. It wasn't unreasonable. There were so many reasons to love him. Yes, he was handsome. And yes, he was strong. But Caleb was also a good man, as different from Glenn as night is from day. He was pragmatic when it came to his job, but he was kind. He didn't hurt people because it felt good to him. While he might be aggressive, he wasn't passive-aggressive. When he was upset, he still talked to me. He made me laugh, even when I didn't want to. He didn't tell me what to do, what to wear, who to talk to. If he told me he was trying to protect me, that's what he was trying to do. He wasn't trying to separate me from people who might see what he really was, how he was treating me, that what we had wasn't normal.

Caleb had never said he loved me. But he saw what

was good in me, even when I tried to hide it. He treated me like something precious. Not untouchable, not some ideal version of myself that I couldn't live up to.

How had this happened to me? I was on the run from the man who'd promised me the world. And I'd fallen in love with an emotionally unreliable werewolf who'd promised me nothing.

It was a shame advice columns didn't cover issues like this.

Pam must have felt guilty for sending me on this depressing thought train, because she stopped in front of me and told me, "I meant it, what I said before. I've known Caleb for a long time now. And I've never seen him look at anybody the way he looks at you."

I shot her a grateful half smile, just as my cell phone beeped in my coat pocket. I pulled out the little prepaid smartphone and saw a new message waiting in my e-mail notifications. Red-burn had sent me a message with the subject line "Package en route." Just then, Caleb and Abe stepped out of the office, laughing and elbowing each other in the ribs. Caleb caught my eye and beamed at me, which Abe used as an opportunity for a shot to the kidneys. Caleb winced, making Abe cackle, and the two of them started punching each other again. I rolled my eyes, but it was nice to be included in that moment. I was relaxed and happy and full, so of course, that was the moment Caleb's incredibly punctual stripper wandered into my line of sight, having just come out of the ladies' room in a revealing parody of a police uniform.

Trixie was a built blond Valkyrie who looked much shorter in her pictures. She was nearly as tall as Caleb, her athletic, busty frame stretching the polyester she wore to the limits of its structural integrity.

I glanced over my shoulder toward Caleb, whose continued wrassling with his buddy prevented him from spotting her. I tried clearing my throat and waving my arms and considered whipping a beer bottle at them, but that seemed like an overreaction. We weren't going after Trixie per se, just the ring she was wearing, so I had no real problem with intervening on Caleb's behalf. But how to go about it? Trixie was considerably bigger than Jerry or Mort had been, and I didn't think she'd have any scruples about hitting another girl. I would need a carefully considered, multifaceted plan.

I hopped off my bar stool and planted myself between this very large lady and her destination, calling, "Hey, Trixie!"

Right, good plan.

Lord, she's tall.

"Honey, you need to move it," she said.

"How do you keep those little star pasties on?" I asked.

"Get out of my way!" Trixie said in a commanding tone.

"Did you take a lot of dance classes when you were getting started, or did you mostly get on-the-job training? Because, you know, I am thinking about going into . . . pole work."

"Sweetie, unless you want me to break that pretty face of yours, you'd better let me through," she said, glaring down at me. "But with a little work up top, I think you could make a lot of money."

"Thanks—hey!" I said, looking down at my little teacup breasts.

Which gave Trixie the opportunity to shove me aside and make for the bathroom door.

I looked across the bar to Caleb, who had finally noticed Trixie. He was trying to push through the crowd, but they were getting rowdy, seeing Trixie and assuming that it was almost time for their show. Trixie was barricaded in by the bodies, and this would be the perfect opportunity to whack her from behind with a pool cue . . . if I was capable of such cowardice. And then she turned on me, and I was pretty sure, given the expression on my face and the cue in my hand, that she knew what I was thinking.

She growled and made a grab at my hair. I ducked out of the way, bobbling my cue as I sidestepped her. She rounded, and I raised my fists, but honestly, I was afraid to take a swing at her. I wasn't sure how I was supposed to play this. From what I'd seen of "bikini boxing" on those tacky testosterone channels on cable, it was more about bouncing around and putting on a show than actually trading blows. Why didn't I switch the TV to one of those more respectable female MMA fights? Why?

Sensing my hesitation, she drew back her arm and plowed her fist right into my face. It hurt, but what disappointed me was the way the punch had me bouncing my ass against the scarred wooden floor. That was demoralizing.

Trixie sneered and turned her back on me to run for the front door. I sprang up from the floor and jumped onto her back to slow her down, but man, she was fast on those big plastic heels.

"Get off of me!" she shouted as I dragged her backward.

"No!" I said. "Give us the ring." OK, now I definitely felt like Gollum. And if she kept batting at my face with those acrylic nails, I was going to look like him.

"I don't know what you're talking about!" she cried, tossing me off of her. My grip on her shirt popped the Velcro closures, splitting it open for all to see as I smacked against the nearby pool table. Instead of taking the time to appreciate how much that hurt, I launched myself at her. I'd hoped the element of surprise would help me knock her back off her feet, but she caught me and damn near threw me over her shoulder.

She swung at the closest thing to her hands: my head. Since she took no precautions against marking my face, I showed her the same lack of courtesy. And I ended up getting tossed to the floor for my efforts. I could see Caleb's anxious face bobbing over the shoulders of those standing closest to us. He couldn't break through the crowd without displaying some serious werewolf strength.

Note to self: Leave the fighting to Caleb. He's much better at it.

I jumped to my feet, delivering an uppercut to her chin. The crowd cheered when I followed through with the elbow so that it caught her cheek as her face whipped forward. She bent forward, clutching her face. I brought her head crashing down on my knee and kicked out at her legs, knocking her off her stripper heels. She used her position to sweep my legs out from under me.

From there, there wasn't much strategy, just the two of us swinging away at whatever we could reach. I think I may have punched her in her spangled red bikini top. By that point, I wasn't able to see so well out of my swollen right eye, so hitting her in the boob was a distinct possibility.

"Come on, ladies, break it up," Caleb said, peeling me off of her and setting me on my feet.

"Crazy little bitch!" Trixie spat.

"Look, all we want is the wedding ring," I told her as Caleb carted me outside of swinging distance. "We just need the ring, and we'll get out of your face."

Trixie nodded slowly, considering. Caleb put me on my feet, and I approached her.

I patted her arm. In a gentler voice, I told her, "If you want, I will personally deliver pictures of you straddling one of those beefy fellas to Lolo, so he knows what he's missing."

Trixie nodded again, but this time, she was swaying on her feet. I didn't think it was because of my vicious blows.

"OK, OK," she panted, slipping the ring off her finger. "Just take it. I didn't want the stupid r-ring . . . any-anyway."

As she dropped it into my waiting palm, a red flush crept across her skin, and her breathing went unsteady and shallow.

I shoved the ring into my pocket. "Hey, are you OK?"

Trixie shook her head, just before her eyes rolled up

and she collapsed to the floor. Her head bounced off the planks with a sickening *crack*.

"Trixie?"

"Come on, get up," Pam called. "She beat you fair and square, Trix. Have some dignity."

I knelt over Trixie, prying her eyelids apart, watching through my good eye to see if her pupils responded to the harsh lights of the bar.

"No, I think she's really sick," I told the bartender as I watched Trixie's lips swell. If this reaction was what I suspected, her airway could swell shut in minutes, and she wouldn't be able to breathe. And contrary to every medical TV show ever made, it's not that easy to improvise intubation with an empty ballpoint pen.

"Trixie!" I called. "Trixie, do you have any allergies?" The only response I got was a muffled grunt. I looked up at the bartender. "Do you know if she has any allergies?"

Pam shrugged. "Just shellfish. You know, shrimp and stuff? But she's really careful to . . ." Pam glanced back at the remains of my sandwich and my hands, which were touching Trixie's neck. "Ohhh."

I raised my crab-contaminated hands away from Trixie's skin and dashed for the bar. I grabbed a prepackaged pair of yellow rubber kitchen gloves from the bar sink. "Is there a clinic in town?" I asked. Pam nodded. "Call them and explain the situation. Tell the doctor that we've got anaphylaxis, plus a possible concussion. We're going to need Benadryl and an epi shot, plus fluids. You got that?"

Pam nodded and dialed the phone behind the bar.

I looked to Abe. "Go into the ladies' room and get Trixie's bag. She probably has an EpiPen."

"I can't go into the ladies' room!" Abe protested.

"It's an emergency," I told him, depressing Trixie's swollen tongue with my gloved fingers. "And you *own* the bar."

"Sorry, right," Abe mumbled sheepishly, before booking across the room to the bathroom door.

Caleb dropped to his knees beside me, watching me with a confused expression. "Is she faking?" he asked.

"You can't fake that," I said, nodding toward her swollen mouth and face. I folded Caleb's jacket and placed it under Trixie's head, tilting her head back to keep her airway open. "She must be pretty sensitive if contact with my hands could make her react like this. Of course, I bloodied her lip, which may mean the shellfish contaminants got into her bloodstream."

Abe jogged back to us with a pink camouflage canvas rolling bag. I unzipped it and dug through a rainbow of sateen bustiers, feather boas, and thongs, until I found a small toiletry bag kept separate from the enormous makeup kit stuffed inside the lid. The black nylon bag was cleaner and newer than the makeup kit and was clearly used less. I unzipped it and found a plastic tube with a purple label marked "EpiPen."

"Does anyone have any scissors or a knife?" I called. "I need to split her pants."

Sheepish again, Abe knelt beside me and reached for the hem of Trixie's uniform pants. He gave the leg of her pants a sharp jerk, and they split up to the knee. He pulled at the tear-away pants, splitting the Velcro to her thigh. My mouth hung open for a moment before I snapped myself out of it and removed the tube's flip-top. I clicked the blue release button and jabbed the auto-injector into her outer thigh, holding it there to make sure the medicine was injected.

I kept my fingers at Trixie's throat, waiting for the telltale spike in her pulse. In a few seconds, the swelling in her lips decreased ever so slightly. Her legs began to twitch and shake, as if she had been zapped with a cattle prod. This was a normal nerve response to the epinephrine, something patients complained bitterly about, along with nausea, anxiety, and bouts of the shakes. Of course, I'd be anxious if I'd had a stranger jab an injection into my bare thigh.

I took another jacket from a patron who stood nearby ogling the red spangly top peeking through Trixie's uniform shirt. I glared at him while I draped the jacket over her chest. She needed to stay warm.

A handsome middle-aged man in a maroon St. Nicholas Clinic sweatshirt barreled into the barroom, black leather medical bag in hand. He spotted the woman on the floor and made a beeline for us.

"What in the hell happened to this woman?" he demanded, examining the swelling and bruises on her face.

"We had a minor difference of opinion before she went into anaphylactic shock," I said.

He looked up at me, blue eyes flashing as if he was about to light into me about her condition. "It doesn't look like you're in much better shape, ma'am," he said disdainfully.

I pressed my gloved hand to my mouth and drew

back yellow latex smeared with blood. Well, that certainly explained the stinging in my lip. I turned to Caleb, who was glaring at the doctor. Maybe he didn't appreciate his tone with me?

"It's not that bad," Abe assured me.

Groaning, I peeled off the contaminated gloves and reached toward the box of proper medical gloves in the doctor's bag. "May I?"

The doctor gave a curt nod. "Ned Mabry."

"Anna Moder," I told him, the name rolling off my tongue on autopilot, then I rattled off a succinct description of Trixie's condition. "Patient engaged in a fistfight that ended with a blow to the back of her head when she hit the floor. Patient has a severe allergy to shellfish and had contact with residue from a crab salad sandwich. Before hitting her head, she developed respiratory difficulty and early-stage swelling of the lips and tongue. I auto-injected a point-three-milligram dose of epinephrine that the patient carried with her in her purse. Swelling has reduced. Patient is responding as expected."

"Thank you, Nurse Moder." Dr. Mabry nodded, checking Trixie's vitals.

"It's *Doctor* Moder," I snapped, irritated that, like a lot of male doctors, Mabry had assumed that a woman with medical knowledge ranked below him. I ignored the way Caleb's eyebrows winged up. *Stupid pride.*

"Pardon me," he said. "I don't know a lot of doctors who engage in fistfights at stripper bars."

"They're exotic dancers," I corrected, becoming more and more irritated with this guy. "And it's none of your business what I'm doing here."

"Well, you've provided appropriate treatment," he said. "I'll take her to the clinic for overnight observation, but she should make a full recovery. I'm open until ten if you want to follow up with her."

I nodded. Trixie was loaded onto a gurney and wheeled away to the clinic. The crowd, which had seen more than its fair share of entertainment that evening, dispersed. I sat heavily on the pool table, swiping at my busted lip with antiseptic. Caleb was at my side in a flash, taking over dabbing duties and then leading me to Abe's office to make full use of his first-aid kit. "You OK?"

"I saw *Million Dollar Baby*. No matter what I say, do not pull the plug, OK?" I told him.

"Maybe we should go to the clinic and let the doctor check you," he suggested anxiously.

I shook my head. "No, I'm fine."

"I guess you would know. You really are a doctor, huh?" he asked.

"That's what the fancy piece of paper I bought on the Internet says."

"Well, even under the circumstances, it was neat to get to see you work. You usually don't speak with that kind of authority and confidence." I opened my mouth to protest, but Caleb added, "It was a good thing. I felt like I was seeing the real Tina. I wouldn't mind seeing more of her."

He grinned and kissed my bruised lip, making me wince. "My face hurts."

"Here." He pressed a gentle kiss to the tip of my nose.

"Oh, my God, she has you so whipped," Abe groaned

from the doorway. He wrinkled his face in disgust. "What did I tell you about being all cutesy?"

"I don't know. Perhaps I can't remember because of the stripping Amazon who pummeled my head!" I shot back, glaring at both of them. "A warning about her being Godzilla in a bikini would have been nice."

"Well, to express our apologies—and our appreciation for not letting our friend die from the food at my bar—here you go." Abe pressed an envelope into my hand. "The fellas wanted me to give you this."

I opened it, amazed at the green profusion of singles that sprang forth from its confines. "What the—?"

"Well, my guys took bets on the fight. You won on fourteen-to-one odds. That's a pretty decent cut of the proceeds."

"Fourteen to one? That's kind of hurtful," I said, staring down at the envelope of crumpled bills. "I tell you what, why don't you give my share to Trixie?" I said, pressing the money back into his hand. "Tell her it's to help with her medical bills. It's my fault for exposing her to the crab anyway."

"You're good people, Tina." Abe nodded and produced a bloody raw steak from behind his back. Before I could protest, he slapped it against my bruised eye.

I yelped. "There's no medical proof that this works."

Caleb snorted. "Steak is Abe's answer to most problems. You know, I keep trying to keep you out of situations where people are swinging at you. And you keep jumping right back into them. I give up. Jump away. Maybe if you're actively trying to get hurt, you'll stay safe, like reverse psychology."

"I really didn't mean for it to happen this time. But it was oddly therapeutic. Getting hit and getting back up," I said. "It's like facing my biggest phobia."

"Don't go doing any more 'therapy' for a while, OK?" he grumbled, before observing in wonder, "You gave Trixie your cut."

"Yeah, it felt weird taking money for beating someone up. Also, there were some questionable stains on some of the bills," I said, shuddering.

It took some convincing to prevent Caleb from actually carrying me out of the bar. He drove me right back to the motel and started the shower, helping me out of my clothes and *tsk*ing over my bruises.

"I'm not going to just jump you this time," he rumbled. "This is me, very slowly, very deliberately, going about the business of us having sex. We're going to talk about your 'no-fly zones' and protection and the possibility of you getting pregnant, since there's a really good chance of *that* happening, what with the werewolf sperm and all—"

I cut him off with a kiss. "Please stop talking."

He nodded sharply, muttering into my mouth, "Oh, thank God."

And with that, he lunged at my mouth, kissing and licking and biting, until he'd explored every inch of it. We slid under the blissfully warm spray, and I winced as it beat against my face. I braced my arms against the wall, letting the water sluice down my back.

Warm hands brushed down the length of my spine.

I jumped, nearly knocking my head into the wall, but Caleb's hand cradled my skull and guarded it from the impact. I turned, my feet slipping a little on the tub surface as I wound my arms around his neck. I pressed my head into the hollow of his throat while his hands stroked my back.

The water cascaded over us, rippling over his skin. I ran my fingers along the line of his ribs, making him jump. I giggled, making him grin as he gently poked at my ticklish sides. He swallowed my indignant squeal. His fingers curled around my hip, and he hitched my legs around his waist. Already encased in a condom, he lined up our bodies and slid forward with aching hesitation. I gasped, and his tongue darted into my mouth, the water moving over our mouths.

I tipped my head back against the door, breathing hard, pinned there like a butterfly. Caleb's hair was dripping over his forehead, inky black, as he loomed over me. His eyelashes stuck together, spiky and wet. I nodded, moving my hips up to meet him. He relaxed, grinding me into the wall, sliding me up and down as we moaned in unison.

Just when we'd worked out an easy rhythm, the water ran cold, and I practically vaulted us out of the shower. Laughing, he carried me to the bed, gently dropped me onto the bedspread, and crawled over me.

As if he wanted to remind me that I was dealing with a dangerous supernatural creature, he bit down on my bottom lip. I dragged my nails down his back, making him hiss. His skin was so hot. It practically radiated against my palms as I stroked his back.

His fingers pressed down over my hips, pulling me back, aligning me with him. I felt him between my thighs, warm and hard and thick. I leaned forward and bit the skin of his hand, the delicate web between his thumb and forefinger.

He yowled in protest, but he didn't stop. His fingers cupped the back of my neck, cradling my throat and pulling me back against his chest, nipping and biting the sensitive skin. His hands trailed over my arms, pressing my palms against the bedspread as his teeth sank just a bit deeper. I cried out, freeing one hand to reach back into his hair, and yanked before he could break the skin.

His hips pushed me into the rhythm he needed without keeping me from what gave me pleasure. His warm, deft fingers trailed down my back, around my hip, and between my thighs, to find that special little bundle of nerves. My hips stuttered as he teased me there, and the very small part of my brain still capable of thinking vowed horrible, anatomically specific revenge if he didn't continue doing exactly *that* for, oh, maybe a month.

A wonderful pressure rippled down my spine, through my belly, and I was falling, rising, spinning, all at once. I lost all sense of balance, falling forward and clawing at the arm around my waist as dark, pulsing shudders racked my body. Caleb pitched forward and nearly knocked me facedown onto the comforter. He hitched me up, hugging me to his chest and balancing me on his lap, while he guided my hips up and down. Because I didn't have the coordination to do that for myself.

I felt him shake and give a long, guttural moan before flopping to his side, pulling me down with him. Our breathing evened out, and I could move my legs again, rolling my ankles from side to side just so I could feel the pleasant little aftershocks that fired down to my toes.

Caleb was staring at me in that analytical way of his, trying to gauge my reaction.

"And suddenly, sex happened," I muttered into the pillow.

Caleb's mussed head popped up over my shoulder. "Slower, sweeter, romantic-comedy sex will happen later, I promise. Sorry most of it was against a shower wall."

"Actually, it's probably the cleanest surface in the room."

He was particularly interested in my tattoos, now that he was seeing them up close. He wanted to know why I'd chosen that design, when I'd started them, and whether I planned to get more. He traced the length of my spine with his lips, biting lightly at the ridge of each vertebra.

"It's my personal star chart," I murmured into the pillows. "It's how I keep track of where I've been."

"Don't most people use stars to keep track of where they are?" he asked, chuckling into my skin, tracing the outline of one with his tongue. I think he was somewhere near the Topeka star.

"Well, I was going to do push-pins, but they weren't as pretty."

"You don't strike me as the tattoo kind of girl."

"I wasn't, but that was sort of the point. Don't you have any?"

"I had a very strict mother," he said, smiling into my skin.

"I think you would look awesome with a tattoo," I told him, rolling over so I was facing him. "You could get a butterfly, right here." I stroked the tramp-stamp area of his lower back. He chuckled again, jerking a little as my fingers stroked a particularly ticklish section of his back. "Or something tribal." He snorted. "The Chinese symbols for love and strength . . . which inevitably will translate to 'cliché tattoo.'"

"It's a little alarming that you came up with those ideas so quickly."

"Spent a lot of time thinking about it."

"You are a very strange girl."

I rolled over, balancing my chin on his chest. "Did you really have a strict mother?"

It seemed a little wrong, asking about his runaway human mom when I knew a little bit of the history. But I wanted to hear more about Caleb from his own mouth, his own version. The story I'd heard about cruel, thoughtless Lydia Graham, who had forgotten the promises involved in mating and left her husband and child to themselves, had been twisted in the telling by so many indignant werewolf housewives that I didn't know if I could trust it.

He blanched a bit at the question. "Oh, I don't know. I mean, she didn't stick around long enough for me to figure her out. She left when I was five. Dad met her when he was traveling in Washington State. He told her that he lived in the middle of nowhere, Alaska, but I don't think she really got it until she moved there. And then she was stuck. Not stuck the way you were," he clarified carefully. "I don't remember them fighting or yelling or Dad being anything but good to her. It was seeing the same people every day, having the same conversations. Dad said he thought it drove her a little crazy. So she waited until I was in school one morning and ran for it."

As a woman who had once run for it, I could sympathize with Lydia and the desperation she must have felt to have taken such a step. But at the same time, how could she leave her little boy behind? I was thankful, at least, that she'd left him with other werewolves so he wouldn't go through his transformation without that support. And in some remote, gloomy corner of my mind, I couldn't help but think that he was repeating his father's cycle all over again, choosing a woman— however temporarily—who would inevitably leave him. Freud would have a field day with Caleb Graham.

"Did you ever hear from your mom?" I asked, running my fingers through his hair.

He leaned into the caress and shook his head. "Wasn't interested. She made her choice."

"And your dad?" I asked.

"He always missed her. He was a good dad. He loved me like crazy, did all of the things a dad was supposed to, but you could tell life was just a little bit less than it should have been for him."

I gave him a little half smile and kissed him. "I'm sorry."

"It is what it is. Yeah, it sucks, and my life could have been better. But there were people in my family who had it a lot worse. So I can't really complain." He rolled onto his side and slid his hand down my stomach, tracing each of my ribs with his fingertips.

"What was it like growing up in the valley?" I asked.

"It was the best kind of childhood for a little kid," he said, sighing. "I spent a lot of time playing in the woods with Samson and Cooper. Maggie was the little sister I never really wanted. We were always chasing something, hunting, running around. Cooper and Samson lost their dads pretty early on, so my dad took them under his wing, so to speak. He taught us how to fix a car, clear a clogged sink, skin a deer with your bare teeth, that sort of thing. "

"Sounds idyllic, in a twisted *Tom Sawyer* kind of way."

"We had to grow up fast. Cooper became the alpha when we were just teenagers. And then that other pack tried to take over the valley, and everything got so screwed up. It just seemed easier to pull away from all that confusion. I knew my dad was disappointed that I moved away, but it just didn't feel right for me to be there anymore."

"Was it Suds who got you into the whole werewolf-tracker-for-hire business?"

"No, and he doesn't know what I am, by the way," he replied. "I was the valley's police force before I left. Usually, the alpha takes on the role along with mayoral duties. But we didn't have an alpha when Cooper left, and I was able to fill in. I liked it. Mostly, it involved keeping the younger wolves in line and corralling my idiot uncles when they tied one on. But every once in a while, some unsavory character would wander into town, thinking it would be a nice place to set up a meth lab, and I would have to explain why this was not a good idea. In following up on the background information for these yahoos, I was amazed at what I managed to discover online. And in a lot of cases, these guys—and sometimes girls—had warrants or rewards for information leading to their arrests. With my extra senses, I could track them, even after they left the valley. I made quite a bit of money that way. And I made some good contacts as I traveled around. So when I left, it seemed a natural fit for me to do it full-time."

"But doesn't it kill you, being away from the packlands for this long?"

"It was hard, at first. I couldn't stay away for long stretches at a time without really pushing myself. But it got easier with time." He gave me a crooked little smile. "What I'm looking for isn't in the packlands."

"Well, that's nice and cryptic, thank you."

"So, your family?"

"What about them?"

"I am assuming that you have one. You weren't hatched. We've established, thanks to your alarming deceptive tactics, that you are an only child. What about your parents?"

"My parents died a few years ago," I told him.

"I'm sorry. What were they like?"

I hesitated and cursed myself for it. He'd shared with me, I reminded myself, and he didn't have to. So instead of giving him the pat answer I'd developed for Anna Moder, I told him about Jack and Marcy Campbell.

"Nice people," I said, smiling when he slid his lips along the ridge of my hip. "High school sweethearts. Mom owned an interior-design business, and Dad ran a construction firm. They loved each other very much. They taught me what marriage was supposed to look like. I just didn't pay close enough attention."

"Well, you'll know what to look for next time," he told me.

"I don't know if there will be a next time for me," I said, yawning.

Caleb's head jerked up, his expression alarmed. "What?"

I sniffed. "I'm thinking maybe polygamy next time around. Civil union with two or three guys. I think there would be less pressure that way."

"Oh, you're hilarious." He groaned, digging his fingertips into my sides, making me jump all over the bed.

"It's not my fault you keep falling for it!" I exclaimed as he tickled my sides. To escape the torture, I went with my only available distraction technique. I kissed him, long and hard, sliding my hands over his and directing them to more interesting, less ticklish parts of my body.

He tapped his finger between my eyebrows. "You've got that look on your face. What are you thinking?"

"Can I see your wolf form again?" I asked. "I didn't get a very good look at you the other day."

Caleb frowned. "Right here?"

"I'll stand way over there, out of range," I promised, scrambling out of bed and wrapping a sheet around my waist as I hid behind the oak nightstand.

Caleb grumbled, but he got out of bed and stood in the middle of the room. He rolled his shoulders and made a sort of squinting face. I giggled a little, which broke his concentration, making him whine, "This is awkward."

"Oh, come on."

He took a deep breath, centering himself. That same golden light spread from his heart, over his skin, dragging his human form in its wake. The light winked out, and standing in front of me was a huge iron-gray wolf, big chocolate eyes twinkling. He made a whuffling noise, as if to say, *Well?*

I knelt in front of him, letting his cold, wet nose tap against my face.

"You're beautiful." I sighed, running my fingers through his thick fur. He nosed against my neck, bumping his head against mine. "Such a big, beautiful boy."

I scratched him behind the ears, cooing over him. He pressed his nose against my shoulder, knocking me back on my butt. I giggled as he hunched over me, licking my face. He phased back to human and was pressing kisses all over my face.

"Well, this *is* awkward." I laughed.

"Too much?" he asked.

I nodded.

12

The Gift Horse Has Some Awesome Teeth

It had taken me much longer than I'd hoped, but we finally arrived in Anchorage. The snow was falling in earnest, giving the already alien city lights an otherworldly glow. Everything seemed far too bright, too neon, too busy. I found myself blinking in the glare of a stoplight.

I gave a fleeting thought to Red-burn and the post office she planned to use across town, but then Caleb asked me to locate Lolo's "construction office" on the GPS system. I declined the honor of meeting him, electing to stay out in the truck while Caleb delivered the wedding ring to a snazzy office building in a nearly empty business park.

Caleb was all smiles when he emerged from the transaction. As part of our payment, Lolo booked us a room at the fairly spectacular Highbury Plaza. We were to stay there for a week, with all expenses paid.

He'd booked spa appointments. We didn't even have to check in, as Lolo's "people" had seen to that.

I got a little nervous at the sight of the tall silver cylinder, one of the highest points on the city skyline. We crossed the chrome and blue glass lobby with our "well-loved" bags in hand and headed straight for the elevators. The moment the doors closed, Caleb lunged, pressing me against the glass elevator wall, and ravaged my mouth. I felt his hands cup my jeans-clad butt and squeaked. "It's a glass elevator! The people in the lobby will see."

"So let 'em see," he growled.

When we'd reached our floor, we slid against the walls of the hallway, kissing and groping and laughing, until we finally found our room. When I unlocked the door, all kissing and/or groping stopped. This wasn't a *room*, this was a suite. It was the fanciest space I'd seen since leaving my "married" apartment all those years ago. Even with the beige, ivory, and slate-blue tones, it was still remarkably feminine. The delicately beige carpet was plush and thick under my toes as I pranced around the room, hopping up and down over the view of the skyline and the mountains. We disheveled the hell out of the immaculately white duvet on the enormous bed, revealing the delicate blue sheets.

I dashed into the bathroom and made a squealing noise that brought an alarmed Caleb running. "There's a separate shower and a bath!" I cried, climbing into the white-tiled whirlpool tub. Every square inch of the bathroom was pristine, recently cleaned white ceramic.

I was reasonably sure there would be no bugs in the

tub. I wanted to bask in the cleanliness, wallow in it. I wanted to eat dinner in that tub, just because I could.

"It's so clean." I sighed. "And it has a separate tub and shower."

"And that's scream-worthy because . . . ?"

"Because sometimes a girl wants to wash her hair in a separate space from where she washes the rest of her."

Caleb frowned. "Girls are weird."

"Hopelessly so," I admitted. "This seems a little too good to be true. Are you sure that Lolo's not setting us up for credit-card fraud or a body hidden in the closet or something?"

"No, Lolo likes to treat people well when they do right by him. If you'd ever met his wife, you'd understand why he was so grateful," Caleb assured me. "She's got a temper on her and doesn't care much who sees her flip out. We didn't just save Lolo's marriage. We might have saved his life."

"Really?"

He nodded. "She tossed a cake at Lolo's head once. Most awkward birthday party I've ever been to."

I considered that for a moment. "So how long is that massage he booked for us?"

He chuckled, wrapping his arms around my waist. "That's my girl."

"Are you going to take a swim in that tub with me?" I asked, kissing his chin.

"I think we'll get to that eventually." He grinned down at me and lifted my hips, locking my ankles at the small of his back. He gave me one long, heated look before devouring my mouth. His hands were everywhere, cupping my face, my ass, teasing my breasts with light little touches around the nipples but never touching them.

Bracing my hands against the open bathroom door, I bucked against him. He ripped my shirt down the front, and my bra followed, fluttering to the floor in ruins. I rocked and rode against him, seeking the friction we both needed so much.

He managed to keep me pinned to the door, unzip his jeans, and roll on a condom without dropping my butt to the floor. He pushed gently inside me. I sighed as my body adjusted, stretching to accommodate him.

And just as I grasped his rhythm, he spun, carrying me across the room toward the bed. *Loved.* I'd never felt so loved and cared for and wanted in my whole life. I wanted this feeling to go on and on, until I was old and gray and no longer able to pull off this position. Wherever I was going, I wanted Caleb to come with me.

Caleb pushed my hair off my shoulder as he rained kisses down the length of my neck, down my spine, pressing his mouth to each individual star before making his way back to my shoulders. He nipped my earlobe as he pressed inside me, working our hips together as he slid his hand around my hip. I pushed back, bracing my arm against the headboard, until I was filled to the hilt. His hands were everywhere—between my legs, on my breasts, at my throat.

A delicious tension wound its way out from my belly, tightening from my breasts down to my toes. Caleb rubbed in small circles, increasing his thrusts as his breath came in short bursts. I threw my head back, yelling when one final thrust of his hips sent a climax rippling along my body. Caleb pulled me up until I was sitting in his lap, my overwrought nerves twitching and firing as he moved underneath me. We collapsed against the mattress, sweaty and sated.

"If you make a joke about me bringing out the beast in you, I will not be held accountable for my actions."

"Understood."

Honestly, we intended to honor our reservation at the steakhouse just across the street. Caleb got dressed up in a white Oxford shirt and khakis. He was tugging uncomfortably at a navy tie when I stepped out of the bathroom. He looked so polished, with his dark hair carefully combed back and the darker caramel tones of his skin highlighted by the crisp white shirt.

"Look at you," I breathed. "You're so pretty."

"Me?" He chuckled. "Do a little twirl for me." I complied with the twirl request, the skirt of the fitted long-sleeved red dress I'd chosen from the lobby shop swishing against my legs. I'd put on weight since the last time I'd bought clothes, which I was choosing to see as a good thing.

We meant to walk out the door and go to the restaurant. We really did. But Caleb was just beaming at me, as if I'd personally hung the moon, and he really liked the way I was wearing that dress . . . and the next thing I knew, we were naked all over again.

Sometime just before the room-service kitchen was

about to close, we managed to put on robes and order dinner. Knowing Caleb's appetite, I ordered big— thick rare steaks, hand-cut fries, macaroni and cheese, chicken and dumplings, not to mention half of the dessert cart. It took three people to deliver our order to our room, plus the sommelier who carried the bottle of semidry red wine I'd ordered. When the sommelier offered Caleb the bottle to inspect, he grinned and motioned to me. I gave it a cursory glance and nodded, smiling warmly at the man.

"A lovely selection, miss," he said, snapping his heels together before pouring us each a healthy portion. He left the bottle on the cart, accepted his tip from Caleb, and closed the door behind him. I took another sip of wine, enjoying the way it rolled over my tongue.

Caleb watched, his head tilted as he studied me. "You used to have this, didn't you?"

"My own private sommelier? Well, not every day, just on the weekends," I teased.

"No, the nice clothes, hotels with wine lists, waiters with accents, the whole thing. You used to have this."

I shrugged. "Well, I lived on the nice side of comfortable, I'll admit. And there are things I miss, like a dependably bug-free shower and knowing where I'm going to sleep every night, but I have to say, I was a lot more comfortable eating burgers at a saloon. With you." I gave him a smacking kiss. "All this, it's nice. But I can live without it."

We ate, sitting on the floor in our robes, in front of the window, with the lights of Anchorage laid out before us. I was toying with an asparagus spear, considering the chocolate éclair left untouched on the dessert plate. It was lying there, all chocolaty and creamy and provocative. It was practically asking me to eat it.

"So, I was hoping you would come home with me," Caleb said suddenly.

The hussy éclair forgotten, I grinned at Caleb and toyed with the belt of his robe. "Well, sailor, I don't think that line works if we're already home for the night, but if you want to do 'strangers in a bar,' I'm up for it."

He laughed, prying my hands loose from his belt without much enthusiasm. "No, back to the valley, which is your home, too, so it sort of works out. I wanted to ask you before, but I was afraid you'd say no. I'm going to be heading back in a few weeks. You could stay with me, in my house. And we could have a life together. I know Maggie would rehire you as the pack doctor. It's difficult to find doctors who can treat werewolves. I doubt she's filled the position."

"But what happens when spring comes and you need to go out on the road again?"

He shrugged. "You can come with me. I work twice as fast when you're around anyway. Or hell, I could work from home. My cousin Cooper has been on me about joining his business, expanding it. I could do that, stay in one place."

"I couldn't ask you to do that."

"You aren't, *I'm* asking *you*. What do you want out of life?" he asked. "'Cause you can't keep running like this. You can't just keep moving on until you're too old and tired to move on again."

Well, that sucked all of the levity out of the conversation.

I knew what I wanted. I wanted to go back to the pack. I wanted to go back to the only real home I'd known since my parents died. And I wanted to stay with Caleb.

"I loved living in the valley. It was an incredible gift that your family gave me, allowing me to practice medicine. It was like regaining the use of a limb. And I belonged for the first time in years. I had a family. People who valued me, looked me in the eye. I was a person again."

"I sense a 'but' coming," he said.

"But it's such a big decision," I said weakly.

"Because you're scared."

I nodded. "That would be a massive understatement, yes."

"By something I've done?" he asked, his expression faltering.

"It's not you. Trust me, it has nothing to do with you. But I believe Glenn when he says he can find me. It's only a matter of time, really. If I came home with you, I could be bringing all that trouble with me, right into your pack. And I couldn't stand it if someone in your family got hurt because of me or if he caused trouble for the pack. It's the reason I left in the first place."

"What if he wasn't part of the equation?"

"What do you mean?"

"I could kill him," Caleb offered quietly, toying with the lapels of my robe. "I could track him down, snuff him out before he even saw me coming. I could make it look like an accident. It would never be traced back to you."

I stared at him for a long, silent moment. It wasn't as if I hadn't considered it. And it would be so easy to let the word *yes* slip from my lips, to let Caleb give Glenn all of the pain he deserved and somehow keep my hands relatively clean. All I had to do was nod, and I would have the ultimate revenge on my bastard ex-husband.

But I couldn't do that. I'd spent most of our time together griping at Caleb about his tendency to act without mercy. I couldn't exactly turn around and ask him to kill for me.

"No."

Caleb protested, "But—"

"No. I love you too much to make you a killer."

Caleb pouted. "Not even a thorough maiming?"

"No."

"OK, then, forget your ex. Forget everything but what you want to do right now, what you know in your heart is the right thing for you. Just for you. What do you want to do?"

I leaned my forehead against his and pressed my lips to his. "I want to go home with you."

Red-burn was going to be so pissed at me when I told her I didn't need that ID after all.

Whooping, Caleb dragged me down to the floor and kissed me. He nuzzled at the place on my neck where he'd bitten me all those months ago, and it tingled a bit. I pulled away, rubbing at my former hickey. Caleb noticed the gesture and pulled himself back up to a sitting position. "So you know how things work with us, right? The mating thing? The claiming bite?" I nodded. "Well, I hope that's something you're willing to consider."

"Are you sure we know enough about each other to be mated?"

"I know that you're strong, you're adaptable, and you're smart, all qualities that make for a fantastic mate."

Somehow I was both touched and slightly insulted that he hadn't mentioned me being at all pretty.

"But I won't put the claiming bite on you until you've finished your business with Glenn. Divorced, separated by church and state, lock, stock, and barrel."

My mouth dropped open. "But that could take years."

He shrugged. "I'll wait."

"Is this some sort of bizarre stall tactic?"

"No, this is about you getting closure before we start something new. I think it's important for you to finish this on your own terms. And frankly, I'd like to put your real legal name on our marriage certificate, not an alias. That means that you can't be married to someone else when we file it. Werewolves don't file a lot of legitimate government paperwork. We take the marriage licenses pretty seriously."

"This is the worst proposal I've ever heard."

"Not true. That honor belongs to my cousin Maggie, whose mating and proposal involved accidentally biting her mate on the ass."

"You're right," I conceded, remembering the number of stitches required to sew up Nick's butt cheek. "That was worse."

"This is important," he told me. "It's something you need to do for yourself, not for me. I can be patient. You can take all the time you need."

I sighed, peering up at him through my lashes. "You're right. I thought the answer was to just keep moving around, but that hasn't worked so far. I have to change tactics. And I would feel a lot better not lying to people every time I open my mouth."

He fluttered his hand over his heart. "A nonromantic response to a nonromantic proposal."

I laughed, whacking him with a pillow, wrestling with him until I pinned him to the floor and pressed a kiss against his throat. I was fairly certain he let me win. "I'll start the paperwork just as soon as we get back to the valley," I promised. "If nothing else, I have to come home with you so I can see the look on Maggie's face when she realizes I might end up her in-law."

13

Pandora Was a Total Idiot

We were leaving. I'd never looked forward to traveling like this. Usually, departures meant distress. Now I was going home.

We would be leaving for the valley in a few days. Caleb was working diligently to close up whichever of his pending cases he could close and to send progress reports to his clients on those still open. Since I was able to type more than five angrily pecked words per minute, I ended up sending out most of them while Caleb dictated.

"I don't suppose you would give up typing for the day and get naked with me?"

"Do you want to leave town without any pesky paperwork hanging over your head?" I asked.

"Hmm, my desire for sex loses out to my hatred of paperwork. Well played, woman." He sighed, hauling himself out of bed. "I need to get the tires checked for our trip and run to the grocery anyway. Surprise, surprise, we're out of condoms again. And those little packs of raisins."

"How about some juice boxes?" I suggested cheekily.

"Well, they might come in handy," he said, considering.

"My big bad wolf." I sighed, rolling my eyes. I kissed him again. "If people only knew."

He swatted my butt good-naturedly. "You're just happy you don't have to buy the condoms."

I pursed my lips, remembering exactly how hot my cheeks got when the clerk at the Ready-Mart gave me the *I know what you've been doing* look over my box of extra-large, ribbed-for-her-pleasure protection. "You're not wrong."

I worked steadily for an hour, doing a little dance when I finished the last report and hit "Send" on the e-mail program.

All I had left to do was pack. I was really looking forward to returning to the valley. I knew I would have to do quite a bit of groveling, but eventually, the pack would accept me again.

Now for the e-mail I'd put off for the last week. I opened the program to sign out of Caleb's address and sign into the secure server I used to contact Red-burn. Just as I was about to click on "Log Out," a new message alert popped into a folder labeled "Pack" with a *ping*. I frowned. I knew there were folders in Caleb's account—heck, I'd arranged most of them—but I'd assumed they were for storage. I didn't realize they could receive directed messages.

I opened the folder and had to search around a bit before I found a subfolder marked "Schuna," bolded and blinking with an unread message. I opened it and saw that the messages were from a private investigator in Seattle named Robert Schuna, the same investigator who'd sent us after a guy named Calvin Dodd. In fact, the new message was from Schuna, with the subject line "Progress Report?"

I didn't remember flagging his messages to go into a special folder. But now that I thought about it, I hadn't seen a new message from him in more than a week.

Frowning at the screen, I tapped my fingers on the touch pad. I thought we'd handled all of Schuna's cases. In fact, I'd sent him his last progress report the day before. Maybe there was a problem with the report? I opened the message.

Graham—

I need another progress report on the Bishop 'missing person' case. The client is getting antsy. Thank God, the guy's in Tennessee, or he'd be camped out in my office, waiting for news. I'd drop his twitchy ass, but he's paying me double. I'm willing to up your stake by twenty percent if you would just find this woman and put us all out of our misery. Send me what you can ASAP, and I'll pass it along to him.

—S.

It took me a moment to realize that the wounded, in-human sound piercing my eardrums was coming from my mouth. Bishop case? Out of Tennessee? It couldn't be true. It couldn't be *my* Bishop case. There had to be some sort of funny coincidence to explain this away.

All of the blood seemed to drain from my hands, leaving them cold and shaking as I tapped at the touch pad and opened the rest of the e-mails. They started two months before, around the time Red-burn sent me the red alert. I opened the attachments and found Glenn's official "case report" listing me as a runaway spouse. He'd told Schuna I had a history of mental illness, substance abuse, and filing false police reports. He'd been trying to get me help, he claimed, and when I found out that he was planning to have me committed to special rehab for the mentally ill, I ran. He just wanted to bring me home and get me help, he claimed.

I clicked through the attachments, finding our wedding portrait, credit reports, transcripts, lists of friends, my résumé and work history—which was amazing, really, considering the supposed mental problems and pill addictions Glenn subtly indicated to my coworkers. The final blow was a picture of me on the beach on our second wedding anniversary. It was displayed on a flyer demanding, "Have You Seen This Woman?" I'd always hated that picture. I was giving the camera my happy-on-the-surface smile, and I looked a little tired around the eyes, but that was to be expected when Glenn had kept me up until five that morning, accusing me of flirting with the waiter who served our anniversary dinner.

Caleb had been hired to find me.

I stumbled into the bathroom on watery legs, collapsing in front of the commode just before I tossed the contents of my stomach. Rivers of tears poured down my cheeks as I threw up, over and over. I balanced my head against my crossed arms, sobbing and sniffling. I grabbed a washcloth, still wet from my shower, and swiped at my face. I collapsed back against the tub.

How could I have been so stupid? He'd been lying to me all this time. Everything he'd said and done had been a cold-blooded calculation to lead me back to Glenn. Pretending not to know my name. Pretending not to know about my connection to the pack, not to know I was a doctor. He'd been pretending, training me to trust him, to let him close, like coaxing a stray cat into your house with a can of tuna. I thought I was being so smart, so guarded, and I'd walked right into his trap.

How could the worst liar in the world have tricked me so thoroughly? I'd *slept* with him! I'd let him see every part of me. I'd told him things I'd been afraid to admit to myself.

I didn't understand why. Was the fancy hotel some sort of trick to make me feel more comfortable or an attempt to soften the blow of betraying me? Or did he just want to screw on soft sheets before giving up his favorite toy? What was his angle? Enjoy one last week with me at this hotel, then pack me up in the truck tomorrow, maybe drug me once I figured out we were driving toward Seattle? Or would he shove a bag over my head and take me to some airplane hangar in the middle of nowhere?

I felt so completely stupid. Did he have a girlfriend somewhere he was going to go home to after he tossed me to the wolves?

Bad choice of words.

The mating. Was the mating real? Had I wanted so much to belong to someone that I let myself believe that we were connected in some spiritual, otherworldly way? Had I made up all those clingy, desperate emotions? My face flushed hot and red, tears stinging my eyes.

I'd been right before. There was no such thing as magic.

He promised he wouldn't hurt me. What complete and utter bullshit. I wasn't his mate. He never loved me. He was probably laughing at me this whole time, humoring me as he coaxed me into trusting him. Why hadn't I questioned that? Why didn't I pay attention to all of those alarms going off in my head?

I had to run. There was no other way. I had to get on the road before Caleb figured out what was going on. He'd made it clear where his loyalties were: his wallet. I could only imagine the kind of money Glenn had offered him. It would be better if I could catch a ride with the next semi I saw. I could get maybe an hour or two head start if his errands took long enough. I could hitch a ride from the tavern down the street, or maybe some of the hotel staff would be willing to help.

I packed as calmly as I could with my heart and mind racing. I took all of my clothes, except the red dress. I crumpled that up in a ball and threw it into a corner. I surveyed Caleb's cache of tools and took some plastic restraints and pepper spray. You never knew what sort of trouble you could get into while traveling. Frowning at what seemed like a trifling amount of protection in my shoulder bag, I also took the collapsible baton. I'd come to think of it as mine, anyway.

And on one last impulse, I grabbed his Taser.

I would need cash. Caleb had socked away a good portion of our earnings in the hotel-room safe. He'd used my fast-approaching birthday as the combination. The thought of stealing from him . . . well, it didn't bother me a whole lot, at the moment.

I dropped my bags near the closet door and was about to kneel in front of the safe when I heard the electronic lock click on the hallway door. I froze.

Caleb was back already!

How the hell did he get his tires inspected that fast? I glanced at the clock. He'd been gone for almost three hours. Apparently, I'd spent more time in the bathroom having a mental breakdown than I'd realized.

The thought of him walking through the front door, all smiles, made me want to swing that horribly heavy hotel steam iron at his face. But that would probably tip him off that I was angry. *Right.* I could act my way through this. I'd faked orgasms that made Glenn think he was some sort of sexual wunderkind. I could play the loving, stupid, unassuming, naive, deceived, imbecilic—

Rein it in, Campbell, I told myself as the door opened. *You can play the loving girlfriend for the next few minutes. Just get him to leave the room, and you're gone.*

I straightened, kicked my bags into the closet, and shrugged into one of Caleb's shirts as if I'd just been slipping into it when he returned. Not pilfering his weaponry and contemplating his demise via steam iron.

His sunny smile tore my heart like wet paper. I forced the muscles of my face into a pleasant expression.

"Took you a while," I said as he dropped his grocery bag and strode across the room toward me. He wrapped his arm around my waist and nudged the closet door with his foot just so he could shove me against it.

"I missed you," he rumbled, pressing my hips against the straining zipper of his jeans to show me just how much he missed me. A rush of longing crashed through me, taking my breath. He was breaking my heart. Even now, I could feel the cracks rippling across the surface.

I cupped my hand around his cheek. As much as I wanted to hate him—and I would—I was going to miss him so much.

"You OK?" he asked, dragging a thumb down my cheek. "Your eyes are all red."

"Fine," I said, my voice a little wobbly. I sucked in a breath to steady it. "I've been staring at the computer screen too long."

"Well, I need a shower. That garage reeked, and I feel like it soaked into my skin. You could join me," he suggested, grinning at me. "In the interest of water conservation and all."

I kissed him, long and deep, drawing it out so that I would remember the feel of his deceitful, shameless lips on mine for the rest of my life. It took everything I had not to bite down and draw blood, to cause just a fraction of the pain he was causing me. I smiled up at him, trying not to wince at the distinct cracking sensation in my chest. "OK, you go get the water warmed up. I'll be right there."

He kissed me right between the eyebrows and dropped me gently onto the bed. "Will do!"

He walked across the room, whistling as he dropped his clothes. I let my head fall back on the mattress. *Get up*, I told myself, pushing myself off of the bed. *Get out the door. Break down later.*

The moment I heard the shower run, I moved back across the room to the closet.

Listening for the sound of water, I quietly slid the closet door open and tapped the combination into the safe's keypad. I winced as each keystroke produced a loud, whining beep. I hoped his werewolf ears wouldn't pick that up.

My eyes slid across the laptop, still open on the desk. I knew it would be so much smarter to delete the e-mail, to give me that much more time as Schuna and Caleb straightened out their miscommunications. But I wanted Caleb to know why I left. I didn't want him to have any doubts.

Eventually, he'd look at the screen, realize what happened, and start tracking me. But before that, I wanted him to realize that I knew what a lying, lowlife asshole he was.

Stop it. You're wasting time. Get your ass out that door and on the road.

I yanked the safe door open, finding a respectable stash of twenties bundled into five-hundred-dollar stacks. I calculated my percentage of Caleb's stash and tucked eight hundred dollars into my pocket.

I pushed myself to my feet and slung the bag over my shoulders. After casting one last glance at the steamy bathroom, I shook my head and made for the door. I had my hand on the door handle when I felt long, wet fingers snap around my wrist.

Caleb was standing behind me, dripping wet, with no towel in sight. His expression was hurt and confused as he looked me up and down, spotting the bags, the jacket, all the signs that I was bolting.

"What are you doing?" he demanded.

I had a hundred responses tumbling around in my head.

Just going to get some ice, honey.

I'm going down to the lobby for some Tylenol.

I'm blowing this Popsicle stand, you lying sociopathic werewolf dick.

But I couldn't seem to produce the words. They seemed to be building up in my throat, threatening to choke me if they poured out of my mouth.

"Tina, what's going on?"

I was practically hyperventilating. All the moments we'd shared, the laughs, the mishaps, every kiss and touch, spun through my head on fast-forward. And rage, white-hot and all-consuming, bubbled up from my belly. I yanked my hand out of his grasp, raised my foot high, and stomped his sensitive instep. Caleb yowled, letting go of my wrist as he hopped away on his good foot.

"What did you do that for?" he demanded, but by

that time, my hand had snaked into my bag and charged the Taser. I clicked the control, swung my arm up, and pressed the prongs to his skin. Without a moment's hesitation, I fired it, sending canned lightning straight into Caleb's chest.

Unfortunately, I hadn't considered how the water covering Caleb's skin would carry the current, and he ended up twitching on the carpet in full-body shock. He shouted for just a second before his jaw muscles locked up. The charge ended, and Caleb looked up at me, eyes wide and golden in their distress. "If this is some sort of kinky 'naughty cat burglar' role-playing game, I am not getting it," he said, panting.

I grunted and gave him another shot, just on principle. This could be considered a breakup, right? Nothing says *I'm just not that into you* like Taser fire.

"S-stop T-t-tasering me!" he shouted, sounding more annoyed than injured. For a millisecond, I felt a little guilty. There's nothing more pathetic than a wet, naked guy flopping all over a hotel carpet while being electrocuted. And then the laptop caught my eye, and I got pissed off all over again. I dropped the Taser into my bag. He sat up, gingerly pressing at the already-healing contact burns on his chest. "What the hell is going on?"

"Read your e-mail," I snarled. Caleb caught my arm, dragging me down to the carpet next to him.

"What are you talking about?" he demanded.

I shrugged him off and tried to stand up, only to have him grab my arm again and stop me. "You know exactly what I'm talking about, you asshole!"

He sighed. "I'm really sorry about this."

"You think *sorry* is going to cover what you did?" I hissed, finally managing to push to my feet.

He shook his head. "No, I'm sorry about *this*." With speed you wouldn't expect from a guy who'd been recently Tasered, he swiped his leg out, knocking my feet out from under me. I flopped onto the carpet next to him with a startled *uuhf!*

My only excuse was that, as with a lot of things about Caleb, I just didn't see it coming.

He groaned, pulling my arm away from his face, where it had apparently flopped with quite a bit of force as I fell. As petty as it was, that made me feel a little bit better.

"I'm sorry I kicked you," he said solemnly, working his jaw to loosen the abused muscles. "But considering the Taser, I think we're even. Now, will you please tell me what the hell is going on?"

"You know who I am," I told him, scooting across the floor to brace my back against the closet door.

"Of course I know who you are!" he cried, rolling toward me. "You told me all about it."

Something about the way the lie rolled off his tongue so easily had me reaching into my bag again. He snatched the bag out of my hands and threw it toward the hallway door. I narrowed my eyes at him. "You're going to sit there and pretend that you haven't known exactly who I am from the minute we met? I saw the e-mails from Schuna, Caleb! I know you've been working on the 'Bishop case' for months."

All of the color drained from Caleb's cheeks, leaving

a waxy werewolf scrambling across the floor to kneel in front of me. "Tina, please."

"Was it all a trick?" I asked, my voice cracking. "Did you really get into a fight with that Marty guy in the parking lot, or was that a setup to get my sympathy? Tell me you didn't blow up my car for no good reason."

"Tina—"

"I trusted you, you sonofabitch! And I don't trust anyone. You promised me, no more surprises. And this is a hell of a surprise. You lied to me. Every time you opened your mouth and didn't tell me what you were really up to, you lied to me. I mean, I get that you're just trying to do a job, that I was an assignment. And after seeing you work, I can respect that it's not anything personal. But why pretend you didn't know me? Why didn't you just tell me Schuna was hiring you to find me? Why pretend you liked me? How could you lie like that? Why not just gag me and toss me into the back of the truck like you do everybody else? It's not like you didn't have the chance. I couldn't exactly overpower you. You let me think . . . how could you let me think that I found . . . just how the hell could you?"

My rant done, I sagged against the door, all of the wind knocked out of me. I hated the tears coursing down my cheeks, hated showing the slightest hint of how much he'd hurt me. But at least I wasn't throwing up on him. I considered that a small personal victory.

His dark eyes flickered down toward my bags. "So you were just going to leave without saying anything?"

"I wanted a head start," I told him. When his jaw

dropped, I added, "You've made it pretty clear you don't care who you're tracking as long as you get paid. You don't care what they did or who's after them—"

"This is different!"

"How?"

"It just is. I can't believe you thought I would just hand you over!"

"Are you really going to try to pull the *indignant* card right now?"

"You know what you mean to me!"

"No, I don't really know what I mean to you. Everything you've told me is a lie. I can thank you, at least, for never saying you love me. You have at least that much shame."

"I've told you I love you in about a dozen ways. But believe me, if I said the words, you'd bolt."

I slapped his hands away when he tried to touch my cheeks. "*Believe* you?" I scoffed. "Because you've proved yourself so trustworthy, right? You didn't even admit you were a werewolf until you had no choice. Oh, my God, is *that* it? Is that why you kept me around? I figured out that you were a werewolf, and you wanted to make sure I wouldn't tell anybody? You—"

"No, stop it. Stop! Look, Schuna hadn't told me anything personal about you." He tried to reach for me again but thought better of it when I unleashed a growl so vicious it rivaled his own on his wolfiest day. "You were an assignment, just like all of my other assignments. When I got your paperwork, I had no idea you were the sweet little pack doctor my cousins had been going on about. I didn't figure that out until you told me. You were just some runaway housewife with a drug problem and a worried husband at home. Schuna said his client just wanted to know where you were, that you were safe. I was supposed to send him the location and then wait for instructions. But you weren't a priority case. I wasn't even following your trail. I was still looking for Jerry when I came across that beautiful 'home' smell. I followed it for days, wandering around that armpit of a town. I saw you working at the grocery store. I did recognize you as Tina Campbell, and I realized the two women I was tracking were one and the same. From that moment on, your case was closed. I couldn't take someone in when she smelled like my pack. I wanted to approach you, to ask how a little human like you could be connected to my pack. But I told myself, 'Not tonight. Just hold on for a while. Watch her.'

"And I watched. I saw that the story Schuna fed me was total bullshit. I saw how sweet you were to everybody who crossed your path, even though it was so obvious that you were exhausted and scared and barely hanging on. I saw you smile . . . and that was it for me. *You* were it for me. I figured whatever was really going on with your husband, I could find a way to help you. I'd finally worked up the nerve to talk to you, which was why I was waiting in the parking lot for you— which I will admit sounds a little creepy, now that I've said it out loud. Anyway, I was waiting for you, and that's when Marty showed up, and the whole thing just sort of snowballed."

He looked at me, obviously hoping to see some softening of my expression. He winced when he saw me glowering at him. "And that convoluted, slightly insane story explains why you continued to lie to me, *how*?"

"Well, how the hell was I supposed to come out with all that without it sounding convoluted and slightly insane? You were already so skittish I was afraid you were going to bolt at any minute. Then you found my tool kit in the truck, and you *did* try to bolt. I'm so sorry I lied, but by the time I thought you might trust me, it was too late for confessions. I knew you'd be so angry that there would be no getting past it. I just wanted to get you back to the valley before I confessed everything," he said, as if he could tell the last few words out of his mouth were not the words of a reasonable, intelligent werewolf.

"Where I would be trapped for the winter and couldn't get away."

He pulled a face that looked remarkably like a wince. "'Trapped' is such an ugly word."

I glowered at him. "I can think of a few more."

"Can I put some pants on so we can discuss this?" he asked.

"You're worried about being naked? Isn't that a werewolf's favorite outfit?"

He shook his head, glancing down. "I feel all vulnerable."

I rolled my eyes and waved toward the bathroom. He bounded up from the floor, having recovered from his Tasering in record time, and threw on some sweats. He offered me his hand, to help me off the floor. I glared up at him.

He sighed and dropped to the carpet next to me. "I've kept us moving just in case Schuna sent another investigator after you. And I've been feeding him fake progress reports. I told him you were spotted boarding a plane from Anchorage to Ontario. And then I told him you'd taken the ferry back to Washington State. Anything to keep him off your trail. We took off after Trixie because Schuna told me he was going to send a second investigator to Fairbanks to help out. I had to get you out of town. Suds is stalling him, telling him that I'm working on another case. By the time we got back to the valley, we'd be snowed in, and we'd have time to figure out something long-term. I've been trying to help you, Tina, I swear."

"Well, it's not working, because Glenn is still driving Schuna nuts with requests for follow-up reports. So, short of killing you or faking my death, this plan is a failure." He opened his mouth, as if he was about to propose something, and I cut him off. "I am not faking my own death."

"I was going to ask why I would have to be killed in this scenario."

I ignored that, because I thought the answer was apparent. "I really don't know where to go from here," I told him. "Everything about us is just one layer of lies after another. We're a lasagna of lies. This is a terrible basis for a relationship."

"No, you're it for me," he told me. "It's always been you."

"I don't want to be loved just because I smell right."

"Well, you do smell fantastic. And I do love you," he

promised me. "Not because you smell right. I love you because you're funny and smart, and you don't know the meaning of the word 'quit.' 'Common sense' and 'self-preservation' are also terms I would like you to look up. I love you because you're stubborn and insanely smart and willing to get into fistfights with strippers to help someone out. I love you because you're so much stronger than you think you are. I love that you can only eat waffles if there is an equal amount of butter and syrup in each square. I love the way you can only sleep if you have a toe sticking out from under the blanket. I hate that you feel like you can't trust me, but I understand that I'm the one who made you feel that way."

"Well, that's awfully generous of you," I grumbled.

"Don't you have anything you would like to say to me?"

"Not that you would want to hear," I retorted. I hated the hurt expression that crossed his face, but I wasn't willing to try to make Caleb feel better or tell him that I loved him. Wanting to hurt him in some way felt like a reasonable thing.

Caleb reached up to touch my shoulder. I moved away, which seemed to deflate him. He slumped against the side of the bed. "So what now?"

"I need time to think," I told him. "I have a whole other life set up for me. I'm not sure where. That's why I had to come to Anchorage, to get the papers and money I needed to get started."

If it was possible, Caleb went even paler. "Tina, no."

"I'm not saying that I'm definitely going to take it. I just need some time to think about everything."

"Everything?"

"Your lies. My lies. Glenn. The werewolf factor. Everything. I can only deal with so much."

"OK." He nodded slowly and got to his feet. I stood, wanting to keep us on the same level. He turned to the closet and threw on a shirt. I watched as he moved around the room, collecting his laptop, toiletries, and clothes. It only took him a few minutes.

A strange sense of desperation came over me as he slid into his coat. *Don't let him go, you idiot!* a little voice in my head commanded. *Stop him. Go with him. Something! Don't just stand there!* Instead, I stood stone-faced by the bed.

"I'm going back to the valley," he said. "You stay here in this hotel under your assumed name for the next week. *When* no one shows up looking for you in that time, you'll know that I'm on your side. *When* no one shows up, I will find a way to get you back to the valley. Hell, Suds will probably come pick you up. I'd rather it be me, but I figure that would interfere with your 'space' thing."

I nodded slowly. It was a fair plan. It gave me an out. But that didn't mean I was happy to see him leave. He went to the safe to retrieve the cash. He counted out a large stack of twenty-dollar bills and put them on the dresser.

"You don't have to do that," I protested.

"You're going to need cash," he reminded me.

"You don't have to do that because I already took eight hundred from the stash."

His eyebrows winged up, and despite the exceedingly crappy situation, I could see the barest hint of a smile quirk the corners of his mouth. "Well, keep that, too. You'll need it." He cleared his throat. "If you decide . . . not to join me, will you stay in Alaska?"

"I don't think I should tell you that."

"Well, if you run again—"

"Don't call it running," I snapped.

Caleb shifted from one foot to the other. "Either way, I'm going to send Schuna a report stating that I've come to a dead end with your case. No more leads. No more information to follow. It's not the first time things haven't panned out on a case. It won't make him suspicious."

I nodded. "I appreciate that."

He moved closer and bent his head to kiss me. I stepped away, shaking my head.

"I can't," I told him, even when my eyes burned and I couldn't seem to draw a full breath. I stared down at the carpet, unable to look at him.

Without another word, he walked out the door.

For hours, I sat on the bed, staring at the door, sure that Caleb was going to walk right back through it. And I wasn't sure whether that would be a good thing or not. I flip-flopped on whether to grab my bags and run for the Canadian border. Finally, I pulled all of my belongings together, went downstairs, and rented a new, more reasonably priced room under "Anna Moder" and created a little rabbit den there. I spent the first day curled in the fetal position under the covers, trying to alleviate the ache in my chest. There was a diner next door to the hotel, and I abused its delivery policy terribly, eating huge amounts of room service. I watched movies on HBO until I could no longer stand the sight of Zac Efron. (It didn't take long.) And I took daily pregnancy tests, all of which were negative.

I didn't stray far from home base. When I decided it was time for professional follicle intervention, I went to the salon on the ground floor of the hotel, where the poor stylists clucked over the damage I'd done over the years with repeated dye jobs. I got a deep-conditioning treatment and new, sassy layers while my toes were painted a frosty cotton-candy pink. I went to the hotel boutique and shopped for clothes that (1) weren't secondhand and (2) weren't ordered over the Internet, which was a novelty. I wore makeup—real cosmetics, not just flavored ChapStick—for the first time in years.

I will admit, I indulged. I dropped my guard and made silly, selfish decisions. I knew I needed to move beyond my physical needs and constant fretting over the immediate future. I had to look at the big picture. I was stalling like hell from picking up Red-burn's packet. It was the polar opposite of self-preservation, but I needed this time to process thoughts such as *Caleb, you jackassed, half-wit jerk-face, I would dearly love to tap-dance on your testicles.* I needed some control over my life. I needed to find my footing and make choices based on preference instead of panic. For so long, I'd based my clothes, my meals, my appearance, on what was available to me. It took some field testing before

I remembered how I preferred my jeans cut or which kind of lip gloss I liked best. (Skinny jeans and a violet-pink shade ironically called "Lupine.")

At least I looked good while I stalled.

Every morning, I would wake up, pack my bags, and practically sprint to the lobby.

I would hitch my bag over my shoulder, prepared to make a blind run to the post office to pick up Redburn's package. I could feel the cold fingers of outside air tracing the lines of my cheeks. And instead of walking out into the cold, somehow, my feet changed direction, and I was standing at the bank of elevators, ready to go back upstairs. And every morning, the staff would look at me with increasingly alarmed expressions.

I was angry with Caleb. There was no question about it. But I'd lied to him, pretending to know he wasn't lying to me, while he lied to me, pretending he didn't know I was lying to him. Neither of us was the picture of healthy communication.

In my minibar-buffeted den, I mulled my options over and over. Run back to the valley, or start another new life, or go back to Tennessee and straighten out the mess I'd made of my old one. The last was more of a not-even-the-least-bit-likely palate cleanser.

A tiny, twisted part of my brain kept telling me I was damaged, messed up in the head. I couldn't even cross a parking lot without having a panic attack. Werewolves needed fierce mates who could stand up to the strange, violent pressures of their world. I would fold under the first test. I knew that pack mating rules seemed unquestionable. But maybe whatever magic governed them would make an exception, since Caleb hadn't gotten me pregnant. Maybe he could go on to have babies with some nice girl from another pack, a girl who didn't have night terrors and trust issues. And yet the very idea made my blood boil.

I didn't want him marrying some other woman. I didn't want her touching him, helping him with cases. Caleb was mine.

Now I just had to figure out how to go about talking to him again without Tasering him.

On the sixth day of my self-imposed Howard Hughes retreat, Red-burn resolved my quandary with a phone call.

"Well?"

"Well, what?"

"What do you think about your new ID? My connection worked really hard to make sure your picture came out nice. And I picked your name myself. I always thought you sounded like a Bethel."

"What are you talking about?"

"Your new ID. Haven't you picked it up yet? Honey, I sent it a week ago, three-day guaranteed delivery. I thought you hadn't called because you were on the move. Or because you were pissed because your new first name is Bethel. But that doesn't matter, because right now, there's an animal clinic in Ottawa waiting for you to take over a vet-tech position."

Sadly, given the amount of time I'd spent working

with both wolf and human anatomy, I was probably qualified for this position. "I haven't had a chance to pick it up."

"What's going on with you?" she asked. "You hassled me for weeks for that ID, and all of a sudden, you don't have time to pick it up? You sound all weird and distracted . . . wait, is there a man in this picture?"

"Sort of."

Red-burn snorted. "Honey, either he is or he isn't."

"He is." I sighed. "I have the chance to build a good life with someone. A life I could live as myself."

"That's fantastic. What's stopping you?"

"This insane roller coaster of a life I live?" I suggested.

"Not good enough."

"For the first couple of months we knew each other, I lied to him about who I was."

"You're in the domestic version of witness protection. You get a pass. Not good enough."

"He lied to me about who he was. And he was a bounty hunter hired by my ex to find me."

There was a heavy pause on the other end of the line. "OK . . . that would be an obstacle."

"Why do I hear glasses clinking?" I asked.

"I'm making myself a drink. You do the same, and we'll talk this out."

I cracked open a tiny bottle of vodka from the minibar and tossed the contents down my throat in one shot.

I hissed loudly, making her snicker on the other end

of the line. "You didn't mix that with anything, did you?"

"No," I whispered hoarsely.

The whole sordid tale poured forth from my mouth in one long run-on sentence. How I met Caleb in the parking lot and helped him through a gunshot wound. (I left out the spontaneous healing.) How we'd bounced around the state fighting crime, sort of. How I'd slowly, almost against my will, fallen in love with him. And finally, how having above-average Internet-surfing skills led to Schuna's e-mail and the Tasering of a lifetime. I don't think I used so much as a comma.

"Well . . . damn," she marveled, stretching the word into two syllables.

"Tell me about it."

"OK, bottom line. If you were never to see this guy again, I mean, no calls. No Facebook stalking—"

"I am the last person on earth without a Facebook page."

She continued as if she hadn't heard me. "No lying in bed half-drunk on merlot, listening to Adele and smelling one of the T-shirts you stole from him. You would never see the barest hint of his existence on this earth. How would you feel?"

I felt like throwing up. Despite the whole brain-melting-anger issue, the thought of never seeing Caleb again was terrifying.

"Having trouble breathing?"

"Yeah," I wheezed.

"Honey, my husband annoys and amazes me on

a daily basis. He may piss me off, but the thought of never seeing him again chokes me up like you wouldn't believe. In the words of the immortal Cher, I love him awful."

"I wish I didn't know what you were talking about," I groaned. "Both the emotional level and the Cher reference. Who quotes *Moonstruck*?"

"Appreciate the classics, whippersnapper."

"Yeah, yeah." I sighed.

"So do you know what you're going to do?"

"No."

"Good," she exclaimed. "Decisions made in haste usually suck. Take your sweet-ass time making your choice, so you know you've made the right one."

14

The Colorful and Creative Threats of the Alpha Female

I took my sweet-ass time to make a decision.

I picked up the phone to call Caleb and then hung up. I highlighted the best route to the valley and then traced another route to the vet clinic. And then I crumpled the map into a ball and tossed it. I couldn't seem to force myself to take those first steps toward my new life. I was so angry with Caleb. Yes, I'd lied to him, but not to hurt him or trick him. I'd lied to protect myself. He'd known who I was all along. He knew that Glenn was looking for me. And he didn't tell me that he was being paid to find me. I couldn't trust anything he told me. I couldn't believe him when he talked about loving me, wanting me for the rest of my life. I'd heard those words before, and they'd turned into shackles, keeping me tied to a man who wanted to make all of my decisions for me. I wouldn't go through it again.

Could I believe Caleb when he said he'd meant no

harm? As progressive as the valley pack could be, female alpha and all, Caleb had grown up in a world where the protective, dominant male instinct was not only accepted but expected. Male wolves were expected to take care of their families by any macho, boneheaded means necessary. Whether that meant throwing themselves face-first into danger or leaving out a crap load of key details, male werewolves wouldn't hesitate as long as they thought their actions would keep their mate safe. While female weres could throw down with the best of them, they tended to be a bit more crafty and manipulative. They were more likely to use sex appeal or casseroles to get what they wanted, or sometimes both simultaneously.

More to the point, Caleb had seemed so sincere when he'd given me his reasons for lying. He'd left me at the hotel with the resources to run. If he was only interested in selling me out for money, he could have hog-tied me like Jerry and handed me over to Schuna as soon as I figured out his connection to Glenn.

I had to admit, the life he was offering me wasn't without its charms. I would be able to return to the valley, the place I'd felt at home in for so long. After a lot of explaining and groveling, I would be accepted back into the pack, the people who had become like family to me.

And yes, I would spend my life with a certain brown-eyed werewolf who made me feel safe and wanted and made my eyelids flutter like window shades. Somewhere in the darkest, deepest recesses of an extremely stubborn and pissed-off soul, I knew I missed Caleb.

There were times I missed him so much that I had to curl under the covers and wrap myself around the aching, hollow feeling that spread from my chest.

I tried to write it off as mating magic or readjusting to living alone after getting used to a warm, solid body next to me in bed every night, but I missed the man for himself. I missed his wry humor and the way he made me laugh. I missed the dozens of thoughtful little things he did throughout the day to try to take care of me, even if it meant annoying me. I missed feeling warm and protected and cared for when I fell asleep tucked under his arm. I even missed his lousy *my woman done me wrong, stole my truck, and gave my dog fleas* country music.

Sometime during my fifth attempt to escape the lobby, I'd come to the conclusion that I was, in fact, in love with the moron . . . which was inconvenient.

I loved Caleb. I loved his kindness and his generosity, which was becoming harder and harder to reconcile with the informational shell game he'd played with me. How could he lie to me for so long? Why hadn't he just come out that first day after the shooting and told me, *Just so you know, I've been hired by your skeevy ex-husband to track you down and drag you back to him, but I think you're my mate, so I'm just going to keep taking his per diem and keep you for myself. More French toast?*

OK, maybe that would have been pushing it. But surely, as we got to know each other, he could have let some hints slip gradually.

And then, of course, I probably would have Tasered him and run like hell.

That was beside the point.

Tasers aside, how had he expected me to respond? Was I just supposed to accept this dishonesty from someone who was supposed to love me? Was I supposed to pat him on the head and tell him I understood?

I bought a cheap, reliable truck with new snow tires at a cash-only used-car lot. Traveling with Caleb had given me a confidence I'd lacked on my first trip to the valley. I could take care of myself. I *had* taken care of myself. And I was careful to keep my baton in Caleb's special coat pocket, its heavy weight giving me a bit of swagger when I stopped to gas up the truck or grab a bite to eat.

It took four days of driving in pretty questionable weather for me to reach Grundy. I beat a respectable snowstorm by a matter of hours and had to stay at the Evergreen Motel overnight to wait for the weather to pass. I prayed in earnest that it was the last motel I had to avail myself of for quite some time.

The road to the valley had been temporarily blocked by a rockslide on the highway pass. I had to promise Leonard Tremblay discreet, no-questions-asked treatment of certain social maladies in return for a snowmobile ride there. Cooper offered to take me, but Mo was suffering from some insanely intense morning sickness, and I couldn't, in good conscience, ask him to leave his mate's side. Nor did I have the heart to tell him that in all of the werewolf pregnancies I'd seen, that level of nausea indicated more than one baby. Possibly three.

After examining Mo and prescribing some ginger tea

and extra-strength iron supplements, I hopped onto the back of Leonard's souped-up, blue-and-purple-flame-emblazoned snowmobile and promised fealty to whatever deity I could think of if I didn't slide off the back. The valley was a winding two-hour ride away. I spent most of it clinging to Leonard like a koala and desperately pinning my scarf against my face to block the freezing wind. Even with temperatures hovering just above zero degrees, this weather was mild compared with what we could expect in the coming months.

Still, it was a great ride. With the snow nipping at our faces and the scenery flying by, I couldn't help but grin like a little kid.

We approached the upper ridge of the valley, where we found Maggie's mate, Nick Thatcher, sitting in a little burrow he'd dug out at the base of a large pine and scribbling into a notebook. Blond, bespectacled Nick could see the entire village from his vantage point, including Maggie's office at the community center. An avid climber, Nick, I knew, would have preferred to do his scribbling from a tree limb overhead, but Maggie had made her stance on snow-covered-tree climbing pretty clear when he had fallen out of that very tree the previous winter and broken his collarbone. As I'd set the delicate winglike bone, Maggie had bounced between fussing and fretting over his pain and threatening to break several of his other appendages "to match."

Nick's cap-covered head snapped up at the sound of the snowmobile's engine. Residents of the valley were protective of its borders, and the nonwolf residents knew to alert the pack about any unexpected visitors. But when he recognized Leonard's blue-and-purple flame motif, his even white teeth showed through the golden-blond stubble on his face.

"Len!" he called as Leonard killed the engine. "What's the news in Grundy? Have you seen Mo lately? How's she feeling?"

"Got a special delivery for you, Doc," Leonard shot back.

I snorted. Nick's PhD was a bit of a stumper for the locals, as they thought they were getting a new MD when he showed up at the Blue Glacier two years before. Even now, I'm not sure our neighbors fully understood the difference between Nick's various anthropology and folk-studies degrees and my time in medical school.

Nick whooped when I pulled the scarf from my head. "Hey, Anna!" He jumped up from his burrow to throw his arms around me. Halfway through his enthusiastic hug, he seemed to remember that I hadn't welcomed this sort of casual snuggling during my time in the valley. Before he could retreat, I gave him a little squeeze, making those baby-blue eyes of his crinkle with pleasure.

"I'm so glad you're back. When you took off like that, you scared a lot of people. Are you OK? Was there some sort of emergency? Maggie's been beside herself."

I snorted. "Oh, I'm sure she has."

Nick's lips quirked. "No, really, Anna, she's—well, I don't want to interfere in pack business. But you need to stop by her office and talk to her."

"I will, just as soon as I—" I stopped myself, suddenly reluctant to talk about Caleb, just in case he hadn't returned to the valley after all. "Settle in."

I saw a faint wince flicker across Nick's features. "Yeah . . . you need to go see Maggie."

"That was cryptic and unhelpful. Thank you, Dr. Thatcher," I told him. "Are you coming with me into town?"

Nick shook his head vehemently. "I'll stay here, where it's safe."

"Thanks a lot," I told him, making him laugh.

Leonard and I slid into town with a flourish in front of the clinic. I never thought I'd be so happy to see a collection of weather-beaten buildings in the middle of nowhere. But I was practically giddy as Leonard untied my bags from the back of the snowmobile. I handed him his cabbie fee (a prescription to treat several different rashes) and called out my thanks before I jogged down the main drag through the village. Leonard waved me off and started the journey back to Grundy, where he could proudly boast to the local ladies that he was disease-free (for now).

I searched for any sign of Caleb on the street, but I couldn't even spot his truck. Mixed in among the more weather-beaten houses were newer homes, constructed over the summer after a smaller pack merged into Maggie's group. There were too many families and not enough housing. Now that the neat little one-story homes were finished, the pack had invested some money in renovating the older buildings, including the community center and the clinic.

Nick had funded the expansion out of his own pocket. Maggie and most of the pack had objected, but he ignored them. You would never have guessed it from his "nerd armor," but Nick was loaded from his involvement in developing Guild of Dominion, an online role-playing game to which he contributed character designs and story lines from his extensive mythological studies. He was pretty unpretentious about the money. In fact, I was pretty sure he had T-shirts that were older than some of my patients. But when he could put his extensive funds toward something good, it made him happy, which was the mark of a good man first, rich man second, in my book.

As the alpha-slash-mayor-slash-sheriff of the village, Maggie kept an office in the large all-purpose building that served as the community center. I made my way down the street, running over the speech I'd prepared in my head. Maggie had always been a bit of a puzzle for me. She was among the younger wolves of the pack, but others followed her without question. She was a good person but about as cuddly as sandpaper, preferring hunting and fighting for the pack to the more maternal roles embraced by the other females. She didn't have time or patience for bullshit, which I respected. Ultimately, she was going to be wicked pissed at me for leaving without notice, but she would know it would be easier to take me back than to try to initiate a new doctor into the ways of the pack.

So I had a little bit of clout on my side . . . but that didn't make me feel any better when I walked through the front door and found Maggie frowning over the village checkbook.

She looked up, and rather than looking surprised or angry, her face went completely wooden. I swallowed a little lead weight in my throat. A calm Maggie was a truly scary Maggie.

"I heard you might be showing up," she said, the corners of her mouth tugging southward.

I offered a nervous little smile. "I heard something about a medical position being available at your village clinic."

"Normally, I would tell you to go screw yourself," she said sternly, glaring at me over the top of her checkbook. "But I happen to need a doctor, and you're less irritating than most of the medical people I know." Before I could respond, Maggie stood and pulled her flannel shirt away from her compact frame to reveal a small but definite swelling of her abdomen.

"You're pregnant," I said, my mouth hanging open a little.

"Well, I'm happy to see your fancy degree isn't wasted," she deadpanned.

I held her jacket open to get a better look, gratified when she didn't swat my hands away. "How many weeks?"

She smirked at me. "Isn't it your job to figure that out?"

"Come to the clinic in an hour, and we'll do an exam. I need to go home, get cleaned up."

"That might be a problem. Tom and his family are living in your house now."

My mouth fell completely open this time. "You gave away my house?"

Maggie threw up her hands. "We're still in a bit of a housing crunch. The only reason we kept Caleb's dad's house open was that we knew Caleb was coming back this winter. We couldn't just wait around for you to decide you were coming back. Tom's family needed the space."

"Great, so I'll be sleeping in the clinic, then."

"I don't think that will be necessary. You can stay with Caleb," she said in her no-nonsense voice. "Once you bat those baby blues at him and he forgives you way too easily." Well, I'd never expected Maggie to take my side in the argument.

I bit my lip. "I owe you an explanation."

"You're damn right you do." Maggie frowned. "Anna—"

"It's Tina," I reminded her, my tone apologetic and glum.

She blanched a little. "Well, that will take some getting used to. Tina, we've always known you'd had some trouble in your life before the valley. People with expensive educations don't take on the Dr. Moder job, isolating themselves out in the middle of nowhere with a bunch of half-crazy, mostly naked people, unless they have a reason to hide. We hoped you'd open up a little, but you did your job well, so we didn't pry.

"But to be honest, I'm not in a good frame of mind to hear your explanations right now. I'm in a bit of a panic about this whole baby thing. I just found out a couple of weeks ago, and everybody keeps telling me, 'Don't worry, it's no big deal, women in our family all have easy pregnancies.' But we've never had a pregnant alpha before, mostly because they were dudes. I'm terrified of shifting, for some reason, even though I know my own mother did it until a month before she had me. I can't so much as look at coffee without barfing like something out of that Monty Python 'wafer-thin mint' sketch. And I'm afraid of lifting anything. Nick actually found me crying in the garage this morning, because I needed to put a gas can in the back of my truck, but I didn't want to lift it, and I didn't want to ask him for help for something so simple. So my husband now thinks I'm insane, which is awesome. So really, I just need you to forget about whatever excuse you were going to give me for disappearing from the face of the earth without a word, and give me an exam to show me that everything is normal and healthy and I am not giving birth to some sort of Cthulhu baby."

I stared at my badass werewolf alpha-lady boss as she burst into tears. "Wow."

"I hate this!" She sniffled. "I mean, I'm really excited about the baby. But I hate feeling like I don't have control over anything, including my hormones. I mean, I watched all of my cousins cry and power-eat ice cream through their pregnancies and thought, not me. Not Maggie-Effing-Graham. I'll be the Chuck Norris of pregnant ladies. And look at me! I don't cry! I hate feeling so girlie and stupid about everything. And I really, really want some peanut butter fudge ripple, but I don't want to ask Nick to go get it for me, because I don't want to hear any of my cousins say 'I told you so.'"

I circled the desk and wrapped my arms around my patient as she sobbed into my jacket. I patted her hair and rubbed her back and assured her that what she was going through was completely normal. I laughed a little as she sniffled into my shoulder, and that earned me a light punch to the kidney.

"Don't laugh at me," she grumbled, squeezing me. "I'm still mad at you."

"I know." I sighed. "But I think this will help me get back in your good graces."

Leaving Maggie to mop up her red, runny nose, I took out her official mayoral stationery and wrote out a "prescription" for her. She read over the paper I handed her. She rolled her eyes. "Five hundred ccs of peanut butter fudge ripple ice cream, to be delivered orally and in secret."

"You tell Nick that if he tells anybody about his ice cream run, I will find a way to erase all of his interview recordings," I told her.

"I like you." She knew exactly what sort of terror the threat to Nick's recordings would inspire in her folklorist husband. "You're kind of high-maintenance and sneaky, but I like you."

"Come to the clinic, and we'll get you checked out. And I'll give you some prenatal vitamins that might help with your coffee issues."

"I might forgive you."

"I missed you, too, Mags."

"Don't push it."

• • •

Stepping out into the snowy street, I noticed a dozen or so pack members oh-so-casually milling around the sidewalk in front of the community center. I stopped in my tracks, waiting for pitchforks or torches to come out. But the expressions on the various aunts' and uncles' faces were more curious than angry. My face flushed warm. How was I going to explain my absence? What had Caleb already told them?

With more mercy than I expected from her, Maggie called out, "Nothing to see here, people. Move along."

The response was instantaneous. All of the loiterers turned their backs and walked off, as if they suddenly remembered urgent business at least twenty yards away.

Clearly, the way to reconcile with Maggie was ice-cream bribery. I looked over my shoulder, toward the pregnant alpha, who was waving me away with one hand while dialing her cell phone with the other.

Caleb lived in a house on the edge of the village, a low-slung, tidy structure with blue siding and white shutters that had belonged to his father before him. I'd never given it much consideration before, but now it seemed that I might be living here. Would there be room for me? Would Caleb and I be happy here?

I dropped my bag in the snow and stared at the front door. The windows were dark. What if the door was locked? What if Caleb had changed his mind and decided he didn't want me there? The "rabbit" in me wanted to yell for Leonard to come back and get me.

This elusive instinct only ramped up as I heard the

muffled thumping of wolf paws hitting packed snow. I turned to see several large wolves cantering into the town limits, nudging and nipping at one another playfully. This was the afternoon patrol, running the boundaries of the valley to check for intruders or hunters straying too far from the nearby nature preserve. I searched the thundering herd for any sign of a large gray male, but before I could spot him, a blur of dark fur and gold light came flying at me. A very naked Caleb landed on his feet just in front of me, scooping me up and crushing me against him. The other wolves made a *huff-whicker* sound, which translated to "Whipped!" among Caleb's werewolf brethren.

I threw my legs around his waist, nearly bowling him over as I covered his face in kisses. Caleb's warm mouth pressed to mine, and he murmured apologies and endearments against my lips.

Several of the loitering uncles whooped and whistled at the spectacle we were making of ourselves. "You owe me five bucks, Donnie!" Uncle Doug yelled. "I told you his truck smelled like the doc!"

I pulled back from Caleb's kisses, so I was sure to be understood. "Just one thing," I told him as I cocked my foot back and kicked him in the shin so hard I may have splintered a metatarsal.

He winced, but he didn't drop me.

"If you ever keep a secret of this magnitude from me again—"

"You'll take away my shins. I understand," he said.

"No, but I will ensure that you are so itchy, nauseated, and pustulated that bruised shins will be the least of your problems. Don't doubt that I have the skills necessary to do it."

"Pustulated?"

"Don't make me get the medical textbooks. The illustrations will make you cry."

He shuddered. "I'll take your word for it. I'm so glad you're here," he breathed into my neck. "I was so scared you wouldn't come back."

"I'm sorry," I said. "I'm sorry I didn't trust you."

He shrugged, jostling me a little as my feet barely scraped against the snow. "I can't blame you. I can't imagine how it must have felt to see that stupid e-mail. I'm sorry I wasn't up-front with you."

"I'm sorry I didn't call you, but I was afraid you wouldn't answer."

"I'm sorry I left you. I should have stayed and worked things out."

"I'm sorry I called you all those horrible names."

"You didn't call me that many names."

"In my head, I did," I admitted. "A lot. Really bad ones."

"So we've established that you're both sorry," Maggie said, shaking her head as she crossed the street with Samson, her unofficial second-in-command.

"What is it about human women that turns the men of this family into complete idiots?" Samson asked. "Idiots who will phase in broad daylight in the middle of the street, where any human visitor could spot them, just so they can hug their mate?"

Caleb gave Maggie a sheepish look. Or at least, as sheepish as a werewolf can pull off.

"So, back for good?" Maggie asked Caleb, although I wasn't sure which of us she meant.

"We both are," Caleb agreed, then turned his attention to me. "Though there are going to be a few things you're going to need to do for us to make this work."

"Like dirty, sexy things?" I offered hopefully.

"Like filing a restraining order and reopening your divorce case."

"That is neither dirty nor sexy."

"I plan on marrying you, Dr. Campbell. And I don't plan on getting arrested for bigamy. Besides, you can't let him chase you for the rest of your days. You have to make a stand sometime."

"He'll take one look at the information on the paperwork, and he'll be able to find me," I said.

"There are steps that we can take, legal and not so legal, to prevent him from finding you. And even if he does, I'll be right here with you. Not to mention a pack of giant werewolves who are pretty darn fond of you." When I frowned, he added, "He won't be able to hurt you, Rabbit. I promise you. You're not alone anymore."

I looked up into his big brown eyes. And I knew that he meant it. I cast a glance over his shoulder to Maggie, who nodded. "OK. I'll do it. I'll file the papers."

"Thank God. Now, would you two please calm your dramatic asses down and go inside? People are starting to stare."

"Maggie likes me," I told him. "I've really grown on her."

"Have not!" Maggie called over her shoulder as she and Samson headed back to the community center.

The other wolves nudged us as they passed, pausing to press their cold, wet noses to my hand in greeting. They trotted off to their homes, careful to phase only after someone let them inside.

Caleb grinned at me. "Let's get you into the house. You have bags to unpack."

He hitched me over his shoulder, and I nearly came face-to-cheek with his bare butt. I yelped, bracing myself against his back to avoid impact. He picked up my bags with his other hand and carried me up the steps. I had only one question left to ask. "How are you not cold right now?"

Our routine changed.

I'd wondered before what life would be like if we stayed in one place. It turned out that life was bizarrely, shockingly normal. We ate together in our kitchen, without waitstaff—or, tragically, people to cook or do the dishes. (Learning to split chores was an interesting, relationship-defining experience. I loved the man, but I drew the line at exclusive bathroom-cleaning duties.) We made up for lack of car time together by logging lots of hours on his couch watching movies. Caleb was a shameless fan of the professional-wrestler-turned-action-star oeuvre, while I stuck with John Hughes. We slept, wound together in a comfortable bed. We learned how to make love leisurely, without worrying about someone in the next room hearing us.

Now that Caleb had decided to stick closer to the valley, I went online for information about opening a licensed, legitimate private-investigation service. When spring came, he would have to travel a little bit, but a good portion of his caseload could be handled over the Internet. Maggie was more than willing to offer Caleb the sheriff's position.

For the moment, Caleb was officially off-duty, so he devoted his energies to getting his dad's house back in order and ready for winter. Normally, this was something he should have started months ago, but the others in the pack were willing to help check the stability of the roof, reseal the windows, and stack cords of wood.

I went back to work at the clinic. The old men and mothers in the village forgave me instantly, flooding my office with arthritis complaints and kids in need of checkups. The pack aunties were slower to warm. I didn't get the cold shoulder, by any means, but the candor and connection I'd once shared with the older ladies of the village had evaporated. I figured that could be reestablished in time. And while they weren't exactly smothering me with affection, they expressed their fondness for Caleb by filling our kitchen with casseroles, beef roasts, and a plethora of pies. I wasn't totally taken off-guard. I'd received plenty of drop-by casseroles from my neighbors and patients. What did surprise me was the recipes, accompanied by comments such as "Caleb has always favored my fried apples" or "Caleb doesn't like his meat too well done, so you're going to need to cut the roasting time by about forty-five minutes." Apparently, I was expected to feed him.

Once I stopped laughing, I informed Caleb that I could make him an omelet if he wanted it, but beyond that, we were going to have to scrape along together for a while. He promised he would show me how to make his dad's tuna noodle casserole.

Although I treasured those days, I knew they wouldn't be enough. I was greedy. I wanted Christmases and Sunday breakfasts and hearing Caleb cursing as he stepped on our kids' Legos in the middle of the night. Kids—I wanted kids. And if Caleb's genes had their say, I would have more than my share of them. For the first time since those early days as Glenn's blushing bride, I found I didn't mind the idea of children. I could see a whole gaggle of dark-haired, blue-eyed little wolves running out our front door for hockey practice and pack runs. They would be beautiful, strong children, with more people to love them than I could count.

I wanted that so much my eyes watered with it.

Caleb was happiest when he ran with the pack. It was as if the wolfy part of his brain was finally in balance with the rest of him. He was the most contented, the most at peace, that I'd ever seen him.

I, on the other hand, grew more twitchy by the day. Somewhere in the back of my mind, I knew these days wouldn't last. A sense of inevitable doom had hung over my head ever since I'd filed the paperwork for a restraining order, using the e-mails and that he'd hired a private investigator to find me as proof of Glenn's bad intent. I'd also refiled my divorce paperwork with the help of Nate Gogan, the sole attorney in Grundy. My divorce proceedings were complicated by the fact that I'd run away. He had earned his retainer that week.

The papers included my current address. It was only a matter of time before Glenn showed up, and I couldn't imagine that would end well for either of us.

Glenn's lack of reaction after being served with the restraining order didn't exactly make me feel better. I contacted Red-burn to update her on my situation and ask her to keep an ear out for any Glenn-related information on the Network's channels, but there had been nothing.

Glenn was unstable, but he wasn't stupid. He would know better than to show up here the minute he received a restraining order, particularly if that sudden appearance preceded my sudden *disappearance*. That didn't mean he wasn't planning. I knew how his brain worked. He'd probably researched every resource he could find for information about my new address. Hell, he probably had a full geological survey of the valley by now. Somehow, knowing he was out there scheming was almost worse than his storming the front door. I kept a game face for Caleb and the pack, even when I felt as if I was unraveling. But in private, when Caleb was running or playing cards with his cousins, I indulged in a little brooding.

I was sitting on the front porch of Caleb's house, wrapped in blankets, enjoying the sight of thick, new-fallen snow, when Maggie, in wolf form, came trotting onto the porch. She was a sleek black female, small but, somehow, still very intimidating.

Other than the fact that she was carrying one baby instead of the expected werewolf multiples, Maggie was enjoying a perfectly normal werewolf pregnancy. Nick was over the moon and insisted on documenting every moment of the pregnancy, videotaping the consultation and the ultrasound. Maggie resisted confiscating his camera until he mentioned taping the stirrups portion of the exam.

I gave wolf-Maggie a weak smile and rubbed behind her ears. In a flash, an irritated, naked young woman was sitting in front of me, glaring at me.

"If you try to pet me again, I will bite your hand off."

I snatched my hand back. "I'm sorry. It's just a reflex. Caleb likes it when I scratch behind his ears."

"I'm going to bite you anyway now."

"Can I offer you a blanket?" I asked her.

"No. Stop running," Maggie said.

"I'm right here."

Maggie rolled her eyes. "But you're still running. You're waiting on the first sign to take off. It's not fair to my cousin. He loves you. And any idiot can see how much you love him."

As much as I hated to admit it when Maggie was insightful, she'd just nailed me. I wasn't being fair to Caleb. He had committed fully, and I had one foot out the door. I was letting years of baggage keep me from judging the situation for what it was. If I was in trouble, I had Caleb. If Caleb was in trouble, he had me and my baton. I was safe. I was protected. I was loved. I would enjoy these precious days of quiet to their fullest. It was time for the rabbit to put away her running shoes.

Something must have changed in my expression, because Maggie added, "That's as mushy as I get. I will

tell you that we have double patrols around the boundaries of the valley, which we can afford to do now that
we have so many extra paws around. I took those photos Caleb printed for us and posted them at the community center. Your asshole ex is our first-ever wanted
poster, thank you very much. And we let Buzz know
that if anyone shows up in Grundy asking questions
about you, he needs to call us. He's the closest thing
they have to law enforcement over there, and it's time
for him to earn his piddling part-time salary."

"Is that how you put it when you asked him for a
favor? Because statements like that could be part of the
reason people don't like you."

Maggie scoffed. "People love me."

I frowned at her but chose not to respond to that.
"So, clearly, you have the in-person issues covered, but
what happens when Glenn starts monkeying around
with your records online or brings the authorities sniffing around, asking awkward questions about pregnancies
that only last four months and an inordinate number of
injuries related to bear traps?"

"You mean, what do we do when he tries to bring
the pitchfork-wielding mob of humans to our door,
screaming for the monsters' heads?" Maggie asked, her
toned laced with unholy glee. "We just put on our best
human faces, all innocent eyes and guileless smiles that
say, 'Oh, gee, Mr. Health Official, I don't know how
our paperwork got so messed up. We're just sweet, unpretentious country folk who don't understand them
fancy computers.'"

"Your smiles say all that?"

"You'd be surprised how often it works," Maggie assured me. "I mean, really, who's going to believe that my aunt Winnie is a werewolf? People want to believe what they know to be true. They'll grasp on to any rational explanation we give them. And if they don't buy it at first, we just keep pushing, finding new stories to tell, until they do.

"I'm not saying it wouldn't cause complications or problems, but as smart as your husband is, he's not enough of an evil genius to blow our cover. We've faced better operators than him over the years. We have devious, slightly more violent methods to deal with him that are best left to your imagination."

"Probably not."

"We can take care of him. Of course, you would have known this if you'd told me about it."

"Hindsight and all that."

"Now comes the part where I threaten to kick your ass from here to Ontario if you hurt Caleb."

I nodded. "Wouldn't expect anything less."

"Seriously, I'd fix it so they'd use your carcass as bait on that *Deadliest Catch* show."

"So to make me feel safer and calmer, you're threatening me with graphic, grievous bodily harm?"

"Yup."

"Little too far there, Mags."

15

This Is Why You Use the Buddy System

With my real birthday on the horizon—not the birthday listed on the "Anna Moder" paperwork—the werewolf aunties insisted on hosting a big joint celebration of my thirty-fourth year and Caleb's permanent return to the pack. It was the first opportunity for the pack to put on a big spread since the first hard frost. I didn't mind being used, as long as it meant Aunt Winnie brought her hash-brown casserole.

So one not-so-special Friday evening, when the roads were clearer than usual, every aunt, uncle, and cousin jammed into the community center to stuff themselves silly under a jungle of tissue-paper flowers produced by Samson's mate, Alicia. Even Mo and Cooper made the treacherous snowmobile trip with their toddler, Eva, to welcome us back into the fold. They were the last of the relatives I'd "fooled" with my false identity. I liked Mo quite a bit, and I hated the idea of her shunning me as a result of perfectly justified hurt feelings.

I should have known better. Mo adjusted to my news the way she had adjusted to most things pack-related: smoothly and with style. She just grinned and threw her arm around me when she and Cooper had made their way through the throng of noshing werewolves.

"Well, now that I know who you are, I'm a little ashamed of myself. I thought I knew another Southern transplant when I saw one," Mo said, grinning, shifting the sleepy-looking toddler so she could extend her hand as if to reintroduce herself. "Leland, Mississippi."

I shook her outstretched hand, and the handshake turned into a hug. "Jackson, Tennessee."

"I can't tell you how glad I am that you're back. Eva bit the new doctor at the Grundy clinic, and now he's less than enthusiastic about seeing her for her checkups. The big sissy."

"She did break the skin," Cooper pointed out, though there was a note of pride in his voice.

"Well, that was the only way she could express 'I do not appreciate the intrusion of your booster-shot needle' with the emphasis she felt was necessary," Mo said primly.

Cooper rolled his eyes but only slightly. "We're glad you're back, Doc."

"I'm glad to be back," I told him.

"And I'm glad you dragged my idiot cousin home with you," Cooper added. "If anybody can straighten his stubborn ass out, it's you."

"Thanks," I said. "I hope I'm up to the challenge."

"Oh, you know you are," Mo said. "If he's anything like Cooper, he'd hand you the moon and stars if you looked at 'em twice. They're shamelessly devoted to their mates, all of them. Even Maggie."

Maggie overheard this and sent a rude gesture Mo's way, which Mo returned without breaking her verbal stride.

"Maggie told me you've had some trouble. And for Maggie to tell me anything means that she's worried. Let them help you, Tina. Trust in them. They'll stand for you until the very end; it's in their natures."

I nodded.

"And if they don't, I'll just knock the hell out of your ex with a fire extinguisher. It's sort of my thing."

I snickered, pressing my lips together to keep from ruining this bonding moment. Mo was known for her prowess with both kitchen knives and fire-suppression equipment, having knocked Maggie unconscious with a fire extinguisher when her sister-in-law had gotten just a little too close to wounding Cooper in a street brawl.

"We gals are in the same boat when it comes to being mated to these yahoos," she said, wrapping her arm around my shoulders. "We humans have to stick together. Maybe we can form a club or a support group. Nick would be perfect for organizing that sort of thing. Hey, Nick!" She called after her brother-in-law, who was in a corner, holding a digital recorder in Caleb's face. Mo easily handed her daughter off to Cooper, who watched his wife scamper off with a bemused expression.

"Runs at a mile a minute, my mate," he said fondly. "And her brain runs even faster."

"I really missed you all," I told him, letting Eva play with the beading on my sweater while she leaned her head against her daddy's shoulder. I stroked her sleek blue-black hair, still marveling at the full mane this toddler managed to grow. She was only two, and it was almost down to her waist. "I know I was only gone a few months, but I feel like I missed so much. Eva's getting so big!"

"But not too big, right?" Cooper asked, anxious. "She's where she needs to be growth chart–wise?"

"She's perfect," I assured him as my fingers brushed over her forehead. I paused. She was a little warm. I checked her nose, which was predictably runny and flush with thin mucus. Her lymph nodes were slightly swollen, and from the way she draped herself against her daddy, you could tell she wasn't exactly bounding with energy.

"Everything OK?" Caleb asked, anxious again.

"Well, it looks like she could be coming down with a cold. Has she complained about her head or her throat hurting?" I asked.

"No, but she's napped a lot today, more than usual," he admitted, rubbing her back.

"Well, it's in the early stages yet, and at this age, she can't really articulate headaches," I said, glancing over my shoulder. "Hey, Uncle Dan, do you have your Maglite?"

Dan proudly held up the little flashlight he kept in a holster at his hip, an idea he'd latched onto after watching too many episodes of *CSI*. "I told you it would come in handy!" he crowed.

"Yes, your moment of triumph has arrived," I retorted, taking the offered flashlight and gently prying Eva's mouth open. I shone the light into her throat and winced at the sight of red, inflamed tissue. "Oh, yeah, that's some sinus drainage you got there, sweetie."

"What do we do?" Cooper asked, his voice slightly panicked. "Do we need to take her to the hospital? Should we call nine-one-one?"

"This is why Mo handles most of her checkups, isn't it?" I deadpanned.

Cooper grumbled a bit. "Yes."

"It's going to be fine. Right now, it's probably just a little cold, one of many little colds she's going to have over the course of her life. But just to be sure, take her back into Maggie's office, and I'll do an exam. I just have to run over to the clinic to get my medical bag and some of the medications she might need. You keep her in here where it's warm."

"Shouldn't we come to the clinic with you?" Cooper asked. "You have all of the equipment there, those defibrillator paddles and the intubation stuff and . . ." He trailed off as I gave him an amused look. "We'll just go wait for you in the office."

"OK, then," I told him, patting his arm. "Let Caleb know where I went?"

Cooper nodded.

I quietly slid into my coat, hoping not to attract the attention of aunties with second helpings. I stepped out into the bitter cold, refreshed by the untouched air, even as it slapped against my cheeks. It was a bit of a relief to get out of the crowd and the noise. As much as I loved the pack, it would take some time before I was used to their exuberance again.

Shivering, I stomped out onto the street, watching for patches of black ice under the shin-deep blanket of snow. The last thing I needed was to bust my butt on slick pavement and lie there in the dark for hours while the party raged on.

Who was I kidding? Caleb would notice I was gone within a few minutes and organize a full-on search party.

I shivered in my jacket, my steps slowing as I crunched through the snow to listen for . . . what? The sound of the whistling between the buildings along the main street? Fat white snowflakes splatting against the wind-shield of Maggie's truck? I shook my head, trudging for-ward, only to stop a few steps later and peer down the street toward the north ridge of the valley.

There was something off. Some organic, nervous alarm skittered up my spine and had me turning on my heel to go back to the community center. I shouldn't be out here on my own. I needed the pack. I needed—

I'd just passed Maggie's truck when I heard soft, steady footfalls behind me, with none of the natural grace of the Grahams. I shuddered, my breath coming in short white puffs in the frigid air. Shards of icy panic wormed their way through my stomach, making it hard to breathe or think.

Whipping around, I turned back toward the north ridge and saw Glenn standing there in all his angry glory, practically vibrating with rage under his thick Gore-Tex coat. The climate had not been kind to Glenn. His overbright brown eyes watered against the cold, prickling wind. His cheeks were fire-engine red. And instead of making him seem pathetic, the wear and tear just made him seem that much more unstable, unpredictable. Any veneer of civility had been torn away to reveal a level of crazy I'd never seen before.

My heart stuttered in my chest as my brain shouted, *Not real! Not real! Not real!*

"Don't you have anything you want to say to me?" he sneered, chapped lips cracking. "I don't even get a hello?"

I stumbled back, barely staying upright as my heel hit a patch of ice.

"Do you have any idea what you've put me through?" he demanded, stumbling forward, grabbing my arm and shaking me like a rag doll. He seemed reluctant to touch me, as if even after all of this time and all of his efforts to find me, confronting me in person was somehow harder than threatening me through a computer screen. "This is all your fault."

Panicked, runaway thoughts kept me from focusing. There was nowhere to hide, nowhere to run. I wanted to curl in on myself, make myself small. "The humiliation of you filing for divorce. Calling the cops on me. Months of searching, paying some stranger to dig into our business. Years of worrying where you were, what you were doing, who you were with. Do you know how humiliating this has been for me?"

In full fury, he didn't hesitate to use the violence he

used to cover up with "accidents" and clumsiness. He grunted, tossing me back into the snow as if I weighed nothing. I skidded across the ice-slick surface of the road, whacking my head against Maggie's bumper.

"Your fault," Glenn spat. "All your fault. Losing those jobs because I was so busy looking for you. You trashed my reputation. You ruined me."

I slowly pushed myself up, gingerly turning my head back and forth. I could feel a warm trickle of blood down my back, where the base of my skull had caught the edge of the truck bumper.

Glenn shoved me back down with the toe of his boot. "What kind of wife does that to her husband?"

"I'm not your wife anymore," I whispered.

"You're my wife as long as I say you are," he growled, stepping on my chest and pushing me down into the snow. He leered down at me, as if he'd been picturing me like this—broken and bleeding under his foot—for a very long time. He gave me one last kick before crouching over me.

I sat up again, bracing myself on the truck. "You can't hurt me anymore, Glenn. This stops now."

He acted as if he hadn't even heard me speak. "We're going to walk out of this valley, take my snowmobile back to that piss-water little town, Grungy or whatever. We're going to go back home, and you're going to beg the hospital to give us our jobs back. You're going to tell them it was all your fault that they fired me. We're going to go back to our life just the way it was. You're going to go back to being the wife you were. Now, pull your hood up, honey, we don't want you to get sick."

Flinching away when he tried to adjust my coat, I stared up at him incredulously. He had finally lost his mind. He thought we were going to go back to where we were when I left? It was insane. Any friends we'd had together had no doubt stopped believing we were a couple years ago. And there was nothing I could say that would get his job back. I doubted I could get *my* job back at the hospital, given my abrupt exit. I shook my head, and the motion upset my equilibrium. "No," I whispered.

He punched me right on the bridge of my nose, where the cartilage connects to the brow. I sank to my knees, seeing stars. "What did you say?" he demanded, standing over me.

"No," I said again, my voice a little louder but shakier. "No! No! NO! NO! NO!" I screamed so loudly that it echoed down the street and off the trees. Glenn viciously kicked me in the ribs, cutting off the werewolf-summoning noise into a squelched cry.

"I see we're going to need a little refresher, honey. I'm your husband. I'm in charge." He delivered another kick to my rib cage. I flopped onto my side, my face buried in snow. The tiny shards of ice burned the scrapes on my skin. I rolled faceup, my coat tangled under my body, and I felt a metal cylinder bump against my leg.

The baton. I'd forgotten that Caleb had sewn a special pocket in the recesses of my coat to store the baton as a just-in-case measure. I thought it had been overkill when Caleb insisted I keep it in my pocket even after we returned to the valley. Who was going to try to hurt me on the twenty-yard walk from the clinic to our house? But now I thought it was just-enough-kill.

As Glenn grumbled to himself about my "fat un-grateful ass," I slid the hand of my uninjured arm into my pocket. My fingers curled around the baton just as Glenn's foot connected with my ribs. The impact knocked me back, spinning me over and over, while the breath fled from my lungs. The baton was still clutched in my hand as I landed in the snow, a heavy weight in numbed fingers.

"When I say stop, you stop." He grunted, kicking me in the stomach this time.

This was never going to stop.

Unable to scream for help, I lay there, cataloguing my injuries—dislocated shoulder, broken nose, frac-tured ribs—and I knew he would just keep coming after me until I was dead. Part of me wanted to give in, to let him just take me. It seemed so much easier than this constant struggle, the nagging fear. I was so cold and tired; down to my soul, I was exhausted. If I got into the car with him now, at least it would be over. He wouldn't have the chance to hurt anybody else.

"When I say get off of your lazy, spoiled ass and get moving, you say, 'Yes, Glenn,' and go where I tell you." Glenn put the weight of his boot on my damaged shoulder. I made a hoarse mewling sound, one that I swore I heard echoed in a canine yelp in the distance. I rolled onto my injured side, trying to protect it. And he laughed. He was enjoying himself, the big man, the little brat who never got enough of my attention. Well, he certainly had my full attention now. My pain and fear were *fun* for him. And if someone was that good at hiding that he was *that* sick, it was not my fault that he'd fooled me. *He* did this, not me. *He* was the one who manipulated and controlled and caused pain, not me. *He* was the asshole, not me.

I was not the problem.

I slung the weight of the baton outward with my good arm, thrilling at the metallic singing sound. Sitting up and fighting against the sick, dizzy sensation that came with it, I brought the baton down with all my strength just above his knee. A deeply satisfying crunch echoed about the street, and Glenn howled. I kicked up, catching him square in the crotch with the heel of my boot.

"I always was a slow learner," I huffed, struggling to my feet. "So is this what it feels like, Glenn?" I slurred, standing over him as he whined and keened over his knee. I cradled my injured shoulder. "Did it make you feel good to stand like this, over me, while I rolled around on the floor like a dog? Answer me!" I yelled, kicking at him, catching him in the stomach.

He moaned and tried to struggle to his knees, but I brought the baton down on his back, knocking him to the ground.

"What you did to me, that's your problem, your damage. You're going to have to live with it, because I'm sick of carrying it around with me. You're never going to touch me again. This is over," I told him, turning toward the community center.

"But you're my wife." He whimpered. "You're mine."

"Not anymore." I walked away, dragging the baton behind me in the snow. My injured arm felt heavy, disconnected, as I stumbled forward. Wiping at the blood running from my mouth, I winced at the split in my lip. Just a few more steps. Just a few more steps, and I'd be back in the hall. I'd find Caleb. I'd be OK.

I staggered forward as I was suddenly knocked to the ground. Rough hands in my hair yanked me to my feet. "You think you could just do that to me?" he demanded, twisting the hair at the nape of my neck and pulling me back against him. I yelped at the sharp stabs of pain throbbing from several different locations. He wrapped his hand around my throat and squeezed, slowly pressing the breath out of my body. "Did you think I would let you get away with it?"

My feet scrabbled uselessly against the crust of snow. The edges of my vision started to turn gray. I swung my baton at his legs, but Glenn used his free hand to swat it out of my hand before snagging my hair again. I fought against the urge to pass out, like swimming against a tidal wave. If I passed out, he would drag me away and do God knew what with me. If I was awake, I could regain control of the situation. Maybe.

Probably not.

A low, loud growl reverberated through the cold air, piercing my chest. Glenn's grip on my throat slackened, allowing my feet to reach the ground. I gulped huge breaths, even as he tightened his grip on my hair.

My vision cleared, allowing me to make out a dozen huge dark shapes as they separated from the shadows, edging their way into a shaft of moonlight. Right at the front of the pack, a big gray male curled his lip over his canines, letting them shine, sharp and silver in the light. If I were Glenn, I would be pissing my pants right now.

"What is this?" Glenn hissed, jerking at my hair, making me yelp. This drew a particularly vicious growl from the gray wolf.

"Did I mention that my new boyfriend's family . . . well, they're pretty special," I said, laughing softly to myself.

The Caleb wolf inched forward, the hair on his back raised, fangs bared. A small black female, Maggie, was at his side. Her stance was calmer but no less menacing. Besides Glenn and me, no humans were on the street. The pack handled pack business.

"Shut up!" Glenn backed away, dragging me with him. I dug my heels into the snow, doing anything I could to make this more difficult for him. I heard the same familiar low growls behind us. And I slowly realized there was a circle of wolves, tightening around me and my crazy ex-husband. They all had their heads lowered, lips curled back. Stalking. The street echoed with raspy growls. Although sick with the pain of my injuries, in the midst of this confrontation, I was as relaxed as a spa bunny after a two-hour massage. I knew I had nothing to fear. I nearly giggled at the absurdity of it.

"Hey, Glenn." I couldn't resist mocking. "Remember when I said we should get a dog, and you 'forbade' me to get one because you didn't want my attentions divided? Sort of ironic, huh?" I giggled, hysteria taking over fully now.

"I said shut up, or I'll snap your damn neck, Tina."

"Oh, do whatever you want to me," I scoffed, spitting a healthy amount of blood into the snow. "You won't even make it to your car. They've got your scent now, Glenn. They'll run you down and leave nothing but scattered bones. You came into the woods, in the dark, thinking you were the biggest, meanest thing to walk here, because you can terrorize a woman half your size. Let me tell you something. You're an amateur. You're nothing. Forget dragons. Here there be giant, pissed-off wolves. And they are not happy with you."

Glenn shook me so hard I was sure I heard my teeth rattle. "Shut up!"

CLANG.

Glenn released his hold on my neck. I sank to my knees, the impact buffered by the snow. I looked back to see Glenn crumpled, facedown, in the street. Mo stood behind him with a fire extinguisher raised over her head.

Glenn moaned, turning onto his back and glaring up at her. "You bitch."

"Not really an insult around these parts, asshole," Mo told him. "You thought Tina was alone? She's not alone here." When he tried to stumble to his feet, she brought the canister down again, just hard enough to daze him. I heard a pleased whickering sound from a large black wolf near Maggie. "Normally, they wouldn't let a human get involved in messy business like this. But they needed someone to speak for the pack, because, well, their jaws are aching to close around your throat right now, and they're otherwise incapable of speech. But she's ours now. And if you come near her again—"

Mo stopped as Glenn leaped to his feet and lunged for her, stumbling on slick ice and unsteady legs. The wolves' growls rose to a fever pitch as she raised the fire extinguisher over her head.

"No!" I cried, snatching the cylinder from her hands with my good arm and swinging it wide, connecting with the side of Glenn's head. He yelped, stumbling mid-lunge, and flopped facedown in the snow again.

Mo's eyes went wide. I dropped the fire extinguisher with a *clang*, wincing as every muscle in my body seemed to seize at once. My dislocated shoulder sagged, useless, at my side.

Glenn's pained moan was muffled by street slush. Mo nudged him over with her boot, so he was at least looking at her when she told him, "If you ever come near her again, the pack will find you. They will make you feel pain like no other human being has ever felt before, and then they will fix it so that your body is never found. It's not an idle threat. They're giant dogs. They're big on hiding bones."

"Still my . . ." Glenn gurgled through the ice and blood crusting his face. "Wife. Mine."

I moved closer to him, despite the loud protesting rumbles of a certain gray wolf practically brushing against my back. I couldn't kneel or bend, because, frankly, I was doing well not to throw up on him. "I'm not your wife anymore. I don't want to see you. I don't want to think about you. And after today, I won't even say your name again. You're not my problem anymore."

I ignored the pathetic little noises Glenn was making, turned on my heel, and walked back toward the clinic to get a Band-Aid for my head.

(At the time, it seemed completely logical.)

But apparently, I turned a little too quickly, considering the blows to my head and the loss of blood. My eyes rolled up, and the world seemed to tilt on its axis and melt into surreal splotches of color.

The last thing I remembered was thinking how much it was going to hurt to land on my bum shoulder. And then a pair of strong, warm arms closed around me, and I felt nothing at all.

I woke up in my own clinic, the late-morning light filtering through the window and directly into my sticky, tired eyes. I immediately clapped them shut, groaning. I tried to press my good hand to them, but the IV lead pulled painfully, and I stopped. I tried to raise myself slowly on the crisp white cotton sheets, my head too swimmy to manage it. I smacked my dry, sandpapery mouth, wincing.

Just lying there in the clinic's lone hospital bed, I could tell I had a concussion, a few busted ribs, and a reset shoulder. My lip was split, and I had a few lacerations. Considering what had happened, I got through relatively unscathed.

Maggie was sitting at the side of my bed, leafing

through a Carol Higgins Clark paperback. I blinked at her, fighting to keep both eyes focused on her face. "Morphine, huh?"

"I sure hope so. That's what the label said."

"Sorry, right now, I can't think much beyond, 'Morphine, yay!'" I giggled.

"Caleb wouldn't let us reset your shoulder without it."

I nodded, hissing as my fingers found the bruises on my neck. "Thank you."

"Thank my mom. She was the only one who knew how to do it or the IV."

I smiled. Gracie Graham had spent the better part of her life patching up her hooligan children, so she was a natural to assist me in the clinic during the occasional emergency. She would have made an excellent nurse if she could have left the valley long enough for college. The fact that she'd set my shoulder, kept me hydrated, used the monitoring equipment correctly, and not killed me with a morphine overdose was testament to her competence.

"You've been out for more than twenty-four hours. It's weird watching someone take so long to heal. I don't know how you humans stand it. I've told Nick he's not allowed to get seriously hurt, ever."

Maggie held a glass of water to my lips, allowing me to gulp it down. The sensation sliding down my parched throat was absolute bliss. She saw me glancing around the room. "Caleb is practically pawing down the door to get in here, but he kept wolfing out every time you twitched or your pulse spiked. Destroyed three chairs and an IV pole, not to mention all those shirts. So we sent him on a run . . . which lasted about five minutes before he was right back at the door, trying to get back in. So we tricked him into going to your house for some extra socks and locked him out."

I laughed, wincing at the dulled pain radiating through my injured ribs. "Ow."

"He's had his face pressed against the glass like one of those freaky cling-film families people stick on their car windows."

I laughed again, repeating the wincing process. "Stop making me laugh."

"Well, I have to keep myself entertained somehow," she said dryly.

"Where did they take him?" I asked, and because Maggie was occasionally intuitive to the point of freakiness, she knew exactly whom I was talking about.

"To the village jail," she said. "It's actually a holding cell for younger pack members having difficulty adjusting to their transition, which means they can get out of control. Disciplinary actions are always handled within the pack, no legal system required. But we dress it up as a jail because outsiders would ask too many questions otherwise. We'll hand him over to the state police once he's healed up a bit—before you get out of here, anyway. Don't want the cops wondering how the hell he got so beat up."

"Pack worked him over pretty good, huh?"

Maggie shook her head. "No, slugger, *you* worked him over with the baton. I will say that Mom is treating him just as carefully as she did you, but he's not getting any of the tender, loving care. I think she enjoys ripping off his bandages a little too much."

"But he knows about the wolves," I said. "He'll tell everybody."

"Tell them what?" Maggie snorted. "That while he was beating and kidnapping his ex-wife, a pack of wolves surrounded him while another woman smacked him with a fire extinguisher? They'll send him to prison by way of the loony bin, which would suit me just fine. Besides, he didn't see any of us phase. And in my official capacity as what passes for law enforcement in this village, I can inform you that he messed up big-time. Violating the restraining order before the ink was even dry, assault, attempted kidnapping. You'll have to testify, but he's going to face real jail time, Doc."

I expected some twinge of guilt, thinking of the man I'd loved enough to marry sitting in a tiny cell for years. But he'd hurt me in so many ways. He was a criminal. He belonged in jail.

"Now, before Caleb batters down the door, I am about to say something you'll probably never hear from me again."

I arched an eyebrow. "You chose to do this when I'm on serious drugs?"

"I'm sorry," she said.

The other eyebrow went up. "Why are you sorry?"

"We'd been watching your ex for three days. He'd been circling the perimeter, trying to get a look at you. The restraining order was pretty specific about distances, and he was staying outside the limits. I wanted to wait until he did something stupid so we could call the state police and press charges that would stick. We had someone watching you every second of the day. But with the party and all, everybody in one spot, we figured you were covered. By the time we figured out that he got past our boundaries . . . I was really scared for you, Doc." She cleared her throat, her big brown eyes shimmering with tears. "We only just got you back, and I was afraid . . . oh, shit, here I go again." She sobbed softly.

I tried to reach up to pat her shoulder, but one arm was immobile and the other was hooked up to an IV. Nick and Caleb appeared at the door. Nick barely suppressed a smile as he hauled his hormonal mate to her feet. "This happens about once a day," he said.

"It does not." She sniffled.

Behind her back, he nodded and mouthed, "Yes, it does."

Caleb pounced on the chair at my bedside as his cousin was spirited away with promises of steak wrapped in bacon. He pressed his face against my good arm, wallowing there a bit before leaning up to gently kiss my damaged lips. He tilted his forehead against mine and sighed, as if he'd been holding his breath for days. "Please don't ever do that again," he whispered.

Taking some small measure of glee in picturing Glenn in an orange jumpsuit, I kissed the bridge of Caleb's nose and told him, "I can almost guarantee it."

"No more secrets."

"That works both ways, you know," I told him dryly.

"No more secrets," he repeated.

"No more secrets," I promised.

"OK, then I can give you this." He opened a small

black velvet box to show me a respectable solitaire set in platinum, with scrollwork designs on the band. Well, it looked like scrollwork at first. Upon closer examination, it was—

"Are those bunnies?" I asked, squinting at the engraving.

"Just one on one side," he said, holding the other side of the band closer so I could see the stylized wolf loping along the opposite side from the bunny. "I did a little reading. Did you know that rabbits can survive in just about any climate? Desert, tundra, forest. And in most cultures, they're the symbol of renewal, because you can count on them, every spring, to crank out a whole new generation of little rabbits."

"I don't think I like where this is going, Caleb. Land your plane," I told him.

He continued as if I hadn't rudely interrupted his nature rant. "So I called you Rabbit at first because you ran, which wasn't all that nice of me. But you're also adaptable, resourceful, and no matter how hard you're knocked down, you just keep coming back. Renewal, Tina. Starting over."

"I get it," I told him. "Just leave the fertility stuff out of it when you tell your family our proposal story. M'kay?"

He grinned and tried to press his case one step further. "I'm afraid I'm going to have to insist on unlimited shared showers and naked Saturdays."

"Every day of the week is Naked Day with you."

"Just humor me, woman."

"Naked breakfast on Saturdays," I counteroffered.

He groaned. "I might have to go to work or something!"

"I love you," he told me, kissing the undamaged corner of my mouth.

I tugged at his sleeve, slowly scooting over so he could cram his large frame into the narrow hospital bed with me. "I love you, too, which is why I am also willing to offer naked Sunday brunch."

He carefully arranged his body around mine and sighed into my hair. "You're the best mate ever."

"I'm working on it."

16 The Valley Gets Even More Visitors, None of Whom We Knock Unconscious

The practically balmy March wind blew gently over my cheeks as I sat on the porch of our house and sipped my tea.

I didn't know what Gracie put in it, and I chose not to ask. But it was a nice, calming blend that helped me unwind at the end of a long day. I was still training my nerves to wind down to a nonpanic state. When someone called me Tina, it still took me a moment to realize they were talking to me and respond. It would be a long time before I would be able to walk into a room without scouting out the exits. And I would always have a problem sitting with my back to a door. But I was slowly and steadily beginning to accept the fact that my ex couldn't hurt me anymore, that my life was my own again.

I started talk therapy with a specialized counselor who worked out of Portland. Samantha Farraday was willing to do sessions via video chat, and we were focusing on linear discussions of "trauma," since my experience was considered "prolonged" by my going into hiding. I liked Samantha. She didn't accept nonsense, bullshit, or rationalizations, which was something I needed.

Caleb was supportive of the endeavor, especially if it meant I felt more comfortable getting married within the next year or so. The claiming bite could come at any time, as far as I was concerned, but Caleb wanted to make sure I was ready. For my part, I was settled. I wasn't afraid. I knew where and with whom I would be spending my future.

I stood on the front porch, watching the sun go down over the lip of the valley. Caleb was on a patrol with the pack and would be home any minute. I finally had a home to call my own, where I was safe and loved. It would take a while to straighten out the official paperwork that would allow me to make life with Caleb permanent. Thanks to Glenn's cyber-antics, there were a lot of debts and criminal charges in my name that needed to be cleared up. Not to mention the fact that I was still legally married.

But as far as the pack was concerned, Caleb was my mate. I was a permanent part of the pack, and I was their own. We weren't thinking about children, but we knew it would happen eventually. We were going to let ourselves be caught off-guard by a *good* surprise for once.

A black SUV with heavily tinted windows crunched down Main Street, drawing stares from my neighbors.

A few of the males tracked the vehicle's progress as it approached the clinic and seemed to be stopping. I arched my eyebrows.

We didn't get strangers here. We certainly didn't advertise the clinic's services outside the valley, so it was unlikely that this was a drop-in patient. I stuck my hand into my pocket, to assure myself that the special sparkly canister of pepper spray Mo had given me was still there.

A tall, willowy woman with red hair and pale skin opened the passenger-side door. She was strikingly beautiful, a sort of redheaded Grace Kelly, in her dark pea coat and celery-green turtleneck. The man who stepped out of the driver's side didn't quite match her elegance. He was tall and lanky, with shaggy dark blond hair and equally pale, Puckish features. His eyes were bright, full of mirth, but it was a naughty sort of humor, which had me checking my other pocket to keep a hand on my wallet. He was wearing frayed jeans and a sweatshirt that said, "It's a bit nippley out."

The woman watched my eyes widen, then followed my line of sight to the man's shirt and sighed. "Damn it, Dick. I told you not to wear that! It's off-putting!"

"It's hilarious!" the man insisted.

"Please excuse my husband. It's a lot warmer in Kentucky. The cold is doing strange things to his mind," the woman said. "I'm assuming this is the clinic? We were looking for a Dr. Tina Campbell."

My jaw dropped open, but I recovered quickly. "Who's asking for her?"

"An old friend," the woman said, grinning, her

sharp-looking white teeth glinting against the porch light. "I recognize your voice, Doctor. I'm so glad to meet you!"

She reached out and pumped my hand vigorously, making me wince at the strength of her grip. The pained expression on my face brought more than a few growls from the werewolves circling ever closer to the clinic. "I'm sorry, do I know you?"

"I'm Andrea Cheney," she said. "You know me as Red-burn."

Though the revelation of my mysterious visitor's identity was a shock, several other mental tumblers fell into place and my mouth dropped open in a more humorous parody of *The Scream*. Suddenly, Red-burn's occasional daytime crankiness and availability for late-night conversations made so much more sense—as did the fact that neither she nor her husband seemed at all surprised by the presence of enormous wolves.

We didn't get many vampires in these parts—or any, really—something about the cold temperatures and weird seasonal daylight patterns. Grundy werewolves, while not particularly surprised when the vampires emerged from their coffins, reserved full belief in another supernatural species until they met one in person. Even Nick, as mad as he was for all things supernatural, was downright dubious about the existence of vampires for years after the Coming Out. He simply didn't believe a creature could hide under the radar for so long without being documented by nosy human scholars like him. Short of being bitten, he held on to some skepticism. And then he met a bunch of werewolves and his mind opened up that much more.

Andrea and her husband's arrival was going to be the talk of the pack all winter.

I squealed and threw my arms around her, drawing giggles from her and the man behind her. The werewolves relaxed but stayed close. "It's OK!" I called. "It's OK. This is my old friend Andrea . . . and . . . ?" I looked to the man with the naughty smile.

"Dick," he said. "I'm this lucky lady's husband."

Andrea rolled her eyes. "Husband, yes. Lucky? Debatable."

Maggie stepped forward. "Red-burn? You sent Eli the e-mails? You're the one who helped An—Tina get a job here?"

Andrea nodded, clasping my arms in her hands and giving them a friendly squeeze. "When I heard that you'd 'come out' and filed for divorce, I had to come by and see you for myself."

"I'm so happy to meet you!" I said, sniffing a little. "I owe you so much!"

"No more than I owed the person who helped me find *my* way out of a bad relationship," Andrea said. She turned to Maggie and explained, "Before Dick, I dated a man who, let's say, wasn't so nice to me. It took a clean break and a rushed move to another state to get clear of him. And now I have a lot of spare time at night, and the Network helps me feel like I'm doing something constructive. Tina's was the first case I handled on my own." She turned back to me. "Did you know that?" I shook my head.

"She talked about you all the time," Dick said. "In a completely undetailed and anonymous fashion." He cleared his throat. "She worried a lot."

"Oh, my gosh, you drove all the way from Kentucky!" I cried. "Come in, come in, you must be exhausted! Can I get you anything to eat or drink?"

Dick shook his head, reaching into the SUV to pull an insulated cooler bag from the seat. "That's OK. We're on a special diet."

Maggie frowned but said nothing. "Can you tell Caleb to come home?" I asked her, leading the couple toward our house.

Dick made a big show of stomping the slush from his boots, but I could tell there was no small amount of glee at coming into contact with actual snow. Andrea told me quietly that their hometown didn't see much beyond sleet, and Dick had been acting like a big, goofy kid ever since they reached the state line. I got the impression that Dick acted like a big, goofy kid regardless of location. I made a mental note to keep him away from Samson.

"What an adorable house." Andrea sighed as she surveyed the small, steady modifications we'd been making to the living room and kitchen. I'd painted the walls a warm, creamy yellow to bring a little sunlight into the rooms. Caleb had cleared out some of his mom's knickknacks to make room for our own mementos, a carved wooden wolf from his cousin Cooper and a framed picture of us smiling into the camera with Suds.

"I'll bet her fella didn't make her install a man cave." She sent a fake pout toward Dick. I wasn't sure what was going on there, and I didn't have the heart to tell Andrea that the whole valley was basically one big man cave.

"A bet is a bet, woman," Dick grumbled.

I giggled, closing the door, mentally estimating how long it would take Caleb to run here to meet our new friends. *Friends. Family. Home.* Three words I hadn't thought I would ever be able to attach to my life again, before I'd come here, to this valley full of werewolves. And now I had all three.

Life, for the moment, was very, very good.

Turn the page to read the

next sexy, spooky, laugh-out-loud

paranormal romance from

Molly Harper . . .

Better Homes and Hauntings

Coming in summer 2014 from

Pocket Books

Nina had been through much worse than seasickness in the past year. Near-bankruptcy. Identity theft. Stolen garden tools. This was going to be an adventure, she promised herself. Nina knew she should walk over and say hello to the others. They were going to be working and living together on the Crane's Nest property for the next few months, until the renovations were over. But at the moment, she could only concentrate on keeping her breakfast down.

The boat hit a particularly rough wave, pitching Nina back against the cabin. She moaned, bending at the knees and propping her arms against her thighs.

A smooth, tanned hand appeared at the corner of Nina's vision, bearing brightly wrapped candies. She startled, drawing up to her full height, and swayed. The other hand steadied her at the elbow. "Whoa, there," a male voice said, a laughing lilt to his soothing tone.

"Sorry about that," Nina groaned, squinting up at the owner of the outstretched hand.

"Seasick, huh?" he said, eyeing her sympathetically over the rims of his mirrored aviators.

"Ever since I was a kid," she said, and glared at the water glittering in the distance. "I ruined every family fishing trip. My brother always told me it would help to keep my eye on the horizon. But I think my brother is a dirty liar."

"Try these," he said, pressing a few foiled candies into her clammy palm. "Ginger drops. They'll help your stomach. And as far as the horizon goes, I think it's better to concentrate on more immediate surroundings.

"Jake Rumson," he said, offering his hand. "I'm the architect who's supposed to be undoing the mess we're getting into."

"Nina," she said. "Linden."

"Like the tree," he said, smiling. "You're with Demeter Designs."

"Like the tree, exactly," she said, a genuine grin breaking through her uneasy expression. She tamped it down quickly. "Not everybody catches that."

"I cheated," Jake whispered, the smooth façade melting a bit to reveal a naughty schoolboy smile. "I got a look at the staff list ahead of time. You're the landscape architect and you're named after a tree and bam— instant mnemonic device."

"Do you use little tricks like that often?" she asked, sipping the water.

"Well, those two made it easy," Jake said, nodding

toward Ben and Cindy, the blond bombshell sunning on the deck. "I didn't need a device to remember Ben Grandy. I was a big fan of his when he played at UConn. Damn shame what happened to his knee—his scholarship, future career, and all that."

Nina nodded. "But he's done well. Even without a degree, he's built a good business for himself. He has a really solid reputation around town. You hired the right person."

"Well, what do you know about Cindy Ellis over there?" Jake asked. "She owns the Cinderella Cleaning Service."

"Never heard of her." Nina lifted her brow. "She's a maid?"

Deacon Whitney, the insanely rich twenty-eight-year-old who'd hired all of them, had never mentioned anything about a maid.

"Not exactly. Ms. Ellis—as she insists I call her—runs a sort of maid-slash-organizational guru service. She cleans and installs these crazy storage systems in some of the swankiest family-owned estates in Rhode Island. Ms. Ellis can organize, store, and reset those furnishings on a seasonal system that even the dumbest millionaire could figure out."

"Are you saying we're working for a dumb millionaire?" Nina asked, the corners of her lush mouth tilting up.

Jake snorted, grinning at her over the rims of his aviators. "First of all, Whit's a billionaire. And second, it wasn't his idea to hire her. The Crane's Nest has been virtually looted by various generations of Whitneys over the years, but there are bound to be a few valuables tucked away where the relatives' enterprising little paws couldn't reach. The family is demanding that Whit catalogue every item of historical or monetary value and save it so that they can do battle over them later."

"So is that why Mr. Whitney wants us to stay on the island full-time? So his relatives can't interfere or influence us?"

Jake carefully considered his response to the question. There were a lot of factors in Deacon Whitney's decision, many of which he had discussed at length with Jake. Whit wanted to be each contractor's first priority until the job was completed. He wanted to prevent the contractors from being distracted by other clients' demands. But his chief concern was the fact that there had already been several false starts to the renovations: he'd lost several contractors and workmen to "frayed nerves," to put it politely. Deacon's theory was that if he could keep the contractors from returning home from the island every night, he wouldn't have to worry about whether they'd lose the nerve to come back in the morning.

A lifelong friend of Deacon's family, Jake had spent the occasional afternoon on Whitney Island over the years and could have listed the strange occurrences, even without the paper-pale vendors stuttering out their tales of terror: Angry thumping footsteps on the stairway between the second and third floors, strange shifting shadows that darted around at the corners of one's eyes. The overwhelming sense that someone was watching you. The smell of rosewater in upstairs bedrooms where no one had sprayed perfume in decades. And of course, the sound of a woman's weeping coming from the widow's walk. He'd experienced all of this and more as Deacon's guest on Whitney Island. And he hated every minute he spent there. But if his best friend in the world wanted him to lie through his teeth so he could resurrect that beautiful, cursed shell of a house, Jake would do it with a smile on his face.

"No, but that's just one more pro for the list," he said, offering her his most charming grin. "Whit wants to finish the project as quickly as possible, and the best way to do that is have your full attention and have the team stay within shouting distance in case there are problems."

Nina chanced a look out at the waves and caught a glimpse of the house they'd come to restore. The Crane's Nest rose out of the water like a drowned debutante, her fine lines eroded and obscured, tangling into the overgrown green expanse of Whitney Island. Nina could see evidence of what had once been an exacting geometric landscaping plan leading up to the rounded porte cochere that hid the massive front doors in a dark cavernous maw. The gardens were long past feral, dry withered grass strangling the remains of statuary and rosebushes. The façade of the house consisted of three levels, a loggia flanked by two-story wings leading into the main structure. The stories were marked by rows of windows, their dark surfaces reminding Nina of the blank stare of dolls' eyes. A ring of tall chimneys crowned a flat slate roof, echoing the pattern of blunt cornices extending from the porte cochere.

Squinting in the glaring afternoon light, Nina traced the line of the roof with her eyes, admiring the wrought iron railing that enclosed the widow's walk. There was potential for a terrace garden there, from what she'd seen of the pictures. She was trying to estimate the roof's square footage when a feminine figure stepped to the wrought iron boundary. Nina gasped. A cold wave of nausea washed through her as the dark shape stared down at the approaching boat. For a moment, Nina thought she could make out the lines of an old-fashioned gown, a slim waist, long, dark twists of hair blowing in the wind. But there was no detail to the face or form, only shadow. Nina shivered and braced herself against the bow, taking deep breaths. When she looked up at the roof again, the figure was gone.

Everybody knew the story of the Crane's Nest and the tragic death of its mistress. It was an urban legend among the local kids who grew up on the outskirts of Newport. Townies like Nina, who spent her time on the less picturesque stretches of beach trying to avoid the summer people, grew up hearing tales of the wailing ghost of Catherine Whitney who wandered the halls of the Crane's Nest, searching for her killer, her lost treasure, a hidden illegitimate baby . . . The details varied depending on who was telling the story. It was a common dare among the high schoolers to go to the island and spend the night at the house. Very few kids managed to make it as far as Whitney Island without getting spooked and speeding back to the mainland. This led to a belief that the island was cursed, and no boat would moor on it.

Nina had lived in Newport for most of her life and this was the first time she'd ever laid eyes on the place. So it was only natural that her fertile imagination would bring the tortured ghost of Catherine Whitney to life after growing up on those stories. Right?

Nina sighed. She had to get a grip. The Crane's Nest job would be the crown jewel of her portfolio. This job would gain her entrée into the Eastern Seaboard's most exclusive circles and the rich potential clients that made up those circles. She would build her business. She would rebuild her life and her credit rating from the ground up. She would stop imagining scary shadow people on the roof. That could lead nowhere good.

"Feeling better now that you're on solid ground?" Jake asked, pressing a cold soda can into her hand. She accepted it gratefully and guzzled the better part of the bubbly elixir before answering.

"Much, thanks," she said glancing over shoulder again toward the still-uninhabited roof. "I swear I'm not this high-maintenance on dry land."

"Hey, you're the first girl to throw up on that boat for reasons unrelated to alcohol. That sets you in a class all your own," Jake assured her.

"That's . . . not particularly flattering," she mused. "Jake, are we the only people on the island? Surely Mr. Whitney sent a prep team ahead of us to clean the staff quarters or stock the kitchen?"

Jake shrugged. "Cindy's crew came out to clean up the dorms for us. And the catering staff from Whit's office stocked the kitchen. But they left days ago. Why do you ask?"

Nina chuckled weakly, sorry now that she'd said anything. "It's just silly. I thought I saw someone on the roof, right before I got sick."

Jake smiled at her, but there was a hitch to the expression, a hesitation that made Nina curious. "We're the only ones here, I promise. There's nobody else. What you saw? It was probably just a trick of the light."

Nina thought better of commenting that tricks of light rarely wore hoop skirts. But before she could come up with a more suitable response, a chopping noise in the distance caught their attention. A tiny black dot in the sky grew closer and closer, the sound of its blades beating a regular rhythm against the wind. The unmarked helicopter landed about forty yards to their left, the displaced air beating a patch of perfectly nice purple gypsy flowers into the dirt. Nina winced at the sight. She doubted the delicate stems would recover from that.

Oblivious to Nina's botanical distress, Jake helped her to her feet. "That's Whit!" he shouted over the noise, that happy grin brightening his face again.

The helicopter landed nimbly on the shaggy but level patch of grass. A slim, long-legged man in jeans and an open blue Oxford shirt emerged from the helicopter. He slapped the helicopter door twice, prompting the pilot to take off. As the wind whipped his Oxford aside, Nina caught a glimpse of Captain America's shield underneath.

Deacon Whitney ran a billion-dollar company and he still wore comic book hero T-shirts.

And of course he would show up before she was fully recovered from a siege of vomiting and possible hallucinations. As the helicopter and its hair-wrecking winds disappeared into the horizon, she did her best to straighten her mussed clothes and look presentable. She took one last breath-freshening sip of her soda and followed the others to greet Mr. Whitney.

Deacon was all long, lean limbs and angular lines, with high, sharp cheekbones and a jawline most matinee idols would sell their mothers for. But his hair was a shaggy, curling mess of light brown, completing the "disgraced aristocrat" look as much as the rumpled business casual clothes. Much as he had when they'd first met at his corporate offices, Deacon gave Nina the immediate impression of being uncomfortable with his surroundings. He'd covered it quickly enough, with easy, unaffected charm and firm handshakes all around, but Nina recognized the look of someone who was stressed and uneasy. She'd seen it in the mirror every morning for months.

Despite the kindred twinge she felt for another neurotic, she was determined to stay as far away as possible from Deacon Whitney. She'd dealt with easy charm before. She'd had more than her fair share of men whose money made the world go round, who thought they were so damn smooth they could lie to your face and get away with it. Nina had no interest in falling prey to that brand of man again, even if it came wrapped in a yummy, geek-chic package.

Jake stepped close and whispered something in Deacon's ear. Deacon frowned and glanced at Nina. Suddenly self-conscious, she combed her fingers through her hair. "Excuse me for just a second," Deacon said.

Leaving the trio of contractors to their own devices, Deacon and Jake wandered down the lawn a bit, clearly having some discussion of details. Deacon seemed unhappy, glancing over at Nina and then at the house, shaking his head. Jake shrugged and, judging from the smirk on his face, had just made some completely inappropriate comment. Deacon rolled his eyes skyward, as if asking heaven why he'd been saddled with this man as his friend. Deacon's expression of exasperation was too well practiced. And Jake was too good at blithely ignoring it.

Jake poked Deacon's shoulder, making Deacon roll his eyes again. So Jake nudged a second time, shoving him toward Ben, Cindy, and Nina.

"Jake just reminded me that 'nice, nondouchebag' employers' greet people by name and make some effort to be sociable," Deacon said, his cheeks flushing slightly. "So, hello, I'm Deacon Whitney, owner of this very large pile of bricks. Please excuse the dramatic entrance, but I've never been fond of boats."

Nina would have liked to have known about the nonboat option. But perhaps there was no nonboat option for nonbillionaires.

"I chose each of you, not because you're the biggest name in your field, but because you presented the most original ideas and I was excited to see what you would do with the place."

"Not me," Jake interjected cheerfully. "I was chosen because of *favoritism*."

Deacon sighed and continued on as if Jake hadn't spoken. "So, thank you for joining me here this summer and giving me your full time and attention in what I'm sure is your busy season. I promise the project will be worth your while. If you have any questions or concerns, don't be afraid to come to me or Jake, here. And if you will follow me, we can get settled into the staff quarters."

Nina had expected Whitney to take them into the main house to bunk in an abandoned guest room. But he led the group down an overgrown pebbled path around the house to a series of low-slung bungalow structures flanking the coach house and the stables.

"The original mistress of the house, Catherine Whitney, ordered the architect to build separate staff residences," Cindy whispered to Nina as they trudged past the jagged remains of the greenhouses. "Even though the other cutthroat but ever-so-elegant Gilded Age ladies kept their servants close in case they had some urgent need for warm milk at midnight."

Cindy Ellis started cleaning inns and B&Bs after her dad passed, she told Nina, working her way up the food chain. Her big break came when Martha Stark's rotten teenage son had thrown a wild party, wrecking several rooms of her mansion on Cove Road while Martha was out of town for the weekend. Normally, Martha would have deferred to her own housekeeper for such a regular occurrence. But Martha was due to host her anniversary party in just a few days and poor

Esther couldn't handle the cleanup *and* the party prep.

Cindy thought her father would be proud of what she'd built, her own operation, with her own staff and the pleasure of assessing each challenge as it came along to determine how she could use it as a way to grow. Even if those problems included a slightly eccentric boss, annoying male coworkers, and what appeared to be an enormous *Scooby Doo* set just waiting to launch spooks at her.

Nina intentionally lagged behind to put a bit more space between them and the men. "Do you know anything about Catherine's . . . ?"

Cindy made an indelicate choking noise as she mimed being strangled. Nina frowned but nodded.

"About as much as you probably heard around the ghost story circles when we were kids," Cindy whispered. "A celebrated society wife flees her much-older husband's luxurious, recently completed summer retreat in 1900, only to be found the next morning floating in the bay not two hundred yards from her front door. She had suspicious bruises around her throat. There were a lot of whispers about the Whitneys' marriage before the murder, and Mrs. Whitney's history of spending so much time with the architect that designed their house didn't help matters. The husband, Gerald, was immediately suspected and put through the indignity of being questioned by the police, but they either couldn't or wouldn't charge him with his wife's murder. Gerald never recovered from the ordeal. The loss of his entire fortune in a series of bad investments sent him into a downward spiral, health-wise. He died in

1903 and their children, Josephine and Junior, were sent to live with relatives. The house was left fully furnished, clothes in closets, objets d'art still on the shelves, everything. The family never managed to recover their reputation or fortune. The house was abandoned, fell into disrepair, and here we are."

Nina stared at her, hazel eyes wide. "Jake was right about you."

Cindy's own eyes narrowed at Jake, who had been frequently checking over his shoulder to make sure the girls were keeping up. "What did Rumson say about me?"

"That you were good at organizing," Nina said, nudging her with an elbow. "That summary of the Whitneys' sordid past was succinct and factoid-packed."

Cindy blushed. "Oh, well, I like to keep things tidy."

"Ladies?" Jake suddenly called from inside the dorm. "If you keep lollygagging, you're going to miss the tour."

The servant quarters were spartan, but it was obvious an effort had been made to make them comfortable. As they walked down the long hall of bedrooms, Jake explained that the original architect, John Gilbert, had designed a series of vents in the ceiling that allowed warm air to rise out of the room and kept the occupants cooler in the summer months.

The individual rooms were eerily quiet, each with two simple iron-frame beds, recently stripped of their ancient feather-tick mattresses. Ben's crews had done basic renovations to three of the rooms, patching up holes in the plaster, painting, and giving the floors a thorough cleaning. Deacon had taken the butler's room, the largest in the building and the only one with a private sitting room. But in what Nina considered a remarkable show of fairness by their employer, each of the "new" rooms was decorated with the same simple queen bed, pale wood dresser, and nightstand. Ben's and Jake's rooms also included drafting tables. Nina imagined the queen beds were an accommodation for the sheer size of Ben's six-foot-"good-God-how-tall-*is*-this-guy?" frame.

Nina spent most of the tour staring up at the wainscoting and crown molding. It seemed bizarre that the architect would devote those decorative touches to a utilitarian building that guests of the Crane's Nest would never see. She looked over her shoulder to see Deacon watching her while Jake chattered about updated plumbing. Just as her brain managed to communicate the "smile like a normal person!" message to her face, he looked away, to the tablet Jake was shoving in his face.

They found the ladies' dormitory, which was a mirror image of the men's building save for the larger bedrooms. The Crane's Nest required more maids than footmen and valets, so the younger women slept four to a room in the same iron bed frames. The recently updated kitchen shared a door with the men's dorm, so the mostly female cooking staff could provide for both sides during their off hours. Nina guessed that the multitude of locks on the ladies' side of the shared door had been employed overnight to protect the servants from temptation.

Nina's first night as a resident of Whitney Island was not a momentous one. Dinner had been a stilted, awkward affair, with the team seated around the long dining table in the men's dorm, scarfing down take-out Japanese food that Jake had ferried across from the mainland in a cooler. Jake tried valiantly to get a conversation going, bringing up Deacon's love for a particular sashimi bar in Boston near his corporate headquarters and funny stories from Jake's family's travels to Kyoto when he was a teenager. But it didn't work. Ben was good for an ice breaker every few minutes, but the minute portions of rice and raw fish seemed inadequate fuel for him and he couldn't seem to maintain a steady stream of conversation. Deacon seemed to thaw a bit when the group started making checklists and plans: cooking rotations, the shower schedule, a first day to-do list to determine exactly how far in over their heads they were with this project. They'd finished dinner and settled down to brass tacks, each presenting their immediate plans for the house—stabilizing/rehabbing the interior structures, salvaging what few furnishings and antiques were left— and how they would work around each other to prevent delays and power-tool-versus-garden-implement hissy fits.

Curled in her solitary bed that night, Nina dreamed she was pulling the sheets tight over a mattress. The mattress was hers. The sheets were hers. But the arms stretching out in front of her belonged to someone else. A large diamond winked from her ring finger, flanked by sapphires. The sleeves of her dress were beautifully cut blue muslin, rolled to the elbow as the soft white hands smoothed the counterpane. She was pleased that she was able to provide clean, comfortable rooms for her staff. She knew how hard the servants worked to keep a home running. And while she certainly didn't need to make up the beds, she found a certain satisfaction in seeing to them herself. She could walk down the rows of rooms, seeing a freshly made bed in each, and know that she'd done *something* productive with her day. Besides, the servants wouldn't arrive for a few days anyway. And it seemed inhospitable to welcome them to their new home with bare beds.

She bent over the far corner of the mattress, tucking the sheet tightly. And when she rose up, she felt a large hand slide down the small of her back and give her backside a pinch. She squealed and the man's other hand clapped around her mouth, pressing her back against his chest.

"Well, look what I found here," an affectionate male voice whispered against her ear. "A pretty piece of skirt already bent over the bed."

A thrill of fear and something more rippled up her spine as those hands slipped around her hips and pressed her bum against a solid male frame. Teeth closed gently over her earlobe, tugging insistently. She relaxed into the masculine embrace, sighing as the mouth moved from her ear to her neck. The hand cupped her chin, tilting her head back toward him. His grip tightened, moving to her throat, squeezing the breath from her lungs. Nina scratched and coughed and fought, but he was just too strong.

Suddenly, the pressure at her throat disappeared.

The scene shifted and she was underwater, watching waves roll over her head. She tried to swim to the surface, but she was held in place by a growing pressure around her legs, tugging her down like an anchor, crawling up her body like greedy grasping hands until it settled around her throat. She reached upward, trying to claw her way toward air, toward light, but was unable to make any progress. Now she saw herself, her arm extended over her head in some obscene ballerina's pose. Her delicate blue muslin sleeve fluttered against the water like an angel's wing, and she watched its motion as it slowly turned brown and disintegrated with age. The sleeve rotted away, leaving a grotesque, decaying limb behind, sloughing and dissolving until all that was left were bleached ivory bones reaching up toward the light.

In her head, she could hear screaming.

Nina bolted up from the bed, clawing at her throat and gasping for breath.

TRY ALL OF DELILAH DAWSON'S NOVELS

WICKED AS THEY COME

STEP RIGHT UP!
TEST YOUR METTLE
—AND YOUR HEART.

A BLUD NOVEL

ALL ABOARD THE
AIRSHIP FOR A
STEAMY, SAUCY
ADVENTURE YOU
WON'T FORGET!

"A wonderfully
fresh new voice!"
—RT Book Reviews

WICKED AS SHE WANTS

A BLUD NOVEL

WICKED AFTER MIDNIGHT COMING JANUARY 2014!

Have you ever heard of Bludmen? They're rather like you and me—only more fabulous, immortal, and hungry for blood.

(They're also very good kissers.)

PICK UP OR DOWNLOAD YOUR COPY TODAY! POCKET BOOKS